Silent Night, Sinful Night

Books by Sharon Page

Blood Wicked
Blood Deep
Blood Red
Blood Rose
Black Silk
Hot Silk
Sin
"Midnight Man" in *Wild Nights*

Books by Melissa MacNeal

Sexual Hunger
Sexual Secrets
"Long Hard Ride" in *Tempted by a Cowboy*
"Naughty Noelle" in *Unwrap Me*
"The Captain's Courtesan" in *The Pleasure of His Bed*
"Getting Lucky" in *Only with a Cowboy*
"Cabin Fever" in *Naughty, Naughty*
Hot for It
All Night Long
"A Lady's Pleasure" in *The Harem*

Books by Chloe Harris

In Deep
Secrets of Sin

Published by Kensington Publishing Corporation

Silent Night, Sinful Night

SHARON PAGE

MELISSA MACNEAL

CHLOE HARRIS

APHRODISIA

KENSINGTON PUBLISHING CORP.
www.kensingtonbooks.com

APHRODISIA BOOKS are published by

Kensington Publishing Corp.
119 West 40th Street
New York, NY 10018

All Kensington titles, imprints, and distributed lines are available at special quantity discounts for bulk purchases for sales promotion, premiums, fund-raising, and educational, or institutional use.

Special book excerpts or customized printings can also be created to fit specific needs. For details, write or phone the office of the Kensington Special Sales Manager: Kensington Publishing Corp., 119 West 40th Street, New York, NY 10018. Attn. Special Sales Department. Phone: 1-800-221-2647.

Aphrodisia and the A logo Reg. U.S. Pat. & TM Off.

ISBN-13: 978-0-7582-6670-5
ISBN-10: 0-7582-6670-7

First Kensington Trade Paperback Printing: October 2011

10 9 8 7 6 5 4 3 2 1

Printed in the United States of America

CONTENTS

WICKED FOR CHRISTMAS

SHARON PAGE

1

Christmas Eve, Hertfordshire, 1812

Miss Amelia Watson could not quite believe she was watching Lord Dante strip off all his clothing.

They stood in the woods behind his family estate. Sparkling snow swirled around them, and the wind swept the blankets of white into fanciful shapes that looked like dollops of cream. The forest had never been so still or so magical. Amelia knew why it felt so special—this was Christmas Eve, after all, a night that, for her, *always* felt magical.

Lord Dante, the gentleman she'd adored for years, had begun with his coat, and she'd stared, openmouthed and stunned, as he'd pulled it off. After all, they were *outdoors*. Yet he had merely winked when she'd gasped, "What are you doing?"

He'd draped his greatcoat over her shoulders to keep her warm. Then he'd handed her his tailcoat. Next to come off: his cravat and waistcoat. She'd gathered up his clothes and breathed in the rich, warm scent of them. Sandalwood, a trace of smoke—he must have smoked a cheroot—and a special smell that was entirely his. It made her want to kiss him all over and discover how he tasted.

Now he was tugging the hem of his shirt out of his trouser waistband. He was preparing to haul his shirt over his head. Snow dusted his golden hair, turning it to the color of caramel where it stuck to his face. On his long eyelashes, the snow melted to water, and he blinked the droplets away. He must be *freezing.*

No. This had to stop.

"You can't take off your clothing," Amelia protested. "We are standing in the middle of a blizzard." In a wind that nipped at her cheeks and made her shiver through her wool cloak.

His smile widened, despite snowflakes melting on his nose. "Then say yes, Miss Watson." He grasped the hem of his shirt and whisked it upward. She saw the prominent muscles of his stomach, the line of golden hair that ran from his navel and disappeared beneath the waistband of his trousers.

They had stolen kisses beneath the mistletoe, and once she had daringly stroked his back under his coat, but she had never seen him undressed before. He was more beautiful and muscular that even her wildest fantasies had depicted. Her throat dried, but she managed to shake her head. "You can't seriously be proposing marriage to me."

She was the governess to Lord Dante's younger siblings. Heirs to earldoms did not marry governesses. That only happened in novels.

He pulled off his shirt. He would be hers to explore and kiss and taste and love, if only she said yes.

"You must be sensible, my lord."

"Amelia, I've wanted to make you my wife for months now. I struggled in vain to do what my family expects. But it's no good. I love you. I must have you. Say yes, love."

"I—" *I shouldn't. I mustn't. I won't.* All the logical answers leaped to her lips but died there. She wanted him. If she couldn't accept a miracle at Christmas, when could she?

He came right up to her, so she had to tip her head back to meet his gaze. Carefully, he took his tailcoat from her arms and pulled it on. He left it open, so it framed the muscles of his broad chest. "There's two pockets in my coat, Amelia. In one, I have a Christmas treat for you."

"Oh! You shouldn't have. I don't have anything to give you."

"You do." His voice became low and intense; his eyes shone brilliantly green. "You have the most amazing gift of all to give to me."

"What?" she asked, perplexed.

"Guess the pocket, love."

She had not given him her answer, but he crooked his finger, coaxing her to do his bidding. So she did. She slid her fingers into his snug right-hand pocket. Her fingers stroked something soft. Velvet. It was a small pouch. She had guessed correctly. And heavens, he must have bought her jewelry. Slowly, she drew it out. He truly should not have. She had *nothing* to give him in return.

"Open it, love. Drop it into my hand."

She did as he asked. Something fell into his gloved palm, something that sparkled like glittering ice. He dropped to one knee and held the most enormous diamond before her. "Marry me, Amelia. Give me my Christmas miracle."

Heavens, he would freeze if he stayed on one knee in the snow any—

"Yes," someone said.

Suddenly she was swept off her feet.

She had been the one to say yes. While her mind had panicked, hastening over a dozen other things, her lips had taken charge, and they had said yes.

Lord Dante held her in his arms. She could not believe he had picked her up so easily. She was rather . . . well . . . *voluptuous* would be the most polite term. She was full-figured, robust . . . in truth, plump.

Heedless of the falling snow, Lord Dante bent his head to hers. Breathlessly, she let her lips part, and when he captured her mouth, she moaned her desire and her love deeply into his. She loved his mouth. Thoughts of it had captured her every waking moment for three years—ever since she had first come to his father's house to be governess to the younger Worthington siblings.

"We'll head to Gretna tonight," he murmured when he stopped kissing her. He had carried her through the snow while he'd ravished her mouth. Lights glowed ahead.

It was a romantic thought, but her practical nature intruded. "We can't. We will never make it to Scotland with all this snow."

"We will, love. Trust me on that. And the blizzard will make it impossible for my family to come in pursuit."

She shivered in his arms. They could escape. They could marry. But what would happen when they returned home? His family would never accept her. "You must put me down. We cannot go back to your house like this."

"We're not going back to the house. Not until we are man and wife. I've taken care of everything." He shot her a possessive look that heated her to her toes. "You are going to be mine, Amelia."

The glow grew closer as he trudged through the whirling snow. She saw the ragged shape of a sloping, thatched roof, the dark outline of stone walls. It was the unused gamekeeper's cottage. There were two paned windows in the small cottage, and they blazed with golden light. Laughing, Dante lifted his booted foot and pushed the door open. Amelia gasped—she'd expected a tumbledown structure, but inside, a large bed was spread with fur throws. In the hearth, a fire crackled merrily. A decanter of wine, along with a tray of decadent fruits, fragrant bread, and steaming dishes sat on a table.

Only one fevered heartbeat passed before Amelia stood in the middle of the cottage, warmed by the fire, slowly taking her clothes off in front of Lord Dante for the very first time.

He watched her strip, and the fire in his intense green eyes made a blush rush over her skin. He came to her and opened the fastenings of her dress. He helped her out of the serviceable wool and deftly unlaced her corset. Then he whipped off his trousers and linens. Her eyes almost fell out of her head. He was *hard*. She knew the word, had a vague idea of what it meant. But she had no idea Dante would look like this. . . .

She had no idea a penis could be so long. Or that it stuck out from a male body, curving upward toward his belly. Or that it had an adorable acorn-shaped top and such large bollocks dangling beneath. He smiled shyly as she stared. He even pirouetted in front of her, a boyish and endearing grin on his face, so she could drink in every inch of him. Then he jumped onto the bed and slipped under the covers. He crooked his finger. "Come, love. Join me."

Amelia gathered her courage. She wriggled her corset down and stepped out of it. Then she swallowed hard and peeled off her shift, revealing her generous hips and her plump thighs. Her breasts bounced heavily as she moved. And when she faced Lord Dante again, now utterly naked, he stared as though stunned by the sight of her.

Her heart sank.

He got up to his knees. The fur throw fell and landed on his erection, and it hung there, wobbling. "Come here, Amelia. *Now*. My God, you're beautiful. So lush and voluptuous and perfect."

Lord Dante pushed the throw down, scrambled across the bed and, another swift heartbeat later, he stood in front of her.

He kissed her, pressing his naked body, every amazing inch of it, against hers. His erection poked into her tummy; his chest was a solid wall against her full breasts. As his mouth lovingly caressed hers, his hands stroked her skin. She felt so wanton. So sinful. She, who had always been the ordinary, plump governess, who believed she would never marry.

Lord Dante gently squeezed her left breast. She squeaked into his mouth. "My lord—"

"Enough of that," he murmured. "You're to be my wife. You are to call me Dante."

"Are you sure about this?" she whispered. "Should we anticipate the wedding?"

"I want to make you mine. We're going to be married as soon as we reach Gretna, but that will take a couple of days. If my family hunts us down . . ." He bent and licked her naked nipple. She squeaked in shock. She had to grip his shoulders as he ran his tongue in slow circles. Around and around her nipple, which instantly tightened and ached. Both her nipples hardened—the other one obviously hoped for the same attention.

"If my family were to catch up with us before we're wed, they will try to stop us. If they make it to Gretna too late, they will try to fight an unconsummated marriage. But if I've ruined you, they'll have to let me marry you. My father, tyrant that he is, would never let me walk away from that obligation."

Obligation. She faltered, pulling back.

He grinned. "I don't mean marrying you is an obligation. But if it means my family has no power to stop our wedding, I want to ruin you now." He clasped her hand and led it to his erect shaft. She swallowed hard, and he wrapped her hand around him. It was like a soft, warm sheath around steel.

"This is our wedding night, love," he said softly. "In my heart, we're already joined."

She nodded. "In my heart, too."

Dante flashed another boyish smile, and he pushed back his tousled blond hair. "Then we should get on with it." Without warning, he swept her into his arms again and carried her quickly to the bed, despite the generosity of her figure. This time his hand cupped her naked bottom, and he somehow managed to carry her while bending over to nibble at her nipples.

Her tummy growled with hunger and nerves, and Lord— no, she meant simply *Dante*—grinned. "Mmm. I suspect I have several appetites to satisfy," he murmured. He laid her with care on the fur throw. She expected him to climb on top. So when he walked to the table where their food was laid, she sat up in surprise. She might be hungry, but she couldn't care less about food. Did this mean, for him, a buffet rated higher than sexual pleasure? He hummed as he filled a plate, and she gaped at him. He would rather eat than have his first encounter with the woman he wanted to marry?

Really, she'd heard the way to a man's heart was through his stomach, but she had never imagined food would take precedence when a man was hard and obviously ready.

He brought the plate to the bed, along with a glass of wine.

"You can't eat in here. Think of the crumbs."

He laughed. "Roll over on your tummy, love."

She did as he commanded. Then something wet touched her low back and she jumped. She twisted to see he had dipped his finger in the wine and was drawing swirls on her back. He bent and licked.

Amelia almost leaped off the bed. To her absolute shock, he poured a thin stream of wine on her tailbone. Droplets spattered on her naked bottom and ran down the cleft between her cheeks. He licked all the drops away; then his tongue dabbed between the twin globes of her bottom, tasting the wine.

Were all wedding nights like this? She had never even read of this in naughty novels.

He kissed her bottom, then cupped the cheeks and murmured, "Lovely."

"My hips are very generous," she said.

"Perfect. Every inch of you is perfect." He held a hothouse grape before her mouth, and she ate it. He fed her this way, with his fingers. It was their first meal together as husband and wife.

He rolled her gently onto her back. He poured a puddle of wine onto her tummy and lapped it up. When he leaned close, she could breathe in the lovely earthy scent of his skin. She could see the curve of his long, golden lashes and the blond stubble on his jaw. He was beautiful. And he was to be hers. Then he arched up and suckled both her nipples in turn. Her senses reeled. Boldly, she whispered, "I would like to drink wine off *your* belly."

Laughing, he flopped onto his back. His hard penis jumped as he did, then slapped his stomach. His stomach looked like a cobblestone road. She lightly traced her fingers over the ridges. It felt so daring to do this. So hard to believe she was *expected* to touch him now. Amelia skimmed her hand up, up to his bare chest. His pectoral muscles were like rock beneath her palms. She gazed at his face and saw he was watching her shyly, breathing hard.

His lips curved in a lopsided smile. "Amelia, love, I'm very nervous."

"You? You can't be nervous."

"I am." He crooked his finger. "Lie on top of me."

Trembling, she did. Her breasts plopped against his chest, her soft tummy covered his rigid penis, and she could not quite decide where to put her legs. Finally, she opened them, settling her plump thighs on either side of his hard ones. He arched up and slanted his mouth over hers. They had kissed beneath the mistletoe in Dante's house, daringly playing with each other's tongues. But this kiss was wilder, more erotic, more intense. It set her on fire, right down to her toes.

His hands caressed down her spine to her derriere, then lower, to stroke her thighs. In one swift, unexpected motion, he flipped them both over. She squealed and they bounced onto the bed, the mattress rippling around them. She loved this—to be captured beneath him, to have his body pressed against hers everywhere.

Was the fire in the hearth burning hotter now? The room felt scorching. Soft fur tickled her naked back as Dante wrapped his arms around her, embracing her, and slid one long leg between hers. She twined around him, a vine clinging to his solidity, her damp body tight to his. She clutched his neck, wrapped her legs around his. This lifted her and placed her private place right against his penis, so her nether curls and her soft lips cradled him. He shifted his hips, moving them gently, so his erection stroked her. She grew scandalously wet with each pass of the long shaft. She could smell her ripe, shocking scent.

He slid his hand between their damp bodies. She gazed up at him, enchanted at the gleam in his green eyes. He glowed, looking at her. It made her feel so . . . desired. So much the way she'd dreamed it would feel to be a wife.

Dante's elegant fingers swirled over her intimate curls. She moaned, almost stunned by how fierce she sounded.

"I should start slowly, love," he murmured. "I should bring you to your first climax with my mouth. But I'm too impatient. I want you too much."

"And we don't have too much time."

He grinned. "Exactly." His fingers, warm and strong, tried to part her nether lips, and she gasped. They were sticky and resisted at first. She stiffened, but he was gentle, and then he pressed his thumb to the place at the very top of those soft lips.

And stroked. Despite his soft touch, sensation slammed into her, making her eyes go wide, her lips part on a cry.

"Goodness," she whimpered.

"Good?" He circled his thumb over the little bud, making it throb and swell and ache.

She couldn't speak. All she could do was moan. In shock. In delight. In amazement. And while she soared close to the ceiling, trying to absorb every stunning sensation, he slid a finger inside her. His gaze held hers as he slid his finger in and out, as deeply as he could. She felt her walls clutch at him, and his finger eased them apart, filling her. So much. How would she ever take more?

She was so aroused she was slick, creamy. She blushed at the wet, sucking noises his finger made as he plunged it in and out.

"Lovely. You're ready for me."

She nodded, unable to speak.

"Not quite," he murmured. His thumb rubbed her nub, again and again. Good—it was so incredibly good. Of their own volition, her hips lifted, rocking into his hand. He rubbed. And rubbed. Each stroke left her dizzier. Each pass had her soaring higher. She clutched at the fur throw. Her hips pounded helplessly. She was growing more and more tense, and she feared . . . something would have to burst . . .

Something *did*. In a wave of pleasure, in a mad pulsing of her muscles, an explosion of light behind her closed lids and a rush of liquid heat through her body. She bucked. She tore at the bedclothes. With her eyes shut tight, she arched beneath him, her body moving beyond her control. Wave after wave of delight claimed her. Oh, oh, *heavens*.

When the waves finally stopped crashing over her, she fell back, weak and tingly, onto the bed. Dazed, Amelia opened her eyes. The first thing she saw was Dante's self-satisfied grin. "Did I please you?" he asked. "I intend to please you so much more. . . ."

He parted her limp thighs, pressing them wide apart. His penis pointed at her most intimate place, and that made laughter bubble up inside her. Nervous giggles that popped into the steamy room like the trapped air in champagne. She felt intoxicated. He lowered to her, the sweet, rounded head of his member touching her private place. It pushed between her wet lips. She had gasped at his finger, and now she was paralyzed by the sudden invasion of the taut head, the thick shaft that followed.

Splaying her hands, she pressed them to his hard chest. Stopping him. "Oh," she gasped.

Lovingly, his lips played against hers. Each soft caress of his mouth helped the pain ease. "I'm sorry, Amelia. This will hurt when I break your maidenhead, but just this time and just for a little while. I think it's madness that it has to hurt you. I promise I'll do everything in my power to give you an orgasm that will make your discomfort worth it."

"All right," she whispered. She tensed, but she trusted him.

He eased forward and she winced. Her fingernails drove into his broad, strong back. She was hurting him, and she didn't mean to, but she couldn't stop.

His hips pushed forward and she cried out. He backed off. But she knew there was no point in delay. "Just push into me," she whispered.

He kissed her hard at the same moment he thrust. Pain lanced her, making her head reel, and she gouged his flesh so hard she must have left scratches. He stayed motionless. She felt him inside, filling her. She felt so full of him. His crotch was tight to hers. They were joined.

Slowly, he moved back, and she felt the unfamiliar stroke deep inside her; she felt every sensation of it. Then he pushed in once more. This time it didn't hurt so much. She relaxed a little beneath him.

He pumped in again, and she bit her lip. He drove faster; he pushed even deeper; he filled her more. He cupped her bottom and lifted her to him, thrusting slowly, deliberately, and with such restrained power it stunned her.

She tried to lift to him. It was good now, the pain a memory, and all she wanted now was to reach up for him, take him inside, and hold him there.

Dante lifted her hips higher, so she couldn't move, so she was at his command. He thrust faster and faster.

She clutched his back, now slick with sweat. She had her legs wrapped around him, and she held on tight. He breathed faster, panting now, and she could see the exertion in the harsh set of his mouth, the tension of his arms.

"Yes," she whispered, trying to pump against him when she could barely move at all.

Then he moved, shifting so his shaft stroked her nub, still swollen and aching from his caresses. He stroked over and over, until she was a brainless thing, until she was nothing more than tingling delight moving with him. *Push to him. Take him. Harder.* She realized she was gasping it aloud. "Harder. Please. *Yes.*"

Her toes curled, her fingers scratched, her hips arched, and heaven dropped down to gather her up. Dimly Amelia saw Dante tense over her. She heard his roar of pleasure. She felt his hips collide with hers and stay motionless. She felt heat. She felt utterly joined to him.

Then she slipped back. Gasping. Whirling. In her heart and soul, she was dancing, though she was still lying upon a bed.

Dante fell off to the side, and he gathered her close. She was hot, sticky, aching, but deliriously happy and spent and sated.

"You should sleep a little," he advised, kissing her mouth gently. "Then we'll travel."

"To be married," Amelia managed to whisper.

"In my heart, we already are," he said.

Dante pushed open the cottage door and stood on the threshold. The blizzard had picked up, and the world was a blur of white. He strained, listening for the sound he'd heard while he got dressed inside and Amelia slept under the fur covers.

He'd thought it was hoofbeats; now he wasn't certain. No one could be riding in the woods through the heavy snow. Had it been footsteps?

It didn't matter if his family caught them. She was essentially his wife now: He'd taken her innocence; he owed her marriage. He wanted her, he loved her, and he was going to have her, and his family could be damned—

Dante.

He jerked to the right. He tried to stare through the snow, but it fell as dense as a plaster wall. He thought he'd heard someone call his name. A gentle breathing came from behind him—Amelia was sleeping.

He should go back to her. But the urge to go outside and search for that sound was something he couldn't quell. He wanted to find out who had called his name. Hell, it was like a compulsion. It would be madness to go out. What he should do was help Amelia dress so they could get to the carriage and begin making their way to Gretna.

But he stepped forward. Who in blazes could be out there? Was his father planning some kind of ambush, prowling up to them through the snow? His father was a proud man, one with a volatile temper, but Dante didn't believe his father would plot to hurt Amelia.

Hell, if his father tried, Dante would do anything to protect the woman he loved.

Suddenly, a dark form materialized in front of him. It was a man, clothed in a sweeping cloak that covered his entire body and a black beaver hat pulled low.

"Who are you?" Dante shouted. Where in the hell had this man come from? Even in the storm, he should have seen the man approach.

Come to me, Dante.

The deep voice growled in his head. No one could speak in someone's mind. But he took a step forward. His feet were moving against his will. He gripped the door handle, but he couldn't stop his legs from taking steps, and as he moved through the thick snow, he pulled the door closed.

He had to protect Amelia. From what, he didn't know. He had an overwhelming sense of danger. He had tucked a pistol in the waistband of his trousers. Drawing it out, he leveled it at the dark figure. The man was backing up, and for some insane reason, he was striding after the man, though he was telling his legs to stop moving.

They had moved ten feet away from the cottage. Twenty feet. Then they were far enough that the cottage was invisible, hidden by thickly falling snowflakes. *Amelia, stay safe,* he thought.

Suddenly the black cape whirled in front of him; then it just . . . vanished. It flapped again in his peripheral vision. Dante spun in that direction. He was turned in circles, aiming at his target, only to have it disappear.

"Stay still, damn it," he growled. His heart pounded. Not in fear, but in anticipation of a fight, in the rush of energy and excitement that came before confrontation. Hell, he was aroused by it. Almost as sexually primed as he'd been for Amelia.

Yes, Dante.

His hand jerked back, so hard he felt his wrist almost snap. Stunned, he loosened his grip on the pistol. It dropped into the snow.

The man materialized a heartbeat later, taking shape right in front of his stunned eyes. The man stood almost seven feet tall. Dante saw long dark hair, whipped by the storm's wind. Glittering eyes that reflected the white snow. Full lips that seemed inhumanly red.

He recoiled, but the man's arms wrapped around him. He couldn't break free.

I have watched you a long time, Dante. The voice filled his head like a choir's song would flood a church.

He struggled. He tried to free his arm to throw punches. The man hissed, his mouth opening wide. Two fangs glinted. Then the man swooped down to him, and those long, curved teeth plunged into his neck.

2

———————

Five years later

Christmas meant a tremendous amount of work. A dozen additional guests would arrive today, Christmas Eve. All the rooms must be cleaned and aired, the beds made with freshly laundered sheets, the grates swept out and readied for blazing fires.

But despite an aching back and sore arms and the feeling she would drop to the floor in exhaustion and never get up, Amelia did not mind the work. If she wasn't busy, she would think of Christmas five years before. She would remember that one wonderful erotic night with Lord Dante. She would remember the horror of waking, of finding him gone, then of learning he had vanished. He had left his home; he had disappeared; he had abandoned her.

After five years toiling as a servant—for a ruined woman could no longer be a governess—she tried desperately not to think of that night. But it haunted her in her dreams.

She dreamed of the smooth silkiness of Dante's sweaty skin

under her palms. She remembered how he had gripped her bottom and lifted her to his every deep thrust. The wonderful feeling of being filled by him. The glorious feeling of an orgasm . . . heavens, it had felt like flying. At night, she would touch herself in a small cot in the attic room, stroking herself to silent climaxes again and again. But nothing had ever been as wonderful as that night with Dante.

And he was gone. His father, the Earl of Matlock, had insisted Dante had run away—probably to the Continent—rather than be saddled with her as his wife.

Sighing, Amelia set down her bucket of water. She got on her knees, gripping a scrub brush, and got to work on the dirty floor. This was her life now. She had dreamed of marrying the man she loved; she had hoped for children. She had loved being a governess and watching Dante's brother and sisters learn. But she would never teach children again. Never have babies of her own now, for no decent man wanted a ruined woman. She was Cinderella in the fairy tale, but with an unhappy ending. She hadn't ended up with her love; she'd ended in the cinders.

"Amelia." One of the other young maids stood in the doorway, a folded piece of paper clasped in her fingers. "Mr. Jones gave it to me."

Llewellyn Jones was one of the guests. From the dreamy look on the maid's face, the girl had noticed his handsome dark looks and vivid blue eyes. Amelia hastily unfolded the note. His strong hand had penned one line. *Meet me at the kissing bough.*

Her heart leaped at the pleasure of seeing Mr. Jones and at the fear of going near the mistletoe again. She avoided the kissing bough like the plague. It made her think of Dante.

Dante struggled within the block of ice that held him. He had barely enough space in the frigid tomb to wiggle his shoulders. But even though Amelia was aboveground, he could hear her. He could hear her laughter. For five years he had been miles away from her, but in his thoughts, he had always been able to hear everything she said. She hadn't laughed once, until now. She was happy.

He had to get the hell out of the ice and see her again.

Had she waited for him? Did she understand he'd been dragged away against his will?

Amelia kicked up snow as she walked. She and Mr. Jones trailed behind the rest of the party. They were gathering greenery to decorate the house on Christmas Eve. The gentleman would cut the Yule log; then it would be loaded upon a sleigh. It was a chance for the gentlemen guests to display their strength to the giggling young ladies. As a lowly servant, Amelia should not be here. But Mr. Jones had specifically asked her to come; he had requested permission from the earl. She had no idea why the draconian earl had been so amenable. It made her wonder who Mr. Llewellyn Jones was.

Five years ago, she'd watched Dante cut down the Yule log. It made her heart ache hopelessly to remember how he'd looked with his sleeves rolled up, a grin on his beautiful lips. Mr. Jones smiled at her. She briskly walked down the path away from him. "I should gather some greenery for decorating inside tonight," she said. It was customary to bring in rosemary, bay, and holly on Christmas Eve.

Mr. Jones offered his arm. Hesitantly, she placed her hand in the crook of it. She was scared to touch him, scared in case she felt something for him. She knew Dante would never come back, but she never wanted to open her heart again.

Mr. Jones took charge, leading them through the snowy woods. Between the bare trees, she glimpsed the moss-covered stone walls and thatch roof of the cottage. She couldn't bear to go there. She tried to pull him back. "No," she managed to croak. "Let us go a different way."

The tall Welshman stopped. His blue eyes gazed softly at her. "Miss Watson, I did not insist you come with me to collect decorations for the house. I had another reason. It is about the disappearance of Lord Dante."

"What? You know something of that?"

"It is my belief that the young lord did not vanish of his own accord."

"What do you mean by that? You mean he was . . . hurt and taken away? Or killed?" Her heart stuttered and she felt instantly sick, dizzy. For five years, she had wanted to believe Dante was alive. Even if it meant he had betrayed her, she wanted to think he was safe . . . somewhere.

"I believe he was attacked. His attacker then took him away."

"Is he alive?" Amelia clasped Mr. Jones's arm. "Do you know where he is? What happened to him? Who took him?" Dante had been strong. A very good shot—she had seen him practice. How could someone have overpowered him?

Mr. Jones laid his hands on her shoulders. "You are so lovely. You might very well be the most beautiful woman I've ever seen."

That startled her. She wore a plain gray wool cloak over her dull servant's gown and an old cast-off bonnet. Yet his gaze held hers with such tenderness. No one had looked at her like this—not since the night she'd shared with Dante in the cottage. She drew back from Mr. Jones's touch. "Please, tell me what you know."

"I don't know how to explain this to you, Miss Watson. Have you heard of vampires?"

"You mean the undead? I've heard tales of them, scary stories told to frighten us around Allhallows Eve." She stared at

Mr. Jones's serious expression. Surely this couldn't be true. "You cannot think he was attacked by vampires? Such things aren't *real.*"

She whirled and ran away—from Llewellyn Jones and from the cottage and all its memories that pierced her heart. Jones followed her. He caught her, making her walk with him, and he told her who he was. A slayer of vampires. He told her story after story to prove such creatures existed. They moved deeper into the woods, away from the jolly party of ladies and gentlemen who were gathering greenery and collecting the Yule log. There, in privacy, Mr. Jones slipped his arm around her waist. "I'm sorry to shock you with all this, but everything I've told you is the truth. My father was a vampire slayer who hunted the beasts throughout Transylvania and the Carpathian Mountains. I grew up knowing such creatures existed. One tried to attack me when I was a young boy."

"Truly?" She shivered as he solemnly nodded his head. Could this *really* be true? She had believed Lord Dante had loved her, and when he'd vanished, she thought she had been deceived—she thought she had been foolish and gullible. But if she now believed Mr. Jones, it meant Dante had not left her willingly. It meant her trust and love had not been misplaced.

She didn't know what to do. Tears gathered and threatened to break free. She fought them. "You think he is dead. If this is true—if a *vampire* caught him—would he not have had his blood drained, his body left there?" It made her sick to even say those words.

"I don't think he was a vampire's victim. I suspect the vampire changed him. Made him into one of them."

Her legs trembled beneath her. Mr. Jones scooped her up and held her to his chest. He was warm and broad. But she was thinking of Dante. He might be alive . . . no, not alive, a vampire. Something predatory and terrifying. She could not believe it.

The afternoon sun dropped completely, sucking the last, lingering purplish orange light from the sky. Snowflakes began to drift down to the hushed world. A world so quiet, Amelia could hear her every labored breath.

Mr. Jones ran his hands up and down her back, stroking her, and he whispered soft, soothing words. She desperately needed something—or *someone*—to cling to. So she grasped his coat and leaned against his chest and let him hold her.

Dante heard her sobs. Each one struck him like the tip of a needle driven deep into his flesh. He could hear a man's deep voice murmuring to her, begging her not to cry. *I have not known you long,* the man said. His voice echoed eerily in Dante's head. The man's voice was low and filled with longing. Dante knew that tone of voice—it was the hopeful, vulnerable rasp of a man in love.

Just a week, the man continued. *But I know that I love you, Miss Amelia Watson. I intend to take you away from this—your sad memories, the drudgery of your life as a servant. I intend to ask you to marry me. But I know, as much as I want you, admire you, love you, I cannot ask you now.*

Love? Amelia? Hell, what was going on? For five years he had hungered to return to her, and she was going to be the wife of someone else? She had forgotten him. She had fallen in love with another man.

What was she going to say? How could she not feel he was near to her? Hades, he was almost under her feet, buried in the frost-hardened ground.

Five years ago he had been taken to an exotic house on a small Mediterranean island—the home of his vampire sire. He'd been changed into a vampire, and he believed he could never come back to Amelia. But finally, a year ago, he knew he couldn't face an eternity without her.

He'd traveled the ocean by hiding in the stinking hold of a

ship, but he had never reached her. His sire had caught him on the road to his home. He had been given a drug that immobilized him. He had been thrown into a hole in the ground, like a grave, and he'd been trapped there, unable to move, as his sire had shoveled dirt on him, on his legs, his torso, then finally his face. He had been buried in the winter last year—a fortnight before Christmas. The ground had been cold and hard, and even when spring had arrived, the ice didn't melt from the earth around his prison. It had stayed solid and frozen through summer, through fall, and into another winter. Apparently, his sire had used some kind of magic to keep him trapped.

I do not know what to do. Soft, melodic, Amelia's voice reached him in his subterranean prison. It wrapped around him, making his heart ache. He was no longer supposed to have a soul, but even without that essential part, he still loved Amelia. He was still capable of love—hopeless love and all the agony that went with it.

He heard the catch in her breath.

I have no mistletoe, said the man she was with. *But I stole one of the berries—I've got it in my pocket.*

You are supposed to take that after *a kiss,* she replied. But she didn't sound hesitant anymore.

Dante struggled in his shallow, narrow grave. Damn this. Damn the demon who had changed him, who had dragged him away from Amelia, from the future they should have had. Damn her for forgetting him.

Fury came in a wave—hot, scalding, steaming rage. It coursed through his cold body, and he could feel his flesh growing warmer, inch by inch. Heat radiated from him. He kicked against the top of his small hollow in the earth. The ground compressed where his toe hit it. Some crumbled onto his leg.

What was happening? He didn't know. He'd tried to claw

his way out for more than a year and had not been able to dig through the earth. But the small hole in which he lay was getting hotter. The ice was melting. Water droplets gathered on the hard dirt above his eyes. One dripped free and landed on his lips.

He shoved outward with his arms. The dirt moved, let his fists punch into it. He was going to get out of here. If he had to dig his way out with his teeth, he was finally going to be free.

And go to Amelia.

Amelia grabbed a bunch of holly and went up the step stool, mindful of her hems. The fragrant scent of the shiny leaves surrounded her. Below her, two maids giggled. They held baskets of rosemary and bay, holly and twined branches of laurel.

She was supposed to make the drawing room look festive and lovely. But her mind was not on her work. She would be punished if she did not do a satisfactory job. Probably denied any of the hearty Christmas dinner and drink.

But she had almost had a proposal of marriage. Llewellyn Jones had gazed deep into her eyes and had told her he wanted to make her his wife. He intended to ask her, once she'd had time to recover from what she'd learned about Dante.

What would she say? What should she say? What did her heart beg her to say?

She didn't know.

Llewellyn had made the truth clear. If Dante was still alive, it was because he was a vampire. He was not really living; he was undead. He had no soul. He was not capable of love. He had turned into a monster. There was no future for her with Dante. If she refused Llewellyn because her heart still yearned for Dante, she would end up alone.

The way Llewellyn had touched her cheek had been so wonderfully gentle. The desire in his eyes had left her breathless. But that one night she'd shared in the cottage with Dante had been filled with magic. She did not think she would ever, ever forget it.

"Ah, the lovely Miss Watson," a masculine voice boomed beside her. She turned, shocked out of her thoughts, and stared down at one of the earl's friends, just as the leering gentleman put his hand on her bottom. Viscount St. Maur waggled his brows at her. He must be over forty.

Her stomach lurched. Many of the earl's friends believed she was like a holly berry, there to be plucked after a preliminary kiss.

"Please, my lord," she begged, as respectfully as she could. "I must have this greenery hung. The clock ticks toward Christmas Day."

"After your work," St. Maur murmured, lust blazing in his bleary blue eyes, "come to my bedchamber. I cannot think of a better gift for Christmas than your lovely tits and sweet little cunny."

She went scarlet. She knew it by the fire in her cheeks. She must be redder than the berries.

"Leave the lady to her work." The growl was Llewellyn's, filled with possessive warning. The slayer lowered his voice. "And if you approach her later, you'll find yourself hanging from the rafters like a bunch of mistletoe."

St. Maur stared at Llewellyn's muscular body, then quickly retreated to get another drink.

Her savior smiled up at her. Amelia's heart wobbled. A proposal of marriage—for her it was a Christmas miracle. Perhaps she had to stop dreaming of Dante and let herself fall in love again.

Amelia couldn't sleep.

She sat up on her narrow cot. When she had fallen from the position of governess to menial servant, she had been given a bed in the large, drafty attic room shared by all the female servants. One of the kitchen maids snored terribly.

But it wasn't the noise keeping her awake. It was thoughts of Dante. She wanted to believe it wasn't true. But Llewellyn had shown her the journals, books, and notes he had kept of his vampire hunting in the Carpathians. It was evidence, he claimed, of the existence of vampires. He had sketches and recordings of eyewitness accounts. It was his job as a vampire slayer, he had told her, to destroy as many vampires as he could. To protect mortals from the soulless creatures who saw them as nothing but prey and food.

Amelia got out of bed. She planned to go down to the gallery. Sometimes she crept there at night. Dante's picture hung there. She would stand in front of it, look up at it, and cry quietly in the dark. Sometimes she would daringly touch it, knowing it was foolish to caress a two-dimensional man, especially the image of one who had abandoned her.

But tonight, she wanted to go and look at him and try to force her heart to let him go.

She stole quietly down the servants' stairs, but at the landing to the second floor, her feet turned against her will and she walked out into the corridor. She could not control her legs. They carried her swiftly down the hall . . . to Dante's bedroom. The only sounds she made were fierce gasps of anger and panic. Why couldn't she stop?

She went into Dante's room. The bed was made with fresh sheets, which were turned back and welcoming. His clothes were still in the wardrobe. His mother had insisted the bedroom be kept ready for Dante, in case he returned. Amelia knew she should leave the room—she *wanted* to—but her feet took her to Dante's bed. Lifting the heavy counterpane, she slipped beneath the cool, white sheets.

Stop this. But she couldn't. Her head hit Dante's pillow. Then she knew nothing at all except darkness.

Well, almost nothing. At some point, she opened her eyes. Even wrapped in a cocoon of inky black, she knew she wasn't alone. Her heartbeat was a rush of sound in her ears. "Mr. Jones?" she asked tentatively. She didn't know why she thought it was Llewellyn—unless he was searching for something. If it was another servant, or the earl or countess, she would be in dire trouble for being in Dante's bed.

A floorboard creaked. Clothes rustled. She didn't hear breathing, but she did hear a subtle crunch, like knuckles being cracked.

"It is not Mr. Jones." Even as the masculine voice rumbled out that name, in tones filled with hurt and autocratic distaste, Amelia knew exactly who it was. Her heart did not beat for seconds.

"Dante?" Now her pulse returned in a dizzying, over-wrought surge. Her blood pumped so fast it made her light-headed. What was he? A vampire or a man? In the pitch-black, she couldn't see him.

Suddenly, a candle flared. It was on the bedside table, yet the footsteps had come from the foot of the bed. She blinked, as even that small circle of light flooded her eyes.

"Yes, it's me, angel."

The bed creaked and finally she could distinguish Dante's broad-shouldered form at the end of the bed. He sat, his hand clasped around the fluted column of the bed canopy. Unblinking, his face set as motionless as a statue, he stared at her.

"God," he said suddenly. "You look so pale. So much thinner. That nightgown, that cap on your head is threadbare."

"I am not a governess anymore," she said simply. "I am one of the maids. I was a ruined woman. I could not be allowed to be near children anymore. Your family intended to turn me out on the spot, with no wages or references. But in the end, they were compassionate and they let me—"

"Compassionate?" he roared. He was looked at her hands.

They were red and chapped, her skin dry and white and scaly. "You were to be my wife. They should have taken care of you."

"They hated me," she said. "They blamed me for making you go."

This wasn't what she'd imagined saying to Dante after five years. She'd had so many fantasies of his return. When she thought she had been abandoned, she'd envisioned facing him with cold pride. Perhaps slapping his handsome face. When she had hoped he'd been dragged away against his will, she had imagined throwing her arms around him, hugging him, kissing him. But now, wondering if he was a vampire, she was having this odd, cool, mad conversation.

Llewellyn had shown her pictures of vampires in his books. They were ghastly creatures. Men who no longer looked like men, with sunken eyes, and curved fangs, and bloodstained mouths. Dante looked exactly as he had when she had snuggled up to him in the cottage bed. Surely that must mean he wasn't a vampire. But that brought waves of both relief and pain. If he wasn't a vampire, it meant he had just deserted her.

Bother this. She was going to be *blunt*. "What happened to you that night?" she asked fiercely. "Why did you go?"

"I didn't go anywhere willingly. I was abducted and taken away."

"You vanished into thin air. The earl sent servants to check all the roads, to investigate at all the inns. They went to the Exeter ports and even to Plymouth, in case you had gone by ship. Or had been taken by ship. Your father searched ceaselessly for you for years. It was only this year that he gave up and stopped looking—"

"He never would have found me," Dante said. He got up off the bed and moved closer, into the circle of candlelight.

He was so beautiful—his hair was shimmering gold, and it fell around his face in long waves. A fallen angel. It had always been the perfect description for him. Beautiful as an angel, with a sensual, naughty side that had everything to do with devilment and nothing with piety. Then she blinked. His eyes weren't green. They reflected the candlelight back at her.

"How did you light the candle," she whispered, "from the end of the bed?"

"I walked from the candle to the bed."

"That's impossible. You couldn't have moved so quickly."

"I didn't leave you, Amelia. You have to know that. And I love you even more now than I did then." Suddenly, he was right beside her, looming over her. But she hadn't seen him move.

His hand closed on her wrist. He pulled her out of his bed and directly into his arms. She cried out in pain at his tight grip. He let her go, cursing.

"Tell me everything that happened to you," she demanded, clutching her sore wrist.

"I can't. On this you will have to trust me. I loved you then; I love you now."

"I need to know. After five years, I deserve to know."

"I cannot tell you," he roared.

He was shouting at her, refusing to give her what she so desperately needed. The *truth*. He had just hauled her out of his bed. He had almost crushed her wrist. What right did *he* have to treat her like this? "What is going to happen now? Did you come back to marry me? Or is that all gone now, in the past that you won't speak of?"

"I can't marry you." He bit off the words.

She recoiled. But again, he grabbed her by the arm—the elbow this time—and he drew her to him. She saw his mouth soften. She saw his gaze flick to the bed. "*No*," she snapped. "I'm not going to let you touch me."

"Five years," he said slowly. "Five years I fought to escape and come to you. Let me tell you this, Amelia Watson. You are not going to marry another man."

His eyes seemed to glow at her. It was as though a blaze of golden light had leaped from them and seared her heart. She wanted him. Her quim began to throb for him. She felt the wet, hot, weak sensation in her belly and legs. Lust washed over her.

He reached out and touched the base of her throat, where her pulse thundered.

His fingertips pressed to her skin, and a bolt of intense heat exploded there. It shot through her, raced down, down to the private place between her legs, and it exploded again. On a wild cry, she felt her body dissolve. The climax took her, shook her, made her legs crumple beneath her.

And while she was still coming, still moaning in pleasure, Dante scooped her up and carried her to the bed.

3

She was shuddering and moaning with ecstasy as he cradled her in his arms. And when a woman climaxed, she grew wet and smelled deliciously of her juices. Dante's vampiric senses flooded with Amelia's lush, erotic scent. His blood rushed down to his groin. His thick, rigid cock strained against his trousers.

But this was more than sex. This was Amelia. Just being so close to her again made his heart thunder with delight, excitement, and nerves. Five years ago, he'd felt all these mixed-up emotions every time he saw her—he'd been as awkward as a boy, as aroused as a man, happier than he'd ever been in his life. Eventually he'd understood what it meant. He had fallen in love.

"You're mine, Amelia, my love," he whispered. She buried her face into his chest, gasping for breath. He smiled down at her. Then regretted it when she tipped her face up and saw his curved fangs.

"Oh my heavens—"

"It's all right, Amelia." But it wasn't. Hell, how could it be when he used those fangs to consume blood? They had launched out as soon as he'd smelled her. But he could control his hunger. He had fed already tonight. Before his sire had imprisoned him, he had learned how to take only a small amount of blood, how to ensure he did not hurt his prey. "Mia," he murmured, and as he whispered the name to her, he knew how perfect it was. As soft and sweet as she was, as exotic and sensual as he knew she could be. It meant *mine*. "I would never hurt you."

Her lips thinned into a disapproving line. Never had she looked more like a governess. "I am not only thinking of *me*. You hurt other—"

"No, my love, I don't." He nuzzled her neck beneath her ear, and his heart clenched as she stiffened in fear. "Don't be afraid." It might not be playing fair, but he used the power of his voice to soothe her. He had been made by a vampire who possessed a strong ability to project a glamour. Those powers had passed to him. He had the ability to easily seduce prey against its will.

He had brought Mia to his room against her will. But he would not use his power to bed her. What he had to do was break through her fear. "If you have heard stories of vampires, I promise, none of them are true."

He carried her to his bed and deposited her onto it. How many nights had he lain here, five years ago, dreaming of her? He used to dream of bringing her to his room for the night and doing dozens of erotic things to her.

She rolled over abruptly and tried to crawl away. He grasped hold of her night rail to stop her and forgot his enhanced strength. He tore the thing right off her. She stopped in shock, gaping down in dismay, while he saw her bared rump, her swinging breasts, and licked his lips.

Maybe she had the powers of allurement too. Whatever it was, in the next moment, he was on his knees behind her, running his tongue over her curvaceous bottom.

She gave a horrified gasp. "Stop! Let me *go.*"

He caught hold of her slender right ankle and held her fast. The more she tried to escape, the more her voluptuous bottom jiggled against his questing tongue. He laved her curves all over, traced his way up to her tailbone and licked there, before he let his tongue dip into the hot, damp valley between her cheeks.

He couldn't stop. She could have screamed to the ceiling, and he would not have been able to lift his mouth from her dewy, naked skin. He never would have been able to step back and let her walk away.

"You are mine," he growled, and he gently nipped the cheek of her derriere as though branding her.

A moan escaped her. But not one of anger or fear. It was a sweet groan of pleasure.

"I did not desert you that night." He ran his tongue down the cleft of her bouncing bottom. She squeaked with shock and suddenly . . . giggled. She was losing her fear and perhaps her anger.

"Something drew me out of the cottage into the night," he told her. "My feet literally took me out into the woods against my will. And there, I was attacked by a vampire."

"That's how . . . how I came to your room. My feet brought me." Her words were labored. And when she half turned toward him, crouched on all fours, he saw her cheeks were pink. "The vampire didn't kill you . . . thank heavens."

He stopped licking long enough to wryly explain, "He didn't want a meal; he wanted a companion. And for some reason, he chose me." Then he gently parted her cheeks and planted a kiss to her puckered anus. Five years as a vampire had opened his world to new and intriguing erotic practices. He couldn't wait to share them with his Mia.

"Who . . . who was he?" The flush had darkened to scarlet and she bit her lip.

"You know, you look incredibly enticing this way," he said softly. And she did, with her full bottom in his face, her graceful legs splayed to support her. Wayward bits of hair were escaping her braid, and they glowed like strands of pure gold in the candlelight.

He gave her one more naughty kiss to her anus as he gently toyed with her cunny. Crisp curls tickled his fingers, and the lips themselves proved as plump and silky as he remembered. She was delightfully wet.

"He was two thousand years old," he said. "He had been an Egyptian king. And he was made into a vampire by a demon who was almost ten thousand years old—one of the first of human kind. Apparently, when they know their lineage, vampires are proud of it."

"Ten thousand years old! But that is not possible—"

"It is. I saw evidence that humankind has lived that long. Longer. Our stories of creation may not be quite as we believe. But that's enough talk for now. For this is a special night. It's Christmas Eve. I remember you told me once you felt it was a night filled with magic. For us, I want it to be a night filled with love." With that, he slid his tongue into the puckered entrance of her rump, past the tight ring of muscle that resisted his play. She moaned, squeaked, squealed. A dozen unique, erotic noises spilled off her lips. His tongue made her wet and slick. She'd bathed herself and she tasted clean, her skin sweet. Gently, he stroked her quim as he teased her bottom, until she panted heavily and her soft moans filled the room. When she dropped her face into one of his pillows to muffle her cries of pleasure, his heart began to thud faster. *Yes.* He wanted to make her come again. After five years apart, he yearned to be intimate again, to be close with her, to share.

"Oh, Dante! No!"

But she suddenly arched her bottom up, and he knew by her thrashing hips that she was coming hard. When she collapsed to the bed, he gave a low chuckle. If he made love to her enough, he could make five years vanish, couldn't he?

He left the bed and moved with his enhanced speed to his bedside table. A brandy decanter was there, and sometime in the last five years it had been refilled. He tipped it to his mouth, swished the liquor around, then swallowed. His fangs still protruded—when he was lusty, they came out and wouldn't retreat.

As best as he could, he hid them from Mia as he returned to her. Lying on her stomach, she clutched the covers. Her braid lay down the length of her slender back. Her skin glowed with sweat, and her bottom still blushed from his kisses and nips.

Gently, he rolled her onto her back. In a heartbeat, he stripped off his clothes. He got onto the bed, his legs splayed over hers, his chest just barely brushing her breasts. As a vampire, he had been introduced to an exotic carnal world. Yet he had never seen another woman as devastatingly lovely as Amelia.

She lifted to him, arching her hips to push against his groin. Needy, sweet little moans escaped her. "I shouldn't . . . but I can't seem to stop myself."

"I love you, my Christmas angel. I always will." He lowered his hips, and his cock nudged between her thighs. In a swift dance, they moved so her legs were wide and he was between them. Catching her mouth in a kiss, he thrust slowly inside her.

After five years of empty hell, he had heaven again.

It was wonderful. It was *devastating*. She wanted to resist him. He had vanished for five years; he was supposed to be *undead*, a monster who preyed on humans and drank blood. But she couldn't resist him. He looked like Dante, the man she had loved, the man she still wanted to love.

Amelia closed her eyes tight and wrapped her arms around his neck. As her fingertips touched warm flesh, guilt and uncertainty hit her for one instant, then flew away, like seeds vanishing on a breeze. He felt hot and beautiful. Against her breasts, his heart pounded in his chest. She let him kiss her; then some madness took hold of her, and she opened her mouth and pushed in her tongue to tangle with his. Like a wanton, she devoured his mouth. She licked him, tasted him, teased him— even thrust her tongue in and out in the same fast, wild rhythm he thrust into her.

Driven by desire beyond control, she arched her hips up to him, to greet every plunge of his hard cock. Her body took charge, yearning for pleasure, questing for release. She heard him grunt as her fingers gouged into him. But she had to hold him tight so she could lift her body to his and slide lusciously along his shaft.

Each thrust brought a collision between his solid, smooth groin and her most aching, throbbing place. Time after time, she received a jolt of sheer pleasure that made her wits whirl. She sought it. Needed it. She wrapped her legs around his waist to take him deep.

Oh, yes. She saw his eyes, an unearthly silvery green, light up as though on fire for her. Then her head lolled back on the bed, for she didn't have the strength to hold it up. She floated like a cloud buffeted about in the sky. All she could do was rise to him, feel the kiss against her most sensitive place, the long, sensual caress of his shaft.

He tipped his hips and drove into her harder. Plunged deeper. She answered with moans, with wildly pumping hips, scratching fingers, and sheer, utter desperation. She banged hard against him, clutching at the sheets as though clawing up a ladder that should take her to heaven.

Pleasure made her whole body curl up, except her fingers, which stretched wide. She sobbed, closed her eyes, and saw fireworks burst. The explosion took her and gave her heaven on earth.

She quivered and trembled and thrashed and wailed and knew only delight. Glorious, shining, miraculous delight. She laughed and could not quite believe she'd made the sound.

Dante kissed her; then he gasped harshly against her lips, his body went stiff, and his hips pushed hard to hers. She drank in his every grunt and groan of pleasure. Tears leaked to her cheeks.

He rolled off her, fell at her side. They lay, without touching, and she closed her eyes. But this time, as the pleasure ebbed away, she didn't doze off into a contented sleep the way she'd done five years ago.

She sat up and buried her face in her hands. What had she done? She had made love to him. True, she'd lost her innocence five years before, but she'd been promised marriage, and she'd given up her virginity in good faith. She could have tenuously dreamed of a future with a husband and a family. But not now. She could not argue she had been duped, or coerced, or forced. For a night of pleasure, she had given up everything. She'd burned her bridges with Mr. Jones.

And all for Dante. All for a man who might be a monster, or who might be lying to her. He had even told her, bluntly, that he couldn't marry her.

She'd wanted him with such madness she hadn't been able to stop herself. *Fool. Fool. Fool.* The word mocked her. She flayed herself with it, beating at her heart and her soul with rage she didn't even know how to express. Christmas had brought her a miracle—a man who wanted to marry her even knowing she had given herself to Dante five years before. And she had just taken that miracle and shattered it into a million pieces.

Tears rushed up. She shouldn't cry. She should go. Or better yet, she should demand that Dante marry her. But what would she get—a husband who was a vampire, who might kill her for his dinner? Or a man who had concocted an elaborate lie and who would abandon her again at the first chance he got?

Oh, dear God. The pure insanity of it hit her. Despite the tears that burned, she gave a wild, hysterical giggle. And that unleashed the waterworks. Sobs ravaged her so much, she had to bend over and hug her knees. The tears came and came.

But even an eternity of tears would not save a burning bridge.

He'd cheated death. He had been taken against his will to a deserted island in the Mediterranean. He had learned to sleep in a coffin and drink human blood. But nothing had hit Dante as hard as Amelia's tears. They took his heart and broke it in two.

He levered up in his bed, but his hands hovered over Amelia's shaking shoulders. Did he touch her? Would his touch help her?

What had made her so willing in his bed? While they were making love, he'd thought it was her desire for him. But her copious tears told him the truth—it was his glamour. She had made love with him but against her true will. Hades, he had never seen Mia cry before. He had wanted her with so much selfish desire, he hadn't thought about what he was doing.

"I'm sorry." Making a swift decision, he put his hands on her shoulders, then slid them down and pulled her into his embrace. "Do you regret what we just did?" What a damn fool question. But it had popped out before he could stop it.

She took a hiccuping breath. "I was an utter fool. You told me you wouldn't marry me. And now . . . Do you drink my blood now?" She pulled back and pushed her braid from her neck, baring it. "You might as well kill me, for I am too stupid to be left to live."

It was like a blade through his heart. "You aren't. The fault is mine. As a vampire, I have a special kind of allure. A glamour, I guess. It drew you to me; it made you desire me, whether you wanted to or not."

"And you . . . you knew this?"

"Yes. I wanted you so much, I didn't care." What was he going to do? Leave her and go where? He was supposed to live for eternity, and at this moment, he understood the full weight of that curse. A lifetime that lasted forever spent without the woman he loved. But he owed her one thing. "I said I wouldn't marry you. That's because I'm a vampire. I can't live a mortal's life. It's impossible." How many times had his sire explained that to him?

"But you came back—"

"To see you. To be with you. I couldn't resist you. And I will marry you." He tried to explain his intentions, his words a jumbled mess of incoherence, apology, hope. "I can't be a true husband to you. But this time, when I leave, I will make everyone believe I have died. That way, you will be given a settlement as my widow. You will have money, a home. You will be able to marry. To fall in love and have a true family." He could either fake his demise or, hell, he could stake his own heart or walk out into the sunlight and make her a widow in truth. But she would be taken care of.

"No. I don't want a sham marriage. I don't want to live a lie."

"Mia, I can't stay in this world. How long before people notice I don't age? For that's what happens to vampires. They never change. Ten years from now, I will still look the same. Even fifty years from now. How do we explain why I'm awake all night and sleep during the day—"

"Many peers do that," she pointed out.

His heart warmed at the display of her feisty nature. "True. Perhaps that wouldn't give me away. But something will. Eventually I'll make a mistake, and someone will guess the truth. Let me marry you. I love you, Mia, and I want to protect you. This is the only way I can do it."

She stared helplessly at him. He worked at her relentlessly. For an hour, he kept repeating it to her. He knew he was wearing her down. But he had to make her agree. Finally she whispered, "All right. Yes. I will do it. I'll marry you. So that you can leave me again, but at least this time I won't be a servant. And this time I'll know I have to stop loving you forever."

Christmas Day

It came with the sparkle of new snow. With the wonderful scent of the Yule log crackling in the great fireplace. It brought smells of roasting and baking from the kitchen, the grunts of men carrying barrels of ale, the giggles of the earl's children— Dante's brother and sisters—as they anticipated treats.

Amelia slid out of bed and hastened to dress. Since it was Christmas, she put on her best gown—one she had worn as a governess. Hopelessly out of date, she had managed to give it new trimming, for Lily, one of Dante's sisters, had given her some ribbon. There was no other reason, of course, that she spent more time than she should to braid, coil, and pin her hair. It was not because Dante would come to the house today, to make his "remarkable" return. He had spent a long time plotting exactly what he would do and what their story must be. He would arrive at the house at nightfall and make his family believe he had just returned from the Continent. He had concocted an elaborate story involving kidnapping and amnesia. Then he would marry her, giving her his name and a title. His courtesy title, as heir to an earldom, was Viscount Darby. Once she married him, she would be Viscountess Darby. She would have a very respectable settlement once she was "widowed." And after she had mourned him, she would be free to do whatever she wished. Even marry. No man would question her lack of innocence if she were a widow.

It was the perfect solution. A gift she could have never dreamed of.

Yet inside, she felt astonishingly hollow when she should be deliriously happy. She had been given a miracle. Dante was giving her hope. And she would have him for a few months, perhaps longer, before he chose to vanish forever.

Enough. She turned away from the small, cracked mirror that hung on the wall of her attic room. She hurried down the servants' stairs, opening the door on the main floor to the delights of Christmas Day.

Dante's three sisters ran through the hallways, giggling wildly, pursued by their brother and other young boys. Twenty-four people were visiting, and their happy laughter could be heard spilling from the rooms. The house smelled of rich smoke and of the crisp, woodsy scent of all the greenery. Silken bows and gold paper decorations, created with enthusiasm by the girls, hung all about.

Amelia hurried to the great hall of the house, and there she felt a waft of cold air. The door stood open, the guests were gathered, and a group of red-cheeked wassailers sung outside on the wide front stoop, hoping to be invited in for food and drink, to be given a few coins.

Out of the corner of her eye, Amelia saw the countess stare at her, sweeping her haughty gaze over Amelia's good gown and her neat appearance. Normally she wore plain brown, with her hair tucked beneath a maid's cap. The countess's eyes narrowed and glared, making the elegant woman look like one of Macbeth's witches. But it was Christmas, a time of charity, a time of goodwill, so she should not think severe thoughts of the countess now. She curtsied, then hastened to the kitchen. Various local people would be coming—for Christmas Day, all were invited to partake in a meal, and the cook and kitchen maids would need help.

Work would keep her from thinking. From imagining the fury of Dante's parents when he insisted on marrying her. From how horrible it would be to marry him, knowing it couldn't last longer than a few months.

The day passed swiftly in good spirits and laughter. It did bring joy to give food to those who had to make do with so little. Amelia had fashioned toys from rags for those children. It twisted her heart to see the beaming smile on a little girl's face as she hugged her new doll to her heart.

And when the door opened to let two families leave into the winter cold, Amelia saw the sun had gone down and twilight had fallen. Her heart stuttered and her fingers trembled. Any minute now . . .

She left the kitchen, then took the stairs to the main hall. Her hands were shaking as they lifted her hems. Any moment . . .

She opened the door and stepped out into one of the paneled corridors, only a few feet from the entrance hall. Suddenly, the door opened, and snow whirled in.

Out of the glittering, frosty gust stepped Dante, hidden at first by a beaver hat pulled low and the high collar of his coat. He doffed his hat, drew off his gloves, and handed them to an astonished footman, as though he had just stepped out for a few hours and had not disappeared for five years. He swung off his greatcoat and deposited this into the hands of another amazed servant.

"My . . . my lord," the man sputtered. "Lord Dante!"

"Indeed it is. And where might my family be?"

Then he looked up, saw her, and smiled. A grin that flashed his fangs. He adopted a more serious expression instantly, and she saw he was taking care to hide his teeth.

"Th-this way, your . . . your lordship," the servant stuttered.

Come, Amelia. Come to the blue drawing room where my family is. I will have to do the pretty and give my mother hugs and try to avoid their questions. I need you to be there. Mia, I don't want to be without you for another minute.

She could hear him speak . . . in her thoughts. Had she dreamed it? But he crooked his finger, winked, then followed the footman. How did he know his family was in the blue drawing room? The servant had not said where they were.

She followed, staying far back. No matter what he said, she did not think she had the right to intrude. His family would be so happy. For them, this would be a miracle.

Just before they reached the drawing room, the butler, Rimple, hurried forward and intercepted them. He bowed to Dante, clasped his hands together in a most un-Rimple-like way, then brushed away a tear. "It is so wonderful to have you return, Lord Dante. Allow me to lead you in to your family."

For Rimple, this was being overcome with emotion. Amelia savored the spurt of delight she felt. It was wonderful to see the happiness on the other servants' faces. But it was swiftly swamped with sorrow. This was only temporary. Dante had made it clear he would leave again, this time leaving no doubt about his "death."

Amelia stood in the doorway as Dante walked in. She saw the paralyzed moment when he called a greeting to his parents, wearing a grin, and they froze in shock. His father had been standing at the window, talking with another earl. His mother stopped in motion, halfway off the settee.

Dante strode forward. Amelia was amazed by his confidence, given how much he had to hide. He gathered his mother in an embrace. Then released her and bowed to his father.

The elderly man moved forward, as though to embrace his son. Then stopped. "No," he said with vehemence. "This will not do. Where in the name of God have you been, son? How can you saunter in here with that obnoxious smile on your lips, when we have spent five years of hell searching for you?"

Ladies gasped at the strong language, but all the guests stared. Amelia stared, too, but only at Dante. How his hair gleamed in the light of the fire. If anything, he looked even more like a Greek god than she remembered, with his strong jaw, the slight cleft in his chin, the aquiline nose, the perfectly sculpted lips. His long lashes, surprisingly dark for a fair-haired gentleman, swept over his eyes. For a moment, his expression hardened and she could imagine he was remembering the old battles he'd had with his father.

She wanted to lurch forward and touch his arm and remind him of the pain his parents had endured. But he suddenly looked contrite and grim.

"Agreed, Father. You deserve an explanation. Let me begin by saying my disappearance was not deliberate or intended in any way. If I caused you pain, I am sorry." With that, Dante launched into his prepared story. He told his family and friends that two burly men had kidnapped him, intending to take him for ransom. They'd hauled him to Exeter, and there he'd escaped and been captured by a press-gang. He'd bribed his way out of forced service on a ship when he made the captain believe his tale about being a kidnapped lord. But he had been left in the Mediterranean. He had made his way north, had encountered thieves, and the attack robbed him of his memory.

Amelia knew none of the story was true, but Dante's ability to charm won the day. His family believed him. His mother and several other women wept into handkerchiefs.

"It took years for me to regain my memory," he explained. "And there is one very important reason why I fought to return home. Someone who haunted me even when I couldn't remember my own name. Love, it seems, has a way of ensuring it is never forgotten."

His mother hastened to him and suddenly grabbed his arm, clinging to him. She glowed at him. His father had always despised him; his mother adored him.

Dante patted his mother's hand, then lifted his head, and his gaze sliced across the room and speared Amelia where she stood. His eyes glittered, reflecting the candlelight, looking unearthly and silver, and she prayed no one saw. That thought kept her rooted where she stood as he came to her.

Then he dropped to one knee and clasped her hand. Wearing a smile that could melt a woman's heart, melt her knees, dissolve any sense she had in her head, he lifted her hand and kissed it. "I came back for Amelia. The woman who is to be my wife."

4

Dante watched as his father stalked toward him.

"Preposterous," the earl barked.

Five years had not changed his father's imposing, barrel-chested build, his disapproving expression, or his piercing agate-green eyes, though it had turned his hair and enormous sideburns gray.

"Impossible," gasped his mother, slanting a look to Amelia that should have frozen his bride-to-be to ice on the spot.

To Dante's delight, his Mia did not look cowed. Her head remained high, her face set in her controlled, governess-like expression.

"Not impossible," Dante countered. He kissed Mia's hand once more and jumped to his feet. "Without my memory of Amelia, without the strength of my love for her calling me home, I doubt I ever would have found my way."

"Poppycock!" his father roared.

"It's not. I intend to marry her as soon as I can acquire a special license. I'd hoped for a happier reunion, Father. Unfortunately, it appears I've disappointed you again. But I will not disappoint Amelia."

A subtle movement in the corner of his eye caught his attention. He turned toward a dark-haired man who lingered by the door frame, glowering. This had to be the man who had tried to take Amelia away from him. He snarled, careful not to show his fangs. He wrapped his arm possessively around his lady's slim waist.

The man's thoughts suddenly launched into his head, even though he had not drawn them out. It was as though this gentleman had sent them. *I know what you are, vampire. You can't have her. You have nothing to offer her. I will destroy you. I know you've been hunting around here. What do you think Amelia will do when she finds out that you have drunk the blood of pretty village maidens and seduced them while you did it?*

Dante recoiled, his gaze locked on the man's blue eyes. He sent a message of his own. *Who in the hell are you? What are you talking about? I haven't touched a village maiden.*

My name is Llewellyn Jones, the man responded, unblinking. *A vampire slayer. And the man who will stake you, marry Amelia, and make her happy.*

Dante lifted a brow. *I'd like to see you try,* he snarled back in his thoughts.

Amelia was going to be his bride. There was nothing the vampire slayer could do to stop it—other than catching him by surprise and staking him. Dante's first problem was the prospect of acquiring a special license from a bishop and having his wedding in a church. Could a vampire go on such hallowed ground? He wasn't sure.

After that . . . he was forcing Amelia to become his wife to give her the protection of his name, and she had reluctantly accepted. How did he make her happier about the prospect of a hasty wedding? He could think of one way. A delightfully carnal way . . .

*   *   *

After an immense Christmas dinner that included roast beef and many mincemeat pies, the guests retired to the largest drawing room. There, a game of Snapdragon had been set up. Raisins had been soaked in brandy in an enormous shallow bowl. Footmen hastened to put out the lights, and then a servant ignited the brandy in the dish.

Flames flew up and the heat warmed Amelia's cheeks. Snapdragon had always seemed like a mad game—the point was to grasp a raisin and eat it without getting burned.

The golden glow from the bowl illuminated the laughing guests as they gathered. Amelia glanced at Dante, who stood in the shadow. He leaned against the wall, staring at her. Staring at her as though she were a treat to be devoured. The thought made her tremble with desire and with uncertainty. He had told her he would never hurt her. Could she believe him? She wanted to. So very much. She also noticed he had not eaten any of the food at dinner.

One after another, the guests tried to snatch a flaming raisin from the bowl. There was much good-natured wagering, shrieks of laughter, and frantic hand waving as people tried and failed. Then Dante moved forward. He slowly lowered his hand into the bowl. He took his time to choose, while flames licked at his hand, while the gentlemen exclaimed in shock and the ladies squealed. With lazy relaxation, he plucked a raisin and held it up between thumb and forefinger, despite the fact it was on fire. He popped it into his mouth and swallowed.

Of course he wasn't afraid. He was immortal. But he left the crowd in stunned shock. They all gaped at him as he walked away from the bowl and sauntered toward her. At his command, she had been elevated from position as servant. She was now known as his fiancée.

He clasped her elbow. "Come with me, love, while they are

all preoccupied, waiting to see who burns his tongue or sets fire to his coat."

She couldn't help but laugh. It was true that this game seemed to appeal to the gentlemen who had drunk copious amounts of liquor at dinner. "Where are we going?"

"A surprise, my love."

He led her down the winding hallways of the house to the gallery, where two footmen waited. One helped Dante into his greatcoat, and as she watched, she suddenly realized another was draping a cloak on her. A cloak lined with glossy black sable, heavy, luxurious, and warm. She was given a pair of fur-trimmed gloves and a thick muff for warming her hands. She stared up questioningly, and Dante said, "A gift for you." When he took her outside and she demanded to know what he planned, he smiled and whispered one word. *Patience.*

A path had been cut through the deep snow, crossing the lawns to the stone stables. The air was crisp and cold. Her boot soles squeaked on the hard snow; her breath cast crystal patterns in the air. The night was too clear and cold for snow, and the black sky above was filled with glinting stars. Ahead, bells jingled and the sweet melody danced through the night air. Dante clasped her wrist and hurried her steps. She rounded the stables and saw a white sleigh waiting for them. Warm blankets were stacked inside, and four snow-white horses pawed at the frozen ground. It was like something from a fairy tale.

"Your chariot." Dante grinned.

As he handed her up, she cried, "I have to know! Where are we going?"

"Our wedding night in the cottage ended in disaster. This time we are going to have a private night of pleasure and nothing will go wrong."

* * *

Soon, Dante brought the sleigh to a stop in front of an elegant manor house that blazed with welcoming light. Icicles hung from the eves, reflecting the glow from the windows.

"It's lovely," Amelia breathed. "Is this house all for us, for one night of sin?"

"Not quite."

He was driving her mad—not just with his teasing, but also with anticipation. Amelia had never known desire could ache so much. She wanted him so fiercely she was indecently wet between her legs. Her nipples were aroused to hard points, and each brush against her shift made her whimper. She was determined to play her own game and pretend his torturous teasing didn't bother her at all.

An impassive servant took her cloak, gloves, fur muff, and Dante's gloves and greatcoat. Then Dante winked. "Come and see how Christmas should be enjoyed."

He cupped her elbow and drew her to a parlor. The most amazing scene met her startled gaze. There was a large group of handsome young men. They were all naked. Completely nude. Amelia had never seen so many bare masculine derrieres and wobbling, erect penises in her life. Well, actually she had seen only Dante's. There were women, too. Beautiful, voluptuous, bare women copulating with the men in a large group. Which meant everywhere she looked, her startled gaze fastened on bouncing nipples and jiggling breasts.

"A Christmas orgy," Dante explained. "Much hotter and more entertaining than Snapdragon."

She glanced at him, too dumbfounded to say a word. His silvery green eyes sparkled like fresh snow, but he looked utterly serious . . . until his lips twitched. Then she gave in to giggles. For the scene before her looked sensual, shocking, mad, and . . . funny. Though her face was flaming, she couldn't help but look and try to determine exactly which man was making love to which woman. In the tangle of limbs, though, it was impossible to know. Heavens, one woman had two men making love to her. The lady was sandwiched between them, and the men's hips thrust vigorously against her. There was one man who had so many women on top that Amelia could barely see him. One woman rode him, one bounced on his face, two flicked tongues over his bronze nipples, and one seemed to be . . . playing with his bottom.

"Did you want to . . ." Her voice was a mere squeak. "Join them?"

"No, love. Come with me."

She stumbled after him up a set of stairs, then to a door at the end of the hallway. Her corset felt like a squeezing band, her heart raced faster than horses at the Newmarket races, and she had gone beyond hot and wet. She felt molten between her legs.

Limned with silver moonlight, Dante drew out a key and fit it into the lock.

"What is this room?" she asked, not expecting an answer.

"A private room I kept here," he said, surprising her. "Even though I was gone for so long, I had paid a small fortune for its use and they preserved it for me. Only I have the key to this lock."

He pushed open the door and led her inside. It appeared to be an ordinary bedroom, though the bed was a large concoction of dark-stained wood and gilt. Dante crossed to the vanity, where a bottle of brandy and glasses sat on a silver tray. Grinning, he lifted the bottle to his lips and swallowed.

She stared. There was something sensual in the cavalier way he drank. He wiped his mouth, still smiling. "Pear brandy. I wanted to give you gifts, love. But I want them to be presents that bring you pleasure. For the first day of Christmas, a bottle of pear-flavored brandy."

Instead of a partridge and a pear tree as in the song "The

Twelve Days of Christmas"? Her father had an old publication of the words and she'd read them as a child.

Dante brought the bottle to her. "Take a sip."

"I saw you swallow the raisin, and now you are drinking brandy. If you can eat and drink, can't you survive without blood?" She asked it desperately. Hopefully.

"No, love. I can drink and eat a little, but I need blood."

She bit her lip, then she drank, lifting the bottle to her lips as he had done. She let the liquor burn down her throat, tasting pears and fire. It was mad—she had just seen an orgy, and still it felt decadent to drink brandy straight from the bottle. But she had to ask him, as much as she didn't want to know, "Who did you bring to this room?"

"I intended to bring you here, but I never had the courage. I've never used it. It has waited for us for five years. Waited for me to have the chance to show you how much I love you." He took the bottle and set it down. "I want to make this marriage good for you, Mia. What's your most secret sexual fantasy, love? What do you dream of, think of, that you would never admit to anyone, not even me?"

"Oh . . . oh . . . er . . ."

"I saw you give gifts to the children. Would you give this to me, as my gift?"

Her blush deepened. Her cheeks felt like fire. "I don't know. I cannot say. It's far too embarrassing—"

"I could try guessing." He began to undress her. When he opened her gown and drew the bodice down from her chest and off her arms, he touched her wrist. He traced a circle around it. "Do you ever dream of being tied up?"

She gasped. She *had* thought of it but couldn't admit it. When she used to desire Dante and thought she, as an ordinary governess, would never catch his eye, she used to dream of what she would do if he suddenly wanted her, wanted her so desperately he ravished her. She knew she wouldn't want to be forced in reality. But in fantasies, it seemed naughty and enticing.

Somehow he had looked into her face and had known. . . .

"It's natural, Mia, and something that arouses many people." He spoke so calmly, she didn't feel so tense and embarrassed. "It allows a woman to fantasize about enjoying wild sex with a man when she knows she isn't supposed to be willing. Would you like to try it?"

"But what would you think of me?"

"I would think that I adore you completely, my soon-to-be darling wife."

"What would we use? There's no rope in here."

He laughed, and she flushed again, realizing how swiftly she'd gone from reluctance to practicality. She'd revealed how wanton she secretly was. But he only looked pleased. He moved to the bedpost, untied something, and suddenly a half dozen lengths of black silk rope fell to the bed. "There, Mia. Rope."

"Wh-what are you going to do?"

"Normally, a woman lies on the bed and her wrists and ankles would be bound, securing her to the bedposts." His voice was a deep, throaty growl.

A shiver tumbled down her spine at what she pictured. She imagined being naked on the bed, with black rope looped around her wrists, her arms secured above her head, her legs spread wide. What would it be like to be his prisoner, to be served up for his carnal pleasure? Heat rushed through her. The aching need heightened between her legs. "B-but we aren't going to do that?"

At the shake of his head, she should have felt relieved. Instead, she felt she had been given a Christmas gift, then had it taken away. "Then what are we going to do?"

"I would like to try something new." His arms encircled her and he undid her corset. He peeled it off her, then whisked off her chemise. She was nude except for her stockings and garters. And her half boots. He looked down at those, smiled, and bent. In a blink of an eye, he'd removed them. She managed to fit in two blinks while he stripped naked. Her gaze dropped—she couldn't help it. She'd always hated gentlemen who stared at women's breasts. Now here she was, mesmerized by the rigid curve of Dante's erection, by the way it swayed, by the glistening moisture gathering at the tip. Curiosity, desire . . . both guided her fingers to stroke the taut head. It bobbed in response.

Softness tickled the sensitive skin of her wrist—he'd tied one of the black ropes around it. Then, with deft motions, he looped the rope around his left hand and bound their hands together. His eyes reflected candlelight, blazing gold.

"You're going to tie us together?"

"I'm thinking." He grinned. "What makes bondage so arousing is the surrender. If I tie you up, you have to surrender to my every desire. You have to trust me."

Just the words made her melt. And the more she felt like flowing honey, like hot cream, between her legs, the harder he got. His erection kept lifting upward, thickening, straightening.

"Bondage?"

"A term to describe these games. Being tied up with ropes, or scarves, or shackles and irons. If we're both tied up, we're surrendering to each other."

"I don't know," she began, but he lifted her into his arms. Clamping his palm to her bare bottom, he carried her to the bed. Their wrists were tied together—a symbol, she thought, of the union they were about to undertake. A marriage of convenience. Tied together, but not really joined. Perhaps it was the Christmas wine, but she felt a sudden yearning for more than just wrists tied together. She twined her fingers with his. She stretched up and licked the skin of his neck. He tasted so rich, so much more decadent than chocolate.

They tumbled to the bed. His chest moved against hers as his silky laughter filled the room. He bent down, twisting his body in impossible ways to tie their ankles together. Then he parted his legs, which forced her legs to spread wide as well. His erection pressed to her belly. Fluid dribbled, tickling her skin. His bollocks brushed the sensitive place between her nether lips, where the little bump, her clit, was nestled. Amelia squeaked in pleasure and shock.

"My cock aches to be inside you. I want to bind us together so I can stay in you forever," he whispered. "It feels so . . . perfect."

She ached, too. It was true—it felt right when they were joined, making love. It was a way she wanted to feel forever. She arched and wriggled both her feet, savoring the way they were trapped. His hips shifted and the head of his cock nudged between her nether lips. Her juices made her slick and wet. He slid in, just a few inches. The thick shaft stretched her enough to make her gasp with surprise, awareness, pleasure.

He kissed her lips, then bent and kissed her nipples. He worked so diligently from right nipple to left that she giggled and moaned helplessly. The deep suction of his mouth sent shockingly wonderful pleasure through her. As if by magic, he drew her nipples to the tallest, thickest, most sensitive points they had ever been. She curved like a bow, lifting to him, pressing against their bound hands and wrists. "Oh, please . . . more," she gasped.

His tongue traced lazy circles around her right nipple, then flicked over the sensitive tip. "Oooh," she moaned. She watched as his tongue plied her nipple in various ways, leaving it tingling and blushing. Then he turned his attention to the left. Each suckle gave a soft, urgent tug in her belly. A tug of delight and need.

He nuzzled and licked her nipples as she tried to lift toward him, tried to take him deeper inside. But he kept teasing her, not letting her have more than the tip of his thick shaft. Yet just his sucking alone was amazing. The tugs deepened. They pulsed. They became stronger, harder, and a powerful tension wound up within her. She was reaching the brink of release.

"Yes," she cried. She wanted him to know how good it was. So he wouldn't stop. He thrust deep into her, and just that one slick glide in her sensitive, throbbing, tingling quim made her burst. Stars exploded in flares of white fire. She had to shut her eyes. She bounced madly beneath him. Pleasure washed over her, danced with her, surrounded and filled her. Until she could no longer moan. Until all she could do was sob in delight.

She floated in the aftermath, falling back to the bed like a feather wafting down to a field. Dante gave a gruff laugh, one filled with pride. She giggled in return.

"We're not done yet, Mia," he murmured. "We can still have much fun." As he withdrew, she saw why. She had exploded in a climax, but he was still stiff, aroused, and ready for more. Her juices had left his cock shiny and wet. With a slice of his fangs, he broke the bonds at their wrists, then released their ankles.

More. Yes, she wanted more. This was their private world, warmed by a cheery, crackling fire. Their private, wonderful place where they could indulge every desire, explore every sin.

Even though she was no longer tied to him, she twined her body around his, her arms tight around his broad back. He chuckled low in his throat and caught hold of her hands. Goodness, he moved swiftly. He twined another rope around her wrists and tied her to one of the bedposts.

"Not all that original, love, but fun all the same."

He lowered between her spread legs. A subtle twitch of his hips and his cock surged in again. He drove into her, then withdrew and shifted, so his lovely, long erection slipped between the cheeks of her bottom. He stroked in and out in the valley between her plump cheeks, then slid back inside her wet, eager cunny. Over and over, he teased her this way, making her moan and squeal.

He caught hold of her right leg and turned her so her legs fell open like scissors. He pounded deeply, so deeply she could only whimper. She could only lie on the bed, since her hands were bound, and take every delicious thrust. He pounded into her and she moaned, urging him on. She was on the brink of something amazing. Beyond any pleasure . . . beyond speaking or gasping . . . all she could do was float with him as his hips lifted her, as he claimed her.

Then a scream of delight exploded into the room. Many wild, untamed screams. *Her* screams. And Dante's soft laughter—somehow over her frantic cries, she heard the low, sensual sound. He was chuckling at her as she went mad with pleasure.

"Come too," she whispered.

"No, love, I want to last—"

"No, please. Join me."

As if those words held their own secret power, she felt him tense above her. He let out a roar like a panther, drove deep, and his hips bucked wildly. "God, yes," he growled.

Dante floated. He was undead, and he would never know a real heaven, but lying on a soft bed after such a powerful orgasm felt close. He rolled over to cradle Mia, but she wasn't there. Bewildered, he sat up. She had scuttled away from him, and she was sitting up, too, her arms wrapped around her knees.

She stared into the shadows, her lips wobbling, her eyes empty and hurt. Then she looked up at him, and her anguish almost ripped his heart from his chest.

"Why do you need this so badly?" she whispered. "Why do you want to coax out my love? Why is it so important to you to think I'm happy?"

He bowed his head.

"In truth, wouldn't it be better if we dislike each other?" she asked. "If we were to bicker and fight all the time? Wouldn't that make it far easier for you to leave? Winning my love may ease your conscience now, but how much pain will it cause us both months from now, when you decide it's time to go?"

"I don't want months of hatred between us." He knew it wasn't much of an answer, but it was the truth. As for her other questions . . . he couldn't contemplate how he would feel when he left. Angry. Bitter. Dejected, furious, wounded, and pained beyond belief. To become a vampire, he had gone to the brink of death. He suspected that would be like attending a picnic compared to the agony of leaving Mia.

"It's more than just my conscience," he said. "You deserve to know how much I love you. You might hate me for leaving, but you'll know, at least, how much pain I will be in."

"There are more than just your feelings involved in this." She got off the bed and walked, naked, to the window. Mia possessed a perfect hourglass shape, lovely shoulders, a neat waist, and a generous flare of hips.

She pulled open the drapes. Moonlight fell upon the white snow. Dante felt the instinctive hunger only a vampire would at the sight of a dark night and a plump moon. He wanted to shift shape into bat form and fly. He wanted to hunt and feed. To deny it was physical agony that surged through his veins. He had to grit his teeth to keep from howling. But he welcomed the pain at this moment.

Mia turned to him, her hair a rippling wave of gold, her eyes flashing with pain. "It's hopeless! Even though I *know* you are going to leave me, all I want to do is get back into bed with you and beg you for more. If you make me yearn for you like this, how will I bear it when you've gone?"

5

On the second day of Christmas, my true love gave to me . . .
Two turtledove feathers to tickle every inch of my naked skin.

Amelia reread the note left on the pillow beside her while she'd slept. Two long white feathers had lain beside it. She quivered as though Dante were already tickling her. Of course he had not answered her question last night. *How will I bear it when you've gone?*

It had been an idiotic thing to ask. She knew exactly what she would feel when he left her, this time for good. She would hurt. She would yearn. She would cry and mourn all over again. Last night, she'd learned nothing would change his resolve. Not anger. Not hurt. Not pretending they could somehow make a marriage work. He had told her he would marry her, but he would not stay. It was as simple as that.

Amelia picked up one feather and drew it across her cheek. She shut her eyes, imagining running the firm tip along Dante's naked back, tracing the remarkable planes of his muscles, then swooping down his spine and stroking the firm curves of his naked arse. She could caress his erect cock. She would like to tease every inch of him, too.

It was daylight—far later in the morning than she had been

allowed to awaken when she was a downstairs maid. Dante would be sleeping now. He had told her he would leave the house for the day and return at dusk, since he slept during the day and could not be exposed to daylight.

Amelia got out of bed and dressed. She didn't relish facing the earl and countess again today. Thank heaven for Christmas guests. Lady Matlock was too refined to make scenes in front of friends and relatives. Since nighttime seemed an eternity away, Amelia donned a cloak and went to the kitchen. She took a piece of cheese and a hunk of fresh bread for her breakfast and ate it as she went outside and walked away from the house.

She was in the woods, dusting the crumbs from her gloves, when she heard a strange sound. A pained grunting. Her heart was a roar in her ears as she crept forward. It could be a trapped animal, and it would be foolhardy to approach. But if it was a creature in pain, she could alert the steward. What terrified her more was the fear it was Dante.

It was a gray-haired man, on his hands and knees in the snow. The trail behind him revealed he had crawled this way for yards, and the smooth white drifts were speckled with blood drops. She gasped as he weakly looked up at her, pale as a ghost, his body shaking. It was the head groom, Thompson. A strapping man of fifty who was normally as strong as an ox.

She hurried to the poor man and crouched by him. "What happened? Were you attacked by an animal? Where are you hurt?"

"Miss Watson . . . help me," he croaked. His lips were purplish blue, his skin as pale as parchment.

She offered her arm to help him stand. He leaned heavily on her and quivered like a leaf in a storm. "Thank ye . . . I were attacked . . . but it were . . . no animal."

"A person did this to you?" she asked, horrified. "Was it someone known to you?"

"Stranger . . . miss . . . not human . . ."

Amelia stopped, aware of the creaking of ice-coated tree branches in the stillness, the loud drum of her heart. "What do you mean 'not human'? What happened, Thompson? You must tell me everything." His shaky hand went to his neck. There were two small bruises on his throat. No, the tiny dark marks were . . . *punctures*. Dear God.

She helped Thompson limp toward the house, but she had a horrible thought. Should she take him back? Would he reveal the truth about Dante? In that instant, she made a choice. She *had* to help this man, even if it meant the household discovered Dante was a vampire. She could not turn her back on someone who needed her help.

As they got closer to the house, Thompson gained more strength. "I were up before light, miss . . . grooming the horses. Heard a sound . . . in the woods. Had . . . to go . . . couldn't stop. A man grabbed me. He . . . had a black cloak . . . hood pulled low. He was so strong . . . dragged me to the snow and sank his teeth into my neck . . . fangs like a wolf. He drank . . . my blood."

"And you . . . you . . ." She stumbled over the question. Surely he would have said if he knew it was Dante. "Did you recognize him? Did you know him?"

"No . . . heard tales . . . from the village. There are demons . . . soulless monsters . . . in the woods. The undead. Vampires."

"Thompson, that can't be possible!" she said firmly, praying she sounded believable. But she felt sick with horror. Was it Dante? Had he attacked the groom?

"It wasn't me, love. I promise you it wasn't. But you were correct—it was a vampire."

Dante was sprawled naked on the bed at the house known as the House of Pleasure. He held the feathers, waiting for her to join him. But Amelia couldn't. She was too afraid. Afraid she would have to face the truth of what he was. Thompson had recovered, but she was frightened.

She crossed her arms over her naked bosom, pacing by the foot of the bed. "It was a vampire, but not you. Who, then? There are more vampires here? I—" *I cannot believe it. I think you are lying.* She couldn't say the words, but they stabbed at her heart.

"I believe it was the vampire who made me five years ago. My sire. He buried me here a year ago. He fashioned a grave for me underground, using earth and the magic he possessed. He imprisoned me." Dante held out his hand. Relief made her knees as wobbly as jelly. She went to him, kneeling on the soft mattress at his side.

"Lie down, Mia," he murmured.

She did, but whispered, "Why did he come back?"

"I don't know." He got up on his knees, his face serious. Worried. He managed to smile, yet she could see he was still troubled. "It's the truth, Mia. I didn't hurt Thompson. Nor did I attack any of the young women in the village who have been reputedly fed upon by a vampire."

The feather skimmed over her breasts, making her tremble. She had to close her eyes as he traced her breasts. She gasped as he used both feathers and flicked them back and forth over her nipples. While he did that, he lowered to his knees and mercilessly licked her clit. Her exploding climax made her scream. He lifted her, laughing, tossed the feathers aside, and carried her off the bed. He lowered them both to the Aubusson carpet. Weakly, she wrapped her arms and legs around him and came again and again as he thrust his cock inside her.

Finally, spent, exhausted, delirious with pleasure, she fell back on the rug. "But . . . but why did he put you in a prison? If he made you, why would he do such a thing to you?"

Dante's eyes reflected the firelight at her, glowing like gold sovereigns. "Can't you guess, love? He wanted a companion. A man to join him in his pursuit of erotic pleasure. Not only did he want us to share women together and go to orgies, he wanted us to be lovers."

Her mouth dropped open in shock.

"Vampires, I discovered, make love freely with both genders. It doesn't matter to them. They enjoy sex for its own sake."

"Did you . . . have sex with him? With other men?"

He ducked his head, looking so vulnerable and wounded her heart lurched in sympathy.

"But I loved you, Mia. I craved you. That was what made my sire angry enough to lock me in a frozen, underground tomb. He hungered for me, but I wanted only you."

He gazed at her beneath lowered lashes, with a shyness that filled her with love. How could she ever part from this man? Yet there was no point in speaking of that. "What was it like?" she whispered, so quietly she doubted he could hear. But he lifted his head, brows arched in surprise.

"What was what like, love?"

A blush flamed over Amelia's skin. "Making love with other men."

The blunt question stunned Dante. He'd thought she would be shocked, appalled, disgusted. Instead, she was scarlet, but obviously waiting, eyes wide, for his answer. Apparently the thought intrigued her—her nipples were two prominent points beneath the silk of her nightdress.

He rolled onto his side and propped his hand against head. He held the feathers, but she plucked one from his grasp. Shyly, she stroked it across his bare chest, drawing swirls around his erect nipples, just as he'd done to her. "Would you tell me?"

"It excites you. I can tell." It was not just the sight of straining nipples or the sultry but uncertain gaze of her heavy-lidded eyes. He could smell the lush wetness of her quim. "Can you guess how men make love?"

Amelia shook her head.

"Men use their hands—jerking each other's cocks vigorously. When men are lovers, they enjoy sucking and licking each other's pricks. A man likes to suck hard on the taut head, drawing the shaft deeply down his throat. Men are competitive by nature. Two men having sex will turn it into a carnal battle, a challenge to see which will make the other come first."

Her blush washed over her body. Her hand strayed down, stroking her clit between soft nether curls. His breath caught as he watched her instinctively arousing herself.

"Of course, the ultimate pleasure for male lovers is sodomy. To bury a cock in a man's tight, hot arse. The grip is remarkably snug, since the muscles of a man's buttocks are so strong."

"And you . . . you did that?"

"When I first became a vampire, I was remarkably randy. I craved sex every moment while I was awake. And I thought you were lost to me forever."

He told her everything, revealing all the things he thought he would never say, not to the woman he loved. "I don't remember very much about the night I was transformed. I remember sweeping you into my arms and carrying you through the snow to the cottage. I will never forget making love to you beneath the fur throws. The sound of your soft breathing as you slept in my arms . . . that I could never forget. For the year I was imprisoned in the ground, I would dream I was back in the cottage with you, and you were sleeping beside me."

He didn't remember the moment of being bitten, and afterward he had lost consciousness. Sometime later, he'd awoken, to find he was lying on a sumptuous bed, shackled hand and foot. He had been dressed, but he'd seen a difference in his skin—it was paler. His muscles had felt strange. He'd sensed a new strength to them, even though he could not use them and could not break free of his chains. Hunger had rushed through him. But it wasn't the growling, gut-gnawing hunger for food. It was a craving that seemed to flow through his very arteries and veins. Suddenly he became aware of so much more beyond the bed and imprisonment. The room in which he was a captive was magnificent—silk hangings on the walls, along with enormous oil paintings done by Italian masters. Gilt and gold gleamed all around him. He could hear the creak of terrace doors, the lap of water against rock, the shouts of sailors in the distance, the cry of seabirds. The air smelled of salt water and greenery. He could smell exotic spices on the breeze and the tang of sex coming from somewhere else in the house. Everything was so intense.

He had shouted in fury, fighting his chains, and within moments a man with long black hair and the face of a fallen angel had entered, literally floating on air. At first, Dante had thought the man was telling him a pack of lies. How could he have been brought to an island in the Mediterranean without remembering a ship? Then his maker had cut his own wrist with his fangs, and at the scent of blood, Dante had almost gone mad with hunger and lust. Within two days, he had finally understood what he had become. It took months before Dante was willing to let go of grief and rage. Before he accepted he could never go home. After that, he had joined his sire in his eternal quest for carnal novelty. They had toured Europe together, and he had racked up hundreds of sexual conquests and experiences. During it all, his heart had remained broken, had ached for Amelia, had ached for love. Finally, he had understood that eternity was not worth living without true love. So he'd come home. "I expected to die," he said softly. "I thought I would be caught and destroyed by villagers or by my sire. Or I would make the choice to destroy myself—"

"What do you mean, destroy yourself?" Mia whispered. She had sat up, facing him.

WICKED FOR CHRISTMAS / 67

"I fully intended to see you one last time, then stand outside in daylight. Sunlight would burn me to ash, love."

"Goodness," she gasped. "That is what you would have done if you had been imprisoned? Perhaps . . . perhaps if your sire desired you so much, perhaps in truth he had fallen in love with you. Maybe he imprisoned you so you couldn't destroy yourself."

He stared at her. How had she seen something he had never dreamed of? "He imprisoned me to save me?"

"Do you think he has come back for you? That he wants you back?" She faced him bravely. "When you leave me, will you go with him?"

"No. When I leave you, I'll be alone for the rest of eternity. But what I will have to do is stop my sire. He hasn't killed yet, but he will."

"How can you stop him?"

"Vampires can be destroyed. Ask Mr. Jones about that. There are various ways. However, sometimes a vampire can't destroy his own sire." He'd spoken thoughtlessly there, and she jumped upon his careless words at once.

"Why not?"

He could invent a lie, but he'd already told her so many truths, he found another coming off his lips. "Not without causing his own destruction."

Fear flashed in her eyes. "And you would be willing to do that, wouldn't you? I can see it in your face. You are willing to die to prevent your sire from killing."

"Of course." He managed a rueful grin. "But only after we are married."

The next night, Dante gave her three French kisses. That was what he called the passionate kisses where his tongue thrust sensually into her mouth. On the fourth day of Christmas, he admitted he'd been at a loss at first, then drew four beautiful necklaces from his coat pocket. Before he gave them to her, they made love—once with him on top, once with her astride him, once against the wall, and once on top of the vanity. After each breathless climax they shared, he gave her first a ruby necklace, then one of sapphires, then emeralds, and finally a beautiful, stunning circlet of diamonds. Each one held an enormous center stone shaped like a bird.

On the fifth night, he secured five gold rings to the headboard and bedposts of their private bed at the House of Pleasure, and they indulged in exotic games of bondage all night. By dawn, Amelia decided it was very pleasurable to be tied up while making love.

She was apprehensive about the sixth day. What could he possibly think of that involved geese? Goose-down pillows? Or feathers again? When she opened a small gold box, she was startled to find six small ivory eggs nestled inside, with gold chains attached.

She knew Dante was trying to make her forget the future. Forget that after he married her in two more days—on the eighth day of Christmas—he would leave. She feared he would not stay for a few months—he wanted to stop the vampire who had made him. Perhaps as soon as they said their vows, he would desert her to hunt down his vampire sire.

She gazed up at him quizzically. "What are these for?"

He winked. "Lift your skirts, love. I'll show you."

He licked the first egg and stroked it against her clit until her legs quivered and she was sopping wet with need. Then—*pop*— he slid the little ivory piece inside her cunny, with the chain dangling out. He did it with another. Then he had her turn around, and he shockingly popped one inside her bottom.

The sensation was stunning. Her legs were as shaky as parchment pages. She couldn't stand, so he carried her to the bed. Then, as she watched, he rubbed warm oil over the remaining eggs and slipped them inside his bottom. Goodness!

His face contorted with pleasure, and he moved over her, so his face was above her quim, his wobbling erection over her face. His bollocks, dusted with soft golden hairs, hung above her. Each movement sent jolts of pleasure from her quim and bottom. She wrapped her hands around his taut thighs and lifted. Opening her mouth, she took his cock deep within.

He bent and nuzzled her quim.

Goodness, again! She could hardly focus on sucking on him when he licked her. But she tried. Tried not to forget to please him as she shook and shivered with pleasure, tried to ensure she didn't scrape with her teeth. He suckled, teased, licked, until she came, moaning and gasping around his thick, rigid cock. He brought her to orgasm three times before he finally surrendered himself.

Laughing, he took out the precious eggs, then put them in a basin of water. He brought another basin to clean her, his hands stroking lovingly with a wet cloth. Then he lay beside her, pulling the covers over them. "Let me stay with you tonight while you sleep."

Oh, this man knew how to break her heart. She rested her head against his chest. His heart beat slowly, but so strong. "I wish you would stay with me every night. Forever."

"There's tomorrow night first, love. One night at a time . . ."

"Swans," Amelia whispered. "What are you planning to do in bed that involves swans? Is it going to be feathers? There couldn't be anything done with the birds—"

"Perhaps I trained them to tease you with the beat of their wings."

"What?"

Dante almost laughed at the panicked, stunned look in her eyes. "No, angel. I planned to make love to you in a heated bath, one decorated with swans, and give you seven special surprises."

"What kind of surprises?"

"If I tell, it won't be a surprise. But I will give you a teasing glimpse at my plan. I'm thinking of tasting you, pleasuring you with my mouth in seven places."

"Seven places," she echoed. "Where?"

"Your lovely mouth. Your nipples—that makes three. Your sweet quim. Your delectable bottom."

"Five," she said breathlessly. "That is five."

"Perhaps the back of one knee. Or your sensitive toes. Or your throat."

"Oh, no," she said swiftly. "Not my throat." Then she flushed with embarrassment and Dante's heart cracked.

The Seventh Day of Christmas

A soft sound woke her.

Amelia sat up, blinking, and the covers fell from her. She was certain she had heard someone whisper her name. But the fire's glow in the hearth lit her room softly, and she could see she was alone.

Had it been Dante?

She slipped out of bed. Something inside her yearned to go outside. It was like an itch that would not be ignored. She had to go.

She drew on a woolen dress and wool stockings, then crept downstairs. The house was quiet. The merrymaking of New Year's Eve was over now that it was almost dawn. Amelia slipped out through the kitchen door, into the rear gardens. Her breath puffed; the cold went right through her. There was no sign of Dante.

But as much as she wanted to turn and go back inside, her feet would not obey.

A brilliant white light glowed in front of her, like an enormous diamond, low in the sky. The Christmas star? No, that couldn't be possible. The light expanded and turned to a rainbow of colors. It burst, so blinding, she had to shut her eyes. Warmth radiated and embraced her.

Amelia...

Her name, spoken softly, forced her to lift her head and open her lids. Three women stood before her. They had appeared out of nowhere! White robes swirled around them. Angels?

"Oh, no, my dear." The tallest, who had dark hair curling down her back, laughed. The sound echoed lushly in the crisp air. "We are most certainly not angels."

"We are vampire queens," the redheaded one said. She crooked her finger, and Amelia's feet took her closer, against her will.

"Do not fear us," said the blonde. "I am Ophelia." She pointed to the dark-haired woman. "That is Cardiamillion. The third of our trio is Lausanne."

"Vampire queens. I did not know there was royalty among vampires. Dante did not tell me—" Amelia stopped. Did they know of Dante? They must. But why were they here?

"Yes, we know of Dante." The blonde rose into the air and floated. The train of her robe rippled behind her. "That is why we are here. To help you plot a way to keep him. You see, it is important that you do not let him leave you."

Amelia blinked. "Why does it matter to you?"

Cardiamillion smiled gently. "It matters to us because the vampire who sired Dante is very dangerous. And we all adore Dante—"

"You do?" she asked sharply. Jealousy, sharp and painful, spiked through her heart. "Were any of you his lover? Were all of you?"

Ophelia shook her head. "No, but we are fond of him. He is so beautiful, and his sire wishes to claim him back. We cannot let that happen. His sire needs Dante's submission to give him power. The power to survive. But you have seen what he does—he brutalizes mortals. He feeds from young women and men and kills them. Dante has learned the skill of taking blood without hurting his prey."

Prey. What a horrible way to think of people.

"If you keep Dante," Cardiamillion said, "if you lure him to stay with you, his sire will wither and die. What Dante must do is openly declare his intention to stay at your side. His sire carries an ancient curse, one bestowed by his very ancient maker. The curse means that once Dante's sire gives his heart to another vampire, he must claim that vampire as his eternal mate. Otherwise, he dies."

Amelia's wits whirled. Eternal mate? Dante's sire had given his heart to Dante? "But Dante is determined to leave me. For my own protection, he says."

"No!" Ophelia cried. "We cannot let that happen. His sire is a rogue vampire. He refuses to obey the rules for existence in the modern, mortal world. He must be stopped."

"You"—Lausanne pointed her long finger at Amelia's heart—"you must make Dante fall so deeply in love, he cannot leave."

Amelia shook her head. She wanted to stamp her feet in the snow. They spoke as if she had a choice. "I *wish* I could. But Dante is stubborn. I don't believe I can convince him to do it. He's resisted so far."

"We are four women," Cardiamillion declared. "Surely we can find a way."

"Miss Amelia Ann Watson, whilst thou have this man to be your wedded husband, to have and to hold from this day forward, for better or for worse, for richer or for poorer, in sickness and in health, to love and to cherish 'til death do you part, according to God's holy ordinance? And thereto to him you give your troth?"

This was the most unnerving moment Dante had ever known. Waiting for Amelia. For her to look to him, to glow like the moon above them, and say, "I do."

And as she smiled at him and those two precious words hung in the cool night air, Dante lifted her into the air and kissed her. Reverend Rutherford cleared his throat and looked away as Dante tipped Amelia back and gave her the hottest kiss he could manage. Soft furs framed her face and tickled his skin. She gave the hungriest, loudest moan as she fiercely kissed him back.

He had given a generous donation to the local church to convince the reverend to marry him and Mia at midnight. He did not dare wed her in the church. For all he knew, he might explode into flame. And given the amount of money he'd donated, he knew the clergyman would overlook the eccentricity of marrying outdoors in the middle of the night.

Finally, he knew it was time to draw back. She looked dazed, and he must look every bit as drugged with desire and delight. He loved this woman, and she was now his wife. But there was business to attend to first. He drew out a bag of coins, an additional gift for the clergyman. "Thank you, Reverend." He deposited the weighty sack into the man's hand. "I'm sorry to have brought you out into the cold. It was a whim on my part—to make a memorable wedding for my bride. I hope I've recompensed the church well for my eccentricity."

"Indeed you have, my lord." Reverend Rutherford bowed to both him and Amelia. "Best wishes for happiness for you both, my lord. My lady." The man stomped his feet to warm them, then hastened back to the manse and no doubt to his warm study.

They were alone in the churchyard. Dante turned to Mia, who blew out a frosty breath. He hoped she wasn't frozen stiff. He wanted to get her to bed at once and begin warming her. "It's our wedding night, Mia. But also the eighth day of Christmas. I was thinking of giving you the gift of eight buxom dairy maids."

"For me?" She eyed him with suspicion. After all, he had told her about the orgies he'd attended with his sire. "Are you certain that gift was not one *you* wanted?"

"No, my love. I have made my vows to you, and I intend to keep them."

He was now a married man. Each smile he shared broke his heart. He didn't want to leave her. He never wanted to leave her. But he had no choice.

He lifted Amelia into his arms, drawing her tight against his chest. The fur surrounding her hood brushed his cheek, and a bittersweet smile curved her lips.

"I was just thinking . . . this is how we began, five years ago," she whispered. "You swept me into your arms and carried me into the cottage so we could have our wedding night."

"We'll have another wedding night now. Mia . . ." There was no way to say it to make her understand how deeply he felt it. So he simply said, "Mia, I love you—"

"Damnation, I'm too late."

The furious shout from the edge of the church grounds made Dante jerk around. He had been so focused on Amelia he hadn't heard the sound of footsteps.

Now the damned slayer Jones stood there, holding a crossbow, wild hatred flashing in his eyes.

6

With care, Dante lowered Mia—his wife—to her feet and glared at the slayer. "If it was your intention to slay me, what has taken you so long?" Quickly, he assessed his options. He scented the air and strained to hear other heartbeats. There were none. The slayer was alone. He could attempt to fight, but it would be hard to combat a crossbow. He could shift his shape into the form of a bat to evade the arrows, then launch an attack on Jones.

He turned to Mia, horror-struck to see her face was as pale as the white fur of her cloak. "Go back to the house, Mia. The church will have record of our marriage. You are my wife now and entitled to a generous portion and all the protection of my family and name."

"Oh, no," she declared. Color rushed over her face swiftly. "I love you, Dante. I did not marry you just for your name. I want you." She spun and faced Jones with furious eyes. "I am not allowing Mr. Jones to hurt you."

He would have applauded her if he were not scared of what the slayer might do. "You just vowed to obey—"

"No woman who promises to obey in her wedding vows actually intends to. In my heart, I promised to stand at your side." She wagged a finger at Jones, who was standing motionless, listening to their debate. "Put down the weapon, Mr. Jones! This is absurd. Dante has done nothing wrong."

He adored her. How was he going to leave her and live an eternity without her? On the other hand, if the slayer shot him with the crossbow, his forever was going to prove short.

Jones stepped forward and peered at Mia contritely. "Vampires are predators, my dear. They have no regard for human life. We are prey to them, and this one has been attacking innocents throughout the village."

"He hasn't," she cried. "His sire has."

Dante saw the quick pulse of tension that flowed through Jones. He heard the slayer's heart beat faster in excitement. Now he knew why Jones had spared him for so long. "You were waiting for my sire, weren't you? You didn't stake me because you believed he would come back for me."

Jones gave a false bow. "Brilliant, vampire. Yes, I let you live to use you as a lure for your sire. I've been hunting him for a long time. As I tracked him across the Continent, I learned about his curse. An ancient curse placed upon him by his sire."

"What in Hades are you talking about?" Dante snapped. "He is a vampire. How more cursed does he need to be?"

Mia turned large blue eyes to him. "I learned about it, too, Dante. The curse means that once your sire gives his heart to another vampire, he must claim that vampire as his mate. If he does not, he will die."

She spoke with calm certainty, but Dante's gut clenched in fear. "How do you know this, love?" That was what frightened him. Had his sire come to her and told her this? Was his sire luring her, trying to destroy her?

"Three female vampires came to me last night. I had an uncontrollable urge to walk outside, and then they appeared in front of me out of thin air. They were vampire queens, and they told me about the curse."

While he focused on his wife, Dante tracked Jones with his preternatural peripheral vision and his acute senses of smell and hearing. The slayer was creeping forward, no doubt seeking a better shot.

"What did they want? What did they ask you to do?" he demanded.

"They did not ask anything of me. Though they did want me—" She stopped, and a scarlet flush flooded her cheeks.

Damnation. "What, Mia?"

"They wanted me to entice you so you would never leave me. So you would not go back to your sire. They want you to openly declare your intention to stay with me."

That was impossible. How could he stay with her when he was a vampire? Eventually, the population would notice he never aged, never went outside in daylight, and never ate food. He'd have the villagers storming his home with torches and pitchforks. Mia could get hurt. What if people believed he had changed her? They could put her to death.

He snarled at Llewellyn Jones. "Give me a wedding night with my bride. After all, Jones, it is Christmas."

The crossbow jerked up. "A wedding night? You had no right to marry her. Hades, you used your bloody vampire magic on her and lured her to marry you. If you had left her alone, she would never have gone through with this farce of a wedding."

"What vampire magic?" Mia asked, confused.

Jones took another step toward her. "Vampires possess an allure, like a glamour, that draws mortals to them. They can influence the minds of humans. And their emotions."

"He told me about his allure. Dante did not use it on me. I married him knowing he is a vampire, and I did it because I love him."

"You love him because he's used his magic on you," the slayer insisted. "Why else would you care for him, Miss Watson? Five years ago, he abandoned you, and since then, he's lived a life of debauchery and sexual excess. He murdered countless innocent people as he and his sire toured the Continent—he took lives so he could have a meal. He ruined you and left you. Now he returns, seduces you, and tells you that once you've married him, he has to go. Where will he go? Back to his orgies. Back to the arms of other women."

Dante wanted to protest. He had no intention of touching any woman but Mia for the rest of his existence. But he hesitated. He could die now at Jones's hand, or he could die when he destroyed his sire; if he somehow managed to survive, he would have to leave her. If she didn't love him, it would be easier for her to let him go.

He turned to the woman who had owned his heart for years, even when he was thousands of miles away from her. "It is the truth, Mia. I was afraid you never would have married me or slept with me unless I used my glamour on you. You may think you wed me willingly, but you didn't. You do not love me anymore. As Jones says, how could you?"

"I know my heart, Dante. And I know you. I know this is a lie."

"Mia, you don't love me because you know the truth. I don't love you. I can't love you. All my life, I've been selfish and arrogant. Jones is right. I'm a rake who uses and abandons women carelessly. All you were to me was a conquest."

Her face blanched in shock. She stumbled back from him. Then her cheeks went scarlet with humiliation and rage. He couldn't read her thoughts—he didn't need to. He could read every curse word she was calling him in her eyes.

He grimaced at the slayer. "Take her back to the house. Tell the family she is my bride, ensure she is treated well. Tonight I will hunt for my sire. And I'll destroy him."

Jones sneered with distaste and distrust. "I doubt you will."

"I give my word as a gentleman. I know why the vampire queens want him destroyed. And I will be the one to see it through. In return, I ask only one thing of you, Jones. Make sure Mia is safe. Protect her. From the queens, from my family."

"Make sure I am safe? I thought you did not care," she said softly. "You cannot hand me over to Mr. Jones as though I am a coat you want to cast off. The choice of what I will do is mine."

Damnation, she had too much of a good, strong, beautiful heart. She was willing to care for him even after he'd hurt her. But he had to drive her away. He had no choice.

He whirled to face her. He triggered his fangs to shoot out. His face contorted into the fierce, monstrous look it took on just before he sank his teeth into the neck of his prey. Mia's scream pierced his heart, but the sight of him, with the face of a true beast, drove her back.

Jones grasped her arm to keep her from falling, while pointing the crossbow at him.

"I lied, Mia. I love you. I have to let you go because I love you so much." It would be the last thing he said to her. Then Dante bowed his head, let his body ripple and twist. He growled like a dog as his muscles shortened; his bones adjusted shape as wings grew out of his back. He gave a powerful flap of his wings and soared into the sky. He did not look at his wife to see how she reacted to his transformation into a large bat. He didn't trust himself to look back.

She'd been certain Dante's parents would think Mr. Jones was mad when he explained that Dante was a vampire. Instead, the earl nodded grimly, without any expression of shock, and allowed Jones to clap him on the shoulder in sympathy.

Amelia stared from the earl to the countess. "I don't understand. You are accepting this story so easily? Without any surprise? Did you know? How could you know?"

The earl sank into a leather chair. They stood in the drawing room, with a fire blazing and dozens of candles lit, and the brilliant light showed the harsh pain on his face. "Jones already explained it to us. In my youth, I worked with the Royal Society for the Investigation of Mysterious Phenomena, searching for artifacts of ancient vampires. It was my 'grand tour,' a journey through India and Africa, searching for the roots of vampirism. I became ill with malaria—a mild case—and returned home. I married and set aside my metaphysical pursuits."

The countess dropped her head in her hands. "We knew vampires existed, but I held out hope that my son had not been turned. He is dead to us. I know that. I know he will have to leave. I will have truly lost him forever."

The countess was so heartbroken that Amelia hastened to her mother-in-law's side and impetuously embraced her. Her wits still whirled—who would have dreamed the earl had pursued the history of vampires—but she said softly, "You haven't lost him. There must be some way he can stay here." To her surprise, the woman did not pull away.

Mr. Jones explained everything: Dante's plan to pursue his sire, his plan to leave. Of course, the slayer told them about his marriage, which Amelia had not spoken about.

The countess raised her head. Amelia was certain the woman would demand she be tossed out of the house. Through red eyes, Lady Matlock surveyed her. "He loved you so much," she finally said. "He was determined to have you at any cost. I was a fool to try to gainsay him."

"My dear—" the earl began, but his wife whirled on him.

"Quiet, Reginald. Our son is deeply in love, and he is behaving as a gentleman by marrying Miss Watson. Do you not see how wonderful this is? He is trying to retain his humanity. He is trying to fight not to be a beast and a demon. Perhaps it means he can stay with the family . . . and Miss Watson . . . I mean . . . Oh goodness, you are now Lady Darby."

The earl looked up, his face gray. He looked as though he had lost all his strength. "My son cannot stay." His lordship glared at Jones. "But you will not stake him. That is the bargain we made. You will spare his life but destroy his sire."

Jones nodded. "Your son will try to fight his sire, and you know what that could mean."

The earl went white. "His destruction."

"I will help him, my lord," Jones said. "I give you my solemn word on that."

Lord Matlock stared blankly ahead. "I know the vampire who created him. He was a young king in Egypt, two thousand years ago. He is vicious and brutal. I am surprised he has not caused more destruction here. I assume the reason he restrained himself is that he wanted to lure my son to his side again. He may be doing this for revenge on me. During my travels, I led vampire slayers to his mate and his children. They were as bloodthirsty as he is. They were all destroyed."

Amelia clapped her hand to her mouth in shock. The countess let out a horrible moan and slumped back. Amelia quickly grasped Lady Matlock's hand, patted her wrist, and shook her gently to wake her. Her mother-in-law stared helplessly at her. "If he wants revenge, he will want to destroy Dante. This beast will want to take my husband's family from him. From *me*."

Amelia stroked Lady Matlock's hand and looked to Mr. Jones. "That will not happen. Will it, Mr. Jones?" It could *not* happen. She'd always imagined Christmas was a magical time— she was not going to lose the man she loved at Christmas! "We will ensure it doesn't!" she cried.

The slayer hesitated, then firmly nodded. His eyes softened as he looked at her. *He loves me.* The thought struck her and she reeled back in surprise. She'd guessed at his interest, but not that it was so strong. Her heart was touched, but Dante possessed her, heart and soul. She was in love with Dante. She would always be, whether he was with her or not. She must save him, so she *could* love him forever.

The Eleventh Day of Christmas

Copper-brown skin. Jet-black hair that brushed broad shoulders. Three tattoos of snakes: two that encircled large biceps and one that ran from the back of his neck, slithered down his spine, and swooped around hard, naked buttocks.

He had finally lured out his sire.

Dante stared at the body of his maker, King Anun, who had ruled Egypt two thousand years ago. His sire had flown here, to this quiet clearing south of the house, as a large bat, which meant he had no clothing. But the cold would not touch him. Anun paced in the snow in front of Dante. "I heard your summons in my head, Dante. I thought, after I chose to imprison you, you would never want to be at my side again. Yet now you tell me you do. That you will leave your fragile mortal to come and travel with me again."

"Yes," he lied. As his maker, Anun could not see into his thoughts. Which was helpful, since he planned to lure the ancient vampire to let down his guard. "You were right. I cannot stay with her. Eventually I would be responsible for her destruction. So I have to leave. I want to return to our life of debauchery, orgies, and pleasure." He grinned. "I missed the fun we had."

Anun paced over the snow, wreathed in shadow, though his muscles glimmered as they moved, reflecting the moonlight. Anun shook his head. "No. I cannot see your mind, but I know you are not driven to be with me. If I cannot have your true devotion, then I require another emotion that it is as strong. Only a powerful emotional bond between us will keep me alive. If it cannot be love, then it must be . . . hate."

Anun held up his hands, and suddenly two trees in front of him caught fire. Flames wrapped around the trunks and flew up into the leafless branches. They licked with golden heat at the black sky. "We cannot pretend to be mortals, Dante. We are powerful beings. That is why humans are prey to us. I could destroy your world in the space of a human's heartbeat. I could send a raging fire to consume your father's land, eat through his villages, burn his people alive. I could drink the blood of those who survive, in one orgiastic night. With a wave of my hand, I could raze his house. If I chose, I could destroy this pitiful little country."

Anun smiled. His features were perfect, without any flaw, like a bronze statue. But he was the most soulless being there was. Dante knew Anun's bloody past—he had killed his own people, feeding on entire families. It pleased Anun to kill the youngest and most innocent first, to cause unbearable pain and grief in the parents' hearts, which he then absorbed through their blood.

"But none of those things would make you hate me enough," Anun mused.

Don't wager on it. I hate you more than you could guess already.

"Your rage in imprisonment let me survive for the last year. But it would not be enough now. I need more. I need your true hatred. There is, I know, one thing I could do that would make you hate me with so much passion I would have sustenance for eternity."

"What are you doing?" a woman shouted in indignant fury.

God, no. He had no right to appeal to God, but Dante was sick with fear. Damned Llewellyn Jones dragged Amelia out of the shadows. She struggled against the slayer, but Jones seemed surprisingly strong for a mortal.

"Anun, no," Dante shouted. "I'll give you the bloody love you need—"

"No, Dante. I used my magic to give the slayer great strength, and in return he is my devoted slave. Something I know you could never be. I have to keep *you* like a tiger in a cage, trapped but always waiting for the chance to rip me apart."

Why had he not sensed Amelia was there? Not scented her? It had to be Anun's magic. Dante lunged for Anun and grabbed him, but his sire lifted his hand and sent a shot of fire that threw Dante onto his back and set his clothes aflame. He shifted shape and soared out of the burning pile of fabric. It turned to ash in an instant.

He swooped for his maker, transformed back to human, and tackled Anun to the ground. They rolled in the snow. Then Anun broke free. He conjured a wall of icicles. With a laugh, he sent them rushing through the air. They slammed into Dante's chest, drove into his skin, but the wounds healed instantly and the icicles fell.

"I can't kill you, Dante," Anun snarled. "But I can drain your strength, batter you until you cannot protect her. Why fight? Why torture her? Does it not hurt her to watch you be brutalized? Let her die now. I will be gentle with her if I kill her now. If I do it later, I will make her death a long, agonizing torment."

"Damn you." He leaped again, but two jagged lightning bolts seared him. His chest was black, red, and oozing, and Amelia screamed. Again the skin quickly healed.

Could he use Llewellyn in some way? He looked into the slayer's thoughts. What he heard stunned him.

I'm not his slave, my lord. I realized he would use Amelia against you and pretended to agree so I could have the chance to defeat him.

Dante quickly spoke inside the slayer's mind. *How did you fight his magic?*

Three vampire queens gave me the strength.

What did they ask of you in payment?

Nothing that will hurt you or Amelia. They want Anun destroyed because of his brutality. In return for helping me, I had to give the Royal Society's word that we would not try to slay any of the queens.

Anun waved his hand and Mia rose into the air, squealing in shock and anger. She flew toward Anun. Dante jumped forward to grasp her, to pull her to safety, but a stream of his sire's power sent him tumbling back.

Even with Jones's help, how was he going to save Mia? She was struggling with Anun, who chuckled with glee, then licked his lips. Dante had to act now.

Jones, you are going to have to stake me.

The slayer reeled back, stunned, his gaze fixed on Amelia. *What?*

Anun pushed Mia's hair to the side, exposing her neck. Dante sent a desperate message to the queens. *I'm going to give my life for this, so Anun will die. I love Mia. For Anun's death, would you give me life again?* Then he shouted, through thought, to Jones, *Do it now!*

Dante saw the slayer pull out a stake. Saw the long strides through the snow . . . the stake coming at him . . . and he threw his body forward to meet the point of it with his heart.

Anun howled in fury, but it was too late. Sharp pain shot through Dante's chest . . . blood spurted . . . the slayer had damned good aim. The shaft of wood tore through his heart, pulverizing it. He managed to twist to see Anun as he fell.

His sire screamed in agony and released Mia. She jumped to safety, the clever woman. As Dante slammed into the snow, Anun exploded into ash that rained through the cold winter sky like snowflakes.

Brilliant golden light surrounded Dante. A trio of soft voices filled his head. *We heard you. We agree to your terms. You are mortal once more, Dante. Free to love. For a lifetime.*

His muscles jerking wildly in the cold snow, his chest was on fire with pain. His heart rebuilt inside him, the agony of it excruciating. Then warmth flowed through him. His skin felt alive, tingling, hurting, stinging, itchy. The rush of mortal sensations overwhelmed him.

Mia's lovely face leaned over him. Tears dripped from her huge blue eyes, landing on his cheeks.

"Mia," he managed. "Are you all right?"

"Yes. Of course I am. You sacrificed yourself for me. But . . . but . . ."

"I managed to make a deal with the vampire queens, love. They saved me. They made me mortal again."

"Mortal? You . . . you aren't a vampire anymore?" She caressed his face.

"No, love. I'm free."

Dante leaned against her as she helped him up the stairs of their home, a manor house on the earl's estate. This was to be their home together, but Amelia barely noticed any details as she led him to the second floor. Footmen hovered everywhere. Several leaped forward to help, but she shook her head.

At the top of the stairs, a youthful maid stuttered, "A . . . bath is being drawn, my lady."

It was so hard to remember she was "my lady." "Thank you," Amelia said.

Dante was so weak, but he seemed to draw on his reserves of strength to keep walking. The bathing room proved to be filled with steamy warmth. Piles of folded towels ringed the huge tub.

Stumbling dazedly, Dante fumbled with the back of her

gown. "No, dear," she said. "The warm bath is for you. To soothe bruises. To wash out your wounds."

"Not a vampire anymore," he said hoarsely. "They won't heal anymore."

"Oh, no, they will. I will see to that. It just won't happen as quickly." Firmly, she undid his shirt, then tugged it over his head. She undressed him with the efficiency she'd used on his siblings when she'd been their governess. That seemed like a lifetime ago. She supposed it was. It had been the lifetime Dante had spent as a vampire.

He had told her many times he loved her. He had risked his life for her. She knew he was not going to leave now. She began to undo his trousers, but he drew her hands away. "I'm capable of taking off my own trousers, love. If you were being driven by wild lust, I'd let you do it, but I don't need you to mother me."

"You are actually . . . pouting. For heaven's sake, why?"

"I . . ." His expression changed. Horror and pain touched his green eyes. "I was so afraid I wasn't going to be able to save you, Mia. You must have feared I couldn't."

She planted her hands on her hips. "And not allowing me to take off your trousers proves you are strong and able to rescue me?"

"You must have hated me for being weak. Now that I'm mortal, I'm very weak. But still able to take off my own trousers."

She laughed. She could not help it. After their fight with his sire, her emotions felt as though they were physical things that had been battered against rocks. And he was worried about showing strength in front of her by unfastening his clothing. She pushed his hands away and tugged down the muddy, bloodstained fabric, down past his lean hips, his strong thighs, down to his boots. "You are the strongest man I've ever known. You had the strength to risk your life for me. And there is something you will have to learn. With you, I am always mad with lust and eager to take off your trousers." She kissed him passionately.

When she moved back, his eyes were blazing. "There's a bed in the adjoining room—"

"After you've bathed. After I have cleaned your wounds and stitched you where necessary." Supporting his right arm, Amelia helped him to the tub.

"Yes, my dear," he said on an obedient sigh. He climbed in and gave another sigh, a blissful one, as water engulfed him. Steam damped his hair, turning it to amber. It stuck to his face, and his green eyes looked up, filled with such hope, her heart ached. "You could join me. We could make love in the water. I could even call for seven swans to be brought in to join us."

"No! You need to be tended first." In true governess fashion, she set to work. The change from vampire to mortal had left him playful. She had to keep slapping his hands away while she bathed him. He kept trying to kiss her. Or pull her into the tub with him. Finally he was done. The dirt and streaks of blood were gone. His skin, she noticed, had turned darker—a lightly tanned color. He stared at his arms. "It is the color it was before I was turned." Then he tried to clasp her around the waist.

"You are not pulling me in with you."

"Then I'd better dry off and come out there to you, love." He gave a rueful smile. "I keep making a hash out of this wedding night business, don't I? Our first attempt didn't end with a wedding. And our actual wedding didn't allow for a wedding night."

"We can have it now." In his exhausted, battered state, she did not want him to try to make love. He needed rest. But she glanced down. Beneath the bathwater, he was incredibly erect.

"I missed giving you your gifts, too," he said. "Tomorrow is the Twelfth Day of Christmas, Epiphany. I owe you gifts for four days."

"Don't worry about that now," she soothed. She poured warm water onto his hair, swishing the wet locks to rinse out all the soap.

"Very wifely." He sighed. "I don't think I ever dreamed you would bathe me and wash my hair. Now that you've shown me how heavenly it feels to have you massage my head, I may command you to wash my hair every time."

"Command? I think you've forgotten that I said I am not so obedient. This, for me, is a partnership. Now, if you were to ask me nicely, I would be happy to wash your hair. If you will do it for me."

"Mia, I will do anything you want."

"Then you should rest."

"No, love. This is to be our true wedding night."

And a few minutes later, they were in their bedroom. Amelia took off her shift, untied her garters, then peeled off her stockings. She turned to him. Naked. Despite a fire, goose bumps washed over her, and her nipples went hard with the cold.

Dante lay under the sheets, his arms pillowed beneath his head. He snored softly. Frowning, she moved softly along the side of the bed. Dante's eyes were shut, dark lashes lying along his cheeks.

She stroked his cheek, smiling. "I love you, Dante. One day we will have our wedding night." She was too cold to slip into bed naked. She pulled on her winter nightgown, climbed under the covers, and snuggled up to him.

Next thing she knew, wintery sunlight was spilling into the room. Dante stood by the window, wearing a navy robe, blinking in the brilliant light.

She sat up, the sheets sliding off her shoulders.

"Good morning, my love," he said. "Since I don't remember

anything about our wedding night, I assume I passed out before I was able to pleasure you."

Amelia shook her head. "I am more concerned about how you feel! You are standing in sunlight—you are definitely certain it will not harm you?"

"I've basked in it for a half hour while you slept, Mia. If it was going to burn me to a crisp, it would already have done so." He gazed at her softly. "I'm free. Thanks to you."

He left the window and walked to the bed—he walked with far more strength than last night. He scooped a square of white off the table and handed it to her. She stared at it, perplexed.

"I was up at dawn today, too excited to sleep," he explained. "So I wrote this for you."

Joy radiated from him—infectious joy that made her heart trip merrily in her chest. "You sound like a child on Christmas morning."

"That is how I feel." He grinned.

She flicked open his note and read:

On the twelfth day of Christmas, my true love gave to me
Twelve lords-a-leaping (magnificent cocks swaying in each
*   other's faces),*
Eleven ladies dancing (massive dildos secured in secret places),
Ten pipers piping (then using long, slender pipes to pleasure
*   me),*
Nine drummers drumming as . . .
Eight buxom milkmaids lick my cunny, nipples, and bottom,
*   and delight me most scandalously . . .*

Her face was blushing furiously, and Dante cupped her cheek—obviously he could see how scarlet she was.

"I'm no poet, but that was what I wanted to give you today. Since we had to face my sire, the vampire queens, and Jones, I didn't get you your gifts." He winked. "I want very much to make your last day of Christmas scandalously erotic and have arranged with the proprietress of the House of Pleasure for you to enjoy all those delights today."

Amelia had to admit arousal bubbled inside her as she merely *imagined* some of those things. "You didn't have anything naughty for the drumming drummers," she whispered.

"I'm sorry, love, but I couldn't think of anything to do with drumming. But I do intend to bestow a dozen wicked pleasures on you today."

She shook her head at her wicked husband. "I already have the most wonderful gift I could ever want. *You.* As for the drummers, my heart is drumming rather hard at the thought of making love with you. These things sound very naughty, but I don't want any other gift but you in my bed. Though, I do have one more thing to ask . . ."

His eyes glowed as he undid the belt of his robe. "What is it?"

"Perhaps we could stay in bed all day?"

Laughing, he jumped back onto the mattress and tossed off his robe. His beautiful, muscular naked body moved over her. He straddled her thighs. "Your wish, my dear wife, is my command. I have no intention of ever leaving your bed. Right now, we are going to have a wedding night, and nothing will stop us."

He levered up on one hand, pushing the covers down with the other. "This is my Christmas wish, love." Then he bent and captured her right nipple in his mouth, suckling through her nightdress. He rolled them over so she tumbled on top of him while he vigorously sucked.

Oh, it was so good. Each tug of his mouth tugged in her cunny, tugged so deeply it seemed to pull at her womb. She was dizzy with sensation. Whirling in joy and desire. She arched to him. "Oh, please, yes, this is so wonderful."

He licked her nipples, which stood up, as firm and thick as

thimbles. Then he licked her collarbones, kissed her shoulders, nuzzled the hollows under her arms, which made her giggle until her throat hurt.

While she was still giggling, he dove between her thighs and suckled her. An almost-instant climax hit her, and she coiled beneath him, gasping, crying out, shouting his name. She fell back to the bed, eyes shut. "Oh, goodness."

"It's good to know I still please you, even though I'm mortal."

"Of course you do. You were mortal for our very first time, and you gave me the most heavenly pleasure."

Suddenly she was scooped into Dante's arms, and he carried her, naked, to the window, where ice made swoops on the panes. "Goodness, it's cold!"

"I'll keep you warm," he vowed, and stood her in front of the window. Wintry sunlight poured over them both.

He embraced her from behind, his arms warm and strong. She rubbed her derriere against his erection, smacking it back and forth. He groaned in agony, cupped her breasts, and thrust deeply inside.

They rocked madly in the sunlight. Pleasure built and built, streaming through her like fire, like sunlight, like joy. When she came, her hands flew forward and smacked against the glass. His hands slapped beside hers, he bucked against her rump, and his hot seed shot deeply inside her.

He panted behind her. "Unfortunately, now that I'm mortal, I'll be exhausted faster."

She wiggled, enjoying his fierce groan.

"On the other hand . . ." She felt him go hard again inside her. He brought her to climax six more times, six wonderful times; then he whispered, "Could you manage twelve?"

"No!" She sighed. "I always knew Christmas was magical," Amelia whispered, and then giggled. And gasped. "Goodness, I'm so sensitive that giggle just made me come."

Dante had to agree. Christmas had provided a miracle, even for a man who was damned. He had been given the most precious gift of all—a future with Amelia.

He led her to bed and lavishly licked her nipples. "If laughter makes you come, I intend to tickle you everywhere."

"Oh, you devil." She sobered a minute, then squeaked as he flicked her nipple with his tongue. "No, I know you must be an angel—a wicked one. For you make me see heaven each time I come."

"I'm just a man, love. One blessed to have the most perfect wife."

Her hand slid between their bodies and wrapped around his hard shaft. All thought left his head, and all his blood rushed to his erection. He managed three words. "Love you, Mia," he whispered.

"I love you, Dante. Now, plunge deeply inside me and give me a very wicked gift."

He obeyed, sliding deep inside her. Their gazes locked, they laughed together. And this time, when he came, Amelia gave him a magnificent glimpse of heaven.

Love and Amelia were miracles, indeed.

She sighed blissfully. "I do love being wicked for Christmas."

Epilogue

Two years later, on December 27, Matthew was born. In two more years, Lucinda arrived on December 28, and Madeline came three years after on the twenty-ninth.

Dante began to wonder if they would be blessed with one child for each of the twelve days.

"Would you be upset if that happened?" Amelia asked. She had just laid Madeline in the bassinet and carefully drew a lace coverlet over the slumbering baby.

"No, love," Dante said softly. "How could I be unhappy to have a large family with you? But what if, when we have twelve children, they all decide to start drumming?"

His wife gave a patient smile. "I don't know. Perhaps we shall have to cover our ears."

"Or hide in bed and start work on the next addition to our family." He grinned. "What would we do with twelve children, love?"

"I suppose we shall be kept very busy loving them."

She was right, of course. "Right now, I'd like to be kept very busy loving you," Dante murmured. He swept her into his arms and kissed his clever, perfect, miraculous wife as her slipper kicked the bedchamber door closed.

NAUGHTY OR NICE?

MELISSA MacNEAL

1

Late November, 1895

> *"It came upon a midnight clear,*
> *That glorious song of old . . ."*

Tess Bennett left the vestibule before she burst into tears. It wasn't Margaret's fault the carolers outside put her in such a dreadful mood: Her housekeeper had been doing everything possible to bring Christmas cheer into their lives. But without Henry and little Claire, this place would never again feel like a home—much less a place to spend the holidays.

> *"And ye, beneath life's crushing load,*
> *Whose forms are bending low . . ."*

What a depressing image! But it reflected her attitude perfectly, didn't it? If she had to spend another day stringing cranberries and popcorn for a tree she didn't want, and watching Margaret and George fail so valiantly at lifting her spirits, she'd simply—

"I'm so sorry, dear. The first year—the first holiday season—is the worst." Margaret placed her warm hands on Tess's drooping shoulders. "Do try to smile and enjoy tonight's dinner, won't you? Mr. Mahaffey will join us at—"

"I don't want to see him." Society wives were expected to be genteel, but some occasions demanded calling a spade a spade—and Reed Mahaffey was digging. "I may have led a sheltered life, Margaret, but I'm fully aware of his motives. He wants to marry into Henry's share of the firm—and mark my words, he'll be *buying* my half of the company rather than screwing me out of it!"

Tess immediately regretted her coarse language, while poor Margaret's cheeks turned the color of the cherry cake she'd baked today. She sighed, fogging the dining room window with her breath. Clouds shrouded the afternoon, hanging over the Mississippi as though it might snow, although that rarely happened here in Memphis. "I'm sorry, Margaret," she murmured. "I'm not myself."

"None of us are, after yellow fever has claimed so many we loved."

"But I *cannot* pretend to enjoy Reed's company. Encouraging his attentions would be the ultimate insult to Henry's memory." Tess turned, detecting her butler's presence in the hall. "George, please give Mr. Mahaffey my regrets before he leaves the office. No sense in his making the trip here for nothing."

"Yes, of course, Miss Tess."

Margaret sagged. "Begging your pardon, dear," she began in a whimper, "but you can't keep hiding yourself away—"

"I'm sorry about your dinner, Margaret. You've made every effort—all my favorite dishes—but there's just no pleasing me right now," she replied quietly. "And I'm sorry about that, too."

Sorry, sorry, sorry, Tess mused as she headed for the stairway. Would she ever stop apologizing for her black mood? The Delaneys craved the company of someone more cheerful this evening: It wasn't as though *she* was the only one who missed her husband and the fair-haired daughter who'd brightened all their lives.

> *"Look now! For glad and golden hours*
> *Come swiftly on the wing.*
> *O rest beside the weary road*
> *And hear—"*

"The angels may sing," Tess muttered, "but I'll believe in those golden hours when I see them! And not a moment sooner!"

Had the spirit of Ebenezer Scrooge overtaken her? Was she doomed to make everyone's life as bleak and miserable as her own? Tess hurried up the sweeping staircase, unfazed by the bright paprika carpet runner she'd bought last week. If Henry's money couldn't bring her happiness, she had no use for Reed's, either!

She entered her room and slammed the door. Acting like a spoiled child, she was—like Claire, having one of her foot-stomping hissy fits.

Images of her six-year-old daughter made her grip a post of her canopy bed as another wave of grief washed over her. *Enough already!*

Tess inhaled deeply. She went to the window, hoping the view would lift her spirits . . . the boats on the river . . . the stately homes across the way . . . *Why is that green carriage coming down the street? It's only three o'clock!*

Tess cleared the fogged window. Yes, indeed, that could only be the Bennett-Mahaffey coach rolling smartly toward the house, with white-gloved Warren Coates gripping the reins.

Panic seized her. Reed was arriving blatantly early, figuring to catch her off balance. And with George already gone . . .

She hadn't a moment to lose! Margaret would admit the dashing Mr. Mahaffey as a part of her own little scheme, and with more than three hours before dinner was to be served—

Tess snatched up her reticule and a hooded cloak. She could *not* be here when her housekeeper announced Reed's arrival! But where would she go?

As her thoughts raced, Tess slipped out of her pumps and padded down the narrow back stairs to the kitchen. The sonorous door chime echoed in the front foyer . . . Margaret's footsteps pitter-pattered to answer it . . . and as the house-keeper's excited welcome rang out, Tess exited through the back pantry door, where they took delivery of their ice and milk. Heart pounding, she put on her pumps. Could the wild idea in her mind possibly work?

Around the back of the house she rushed, waving her arms to catch Mr. Coates's attention. Her husband had trusted this sturdy fellow to deliver bank deposits and investment checks. Would Warren play along with her now, or would he betray her?

"Why, good afternoon, Mrs. Bennett! I—"

"No time for chitchat, Warren!" she said, pointing toward the house. "You *must* get me away from here before Reed knows I've slipped away. I can't endure an afternoon of that man's romancing. We all know what he's really after, don't we?"

For a heart-stopping moment, the driver gazed at her as though he might put her in her place: the widow of Memphis's most esteemed cotton factor had no business playing cat and mouse like an impudent child. Tess gazed at him, clutching her cloak, imploring him with the blue-eyed smile that had derailed many a Memphis gentleman's train of thought.

Warren chuckled gruffly and hopped down to open the carriage door. "He's not the most *subtle* Romeo, is he? When I suggested that such an early arrival wouldn't impress either you or Mrs. Delaney, he told me to keep my opinions to myself." Coates waited for her to settle on the soft leather seat. "Where shall I take you?"

"I haven't the slightest idea. But we'd better go before they realize I've escaped!"

"Right you are, ma'am. Warren Coates at your service."

As the carriage lurched, the rapid *clip-clop, clip-clop* of the horses' hooves made Tess's heartbeat accelerate with a happiness she hadn't known since . . . well, since before she'd lost her husband and child. She was running away. Having an adventure!

And what'll you do when they discover you're gone? Reed won't be happy when he learns the company driver was your accomplice.

It suddenly didn't matter what anyone thought—or what Mr. Mahaffey did. She was *tired* of following everyone else's rules, and she was *damn* sick of feeling so useless, so alone in her own home. If she didn't want to suffer through the holidays in this black dress, why should she? Surely there was a place she could celebrate Christmas—honor Henry and Claire's memories in her heart—without Southern society looking down its nose at her. There had to be something more to life than matrons who smothered her in their honeyed pity and ambitious men who wanted what Henry Bennett had left behind.

Tess rapped on the carriage ceiling.

The slot above the opposite seat slid open. "Yes, ma'am?"

"Take me to the train station."

She could imagine the furrows in Warren's forehead. "The train station, Mrs. Bennett? Might I ask—"

"You know how Henry always spoke of crossing the country by rail? Hiring a private Pullman car to take in the scenery from its picture windows?" she replied, her excitement rising. "The advertisements look so enticing—special holiday trips through the Rockies and such. I'm going to *do* it. No time like the present—and no present like time away from Mr. Mahaffey! Don't you agree?"

The coach turned down the next busy street, and within minutes they stopped. All around the railway station, people strode with a purposeful air, some dressed in high style with a manservant wheeling their trunks on a cart, while others appeared to be penniless immigrants. But they were all *going* places. Tess had never in her sheltered, privileged life set foot away from home without servants or without her father or Henry making her travel plans. What if she boarded the wrong train or—

What if Reed catches you? You'll never be out of his sight again.

Tess straightened her shoulders, fixing a grin on her face. She couldn't let her driver see her fear as he handed her down from the carriage. "Thank you so much for understanding, Warren," she said in the firmest voice she could find. She reached into her reticule. "I hope you'll accept this gift as my—"

"Keep your money, my dear." He gently closed her hand around the greenbacks. "Allow me to assist with your ticketing, and then I'll deal with the Delaneys and Mahaffey."

"What will you tell them?"

"I'll make up something."

An unladylike snicker escaped her as she grabbed him around the shoulders. The old fellow hugged her, beaming. "Henry always spoke of a mischievous streak—a sense of purpose that set his wife apart from other women. He would be proud of you, Miss Tess."

Her heart swelled, but it was no time for tears. "I'd be eternally grateful if you'd arrange my fares and transfers, Warren. I'll keep you posted on my travels."

"And I shall assure the Delaneys I've seen to your safety, without hinting at your whereabouts to Mahaffey." He gave her another purposeful look. "If you need anything—anything at all, dear lady—I'm but a telegram away."

She swiped at her eyes. "What if Reed fires you? I'd hate to think I cost you your position."

"Plenty of firms need dependable drivers. Hasn't been the same since Mr. Bennett passed, anyway." He bussed her knuckles. "Come inside where it's warmer. I'll have you on your way in no time."

Once Warren left her beside a long wooden bench to go to the ticketing window, she had a chance to think about this unexpected turn she'd taken. *How will you cross the country in a luxury Pullman with only the clothes on your back? You don't even know how much money's in your reticule! Who do you think you are, believing everyone will grant your every wish like Henry—and Warren Coates—have?*

Was it the airlessness of the crowded station, or did she feel faint? No time for turning tail, though. Tess lowered herself to the bench and inhaled to clear her head. No time for feeling like a weak-kneed sissy, either. And what was taking Coates so long? As she gawked over her shoulder to view the line at the ticket window, something slithered across her feet.

It was a newspaper page, caught in the current of people coming in from the cold. As a train whistle blasted and a *hisssss* of steam rose around the platform outside, Tess froze in the moment . . . as though she'd been *meant* to peruse this segment of the *Rocky Mountain News*. How odd. She hadn't read a paper since she'd sent copies of Henry's and Claire's obituaries to family back East.

Tess quickly scanned the columns of print, not sure why she felt so driven, so destined, to find whatever beckoned her. Pulse thumping, she turned to the other side and—

Santa seeks a special helper.

The advertisement was positioned in the Help Wanted section. Why on earth did she linger over this page when she'd never worked a day in her life?

> Santa seeks a special Helper: Excellent compensation and a sweet future indeed for an Applicant who's both Naughty and Nice—and who believes in Magic! Only those of childlike mind and stature need apply. Box 8, Cascade, Colorado.

Tess blinked. Warren was now at the ticket window, so she quickly turned her attention to the quaintly phrased text again. *Both Naughty and Nice... believes in Magic... childlike mind and stature.* Whoever wrote this had a whimsical mind and a different perspective on the world than, say, Reed Mahaffey. Her heart thrummed: She *was* petite—a Dixie pixie, Henry had always called her. And she so wanted to believe in whatever magic had whisked her from the house to the train station.

But naughty and nice? The idea sent a delicious tingle through her body: She'd been told all her life she was nice—mostly when somebody wanted something. But *naughty?*

Her grin flickered. Tess studied the signs and arrows posted on the walls and then scurried toward a small office a few yards from where Warren counted out money to the ticket agent. "I need to send a message, please," she said breathlessly. She thrust the newspaper beneath the window bars, jabbing the address with her finger.

The telegrapher handed her a pencil and paper. "Please write legibly and—"

Tess's hand flew at the speed of her thoughts: *Don't you dare hire anyone but Tess Bennett! I'll be in Cascade shortly and you'll see why!*

The man in the booth paused, his fingers poised over his telegraph key. Then he gazed quizzically at her. And was it any wonder? Why on earth had she presumed to . . . She had no idea who had written such an ad or what she might be getting into when she disembarked.

Does the train even go to Cascade?

Tess blinked. She clearly needed to consider the consequences of her bold, brash actions. A woman traveling alone had no safety net—no Warren Coates to turn to, should this ad have been penned by a man with nefarious ways of putting women to work.

But the expression on the telegrapher's face, and the fact that Coates was searching the crowd for her, pulled out all her stops. "Please, sir! I've a train to catch!" she urged him sweetly.

"Thirty cents, if you please."

As she dug in her reticule, Tess's mouth went dry. Wasn't that awfully expensive for such a simple message?

As though spending thirty cents is a hardship. Get over yourself. And get on with this Christmas adventure, naughty girl!

2

"Excuse me, sir, but does this train stop in Cascade, Colorado? I don't see that town on my ticket." From her seat beside the picture window in the observation car, Tess smiled up at the uniformed conductor. After a lovely four-course dinner, she'd spent several minutes gazing at the distant sunset while snowflakes drifted around them, catching the day's last light.

The agent smiled indulgently. "No, ma'am. The closest station to Cascade is Colorado Springs."

Tess's heart lurched. She studied her itinerary again. "And . . . is Colorado Springs near Denver, then?"

"Oh, no, ma'am. That's a different line, requiring a transfer. Shall I look at your ticket?"

Her mouth went sour. Not even two hours from Memphis and her adventure was going awry. *And isn't that what you deserve for going off on your own tangent, Dixie Pixie? Had you followed Warren's plan instead of answering that ad—*

"Might I be of service, miss?" A mustachioed gentleman and the man beside him nodded cordially from across the aisle.

"Didn't mean to eavesdrop, but my partner and I are quite familiar with the Springs. Cascade's only a stagecoach ride away."

"Unless the roads are snowed shut," his friend added. His gold-rimmed spectacles twinkled when he grinned. "This time of year, that's quite common, you see. Not many folks live in Cascade, and those who do spend a good bit of each winter holed up in their homes."

This wasn't what she wanted to hear. These two looked respectable enough in their vested suits, with their brandy snifters and cigars, but she'd been pondering the pitfalls of traveling as a woman alone. Her trusting nature could get her into trouble if she believed everything every nice-looking man told her.

Tess sat straighter, which subtly thrust out her breasts. Henry had always said attitude was everything: He'd *believed* himself the most competent cotton factor in the Memphis region—and had worked diligently to prove it—so everyone who dealt with him considered him the best as well. Never mind that she was dressed in mourning and obviously beyond familiar boundaries. She would not whimper and board the next train home. She would prevail!

"I have it on good authority that Santa himself lives in Cascade," Tess asserted demurely. "And if Saint Nick delivers toys around the globe in a single night, in a sleigh pulled by reindeer, his magic will direct me to his door!"

The conductor coughed: He figured her for a real twit now. That line about Santa probably wasn't a sound strategy for a woman alone. *Or maybe it's the best thing you could've said. If these fellows think you're stupid, they won't go sniffing after your business in Colorado.*

The railway agent returned her ticket, smiling kindly. "I'll telegraph ahead to see what I can do about rerouting you, Mrs. Bennett. Shouldn't take but an hour or so to secure you a seat on—"

"If the lady will allow us, we shall accompany her," the man across the aisle said. "We're bound for Colorado Springs, anyway, and I know a trustworthy coachman who will see her safely to her destination in Cascade."

Tess smiled radiantly. As often happened, she had situated herself in just the right place at the right time: that same sort of magic alluded to in the advertisement! "How lucky can I get?" she exclaimed graciously. "Not one but *three* gentlemen lighting my way. I can't thank you enough—because I don't yet know your names."

"Spencer Penrose, known to my friends as Spec," the first gentleman said as he rose from his seat. "And this is my partner, Charley Tutt. So pleased to make your acquaintance—Mrs. Bennett, is it?"

"Yes, but please call me Tess. 'Mrs. Bennett' reminds me of my mother-in-law."

Mr. Penrose's hearty laughter filled the observation car and made people smile when they turned their heads. As he bowed debonairly over her hand, his face radiated a boyish sense of fun. Mr. Tutt, too, gripped her hand; he seemed to think she was witty rather than critical of Henry's mother.

And the conductor, whose eyes had widened, seemed *much* more interested in her now. "Francis Turley at your service, ma'am," he said crisply. "I shall return with your new ticket in minutes."

"Thank you so much, sir." Tess watched him walk quickly through the door, toward the front of the train. Who might these two other gentlemen be, that Mr. Turley had snapped to attention at the mention of their names? Maybe she should behave like a proper lady before she put her foot in something she couldn't shake off.

"Won't you join me?" she asked, gesturing to the seats directly across from her. "It was awfully kind of you to offer me an escort, after the way I spouted off about Santa and his magic. You probably think I'm behaving childishly."

Spencer Penrose smiled like a cat who'd swallowed the proverbial canary, while Mr. Tutt took a long sip of his brandy to cover a knowing grin. What had she gotten herself into now?

"Santa *does* live in Cascade, Tess," the man in the stylish tweed suit assured her. "Charley and I are his close personal friends."

"Well, if indeed Ed—er, *Santa*—has any close friends," the other fellow chimed in as the two men took their seats. "What with all his charity events and spending time in his workshop with his, um, *elves*..."

"At the very least we're on his *list,* Charley," Spec insisted with a purposeful look at his partner. "Very near the top of the good boys and girls. So at our first opportunity, we'll send him a telegram to say you'll arrive safely and soon, Tess."

"Regardless of those snowy roads I mentioned earlier," Charley added with a nod.

Tess followed their patter, trying to read between the lines. What was this about, really? Had she unwittingly spoken in some sort of code when she'd mentioned Santa living in Cascade?

And why were they insinuating that this Santa had no close friends? Was it because of the sparse population of Cascade? Or did the man who'd written that advertisement pose a threat she should know about before she continued her adventure?

Tess blinked, wondering if Warren had assured Margaret and George of her safety...wondering how Mr. Coates had appeased his boss as well. Her stomach tightened around the rich dinner she'd eaten. Perhaps she should've stayed home to face Reed Mahaffey rather than running off on such a whim....

"You seem perplexed, my dear. Have I said something that alarms you?"

Tess focused on Spencer Penrose to quell her rising doubts.

He looked very successful: well groomed yet comfortable in his vested suit. Comfortable about who he was and what made his world go around. All of the truly wealthy men in Memphis had this same air about them: an understated way of doing things for others, without touting their money.

She sighed. Better to confess than to suffer the consequences of a split-second decision. Tess pulled the folded newspaper page from her reticule. "At the risk of looking ridiculous . . . I came west on the spur of a desperate moment. I saw this ad, and again—not thinking things through—I sent a telegram saying I'd be arriving soon."

Spec and Charley sat with their elbows on their knees, listening intently. "And?" Spencer's thick mustache flickered.

"You seem to *know* this . . . this Santa, but how can I be sure I haven't signed on for something . . . indecent? Or even dangerous?" she queried in a small voice. "I'm the widow of a successful cotton factor. I have no business running away from—"

"Sadness? Painful memories?" Charley asked quietly. "Unbearable holidays in an empty home?"

"Or perhaps the unwanted attentions of a man who's after your husband's money?" Spencer Penrose glanced at the ad, smiling kindly. "It's your business why you left home, dear Tess, but I assure you there's nothing indecent or dangerous about the man who posted this."

"Well, he has his particular . . . *tastes* in employees," Charley pointed out.

"But those employees love him so much they'd never leave him," Penrose said as he studied her. "You'll be the perfect addition to his staff, Tess. He's already working his ingenious, childlike magic—casting it out like a net woven of cotton candy—to attract just the right helper for his Christmas charity events."

Tess let out the breath she'd been holding. "So he's legitimate?"

"Oh, more than that, he's generous and sweet-natured—"

"Hardworking and admired. Loved by all who know him."

"And whoever you're running from won't catch you, way out there in the Rockies," Spencer concluded. "However, if *I* were pursuing you, dear Tess, I wouldn't let deep snow or the treacherous, winding roads—"

"Or wind or sleet or dark of night."

"—stand in my way of finding you," Penrose concluded with an intense gaze.

Tess sat very still, fixed in Spec's gaze, aware of a thrilling little undercurrent that made her insides tighten. Was he flirting with her? *Attracted?* Or did he carry on this way with every woman he met? "Matter of fact, there *is* a man vying for my attentions in Memphis," she admitted quietly. "But he mostly wants to control all the shares of the partnership, now that Henry's gone."

Both men smiled endearingly. "I'm sorry for your loss, Tess," Mr. Penrose said as he reached for her hand.

"But there's not a man alive who wouldn't want you, regardless of your financial standing," Charley Tutt joined in. "Perhaps it's the best thing that could've happened, your taking off for Cascade to work with . . . Santa. You'll be safe and warm—"

"Well paid and befriended by all," Spencer agreed.

"Protected from your husband's partner well into spring. Yet, should you require assistance from your attorney back home, or need to send him directions concerning your accounts," Charlie continued, "he's but a telegram away. Colorado may be a far frontier, but—thanks to the development of the gold mines in nearby Cripple Creek—we have all the modern conveniences."

"You'll be *fine,* my dear," Spec assured her as he gazed raptly into her eyes. "And should you need the least little thing, I shall be at your service!"

Tess blinked. Their rapid-fire conversation had left no time to read between their lines, yet their goodwill amazed her. She grinned as both fellows pulled vellum cards from their coat pockets. "I . . . I don't know how to thank you."

"Oh, we'll find a way," Charley teased as he rose to go.

"Every man takes his turn at being the giver and the receiver," Spec chimed in. His head turned as the *whoosh* of the doors announced the conductor's return. "Mr. Turley has found a way to reroute you, I'll wager. We'll wait at the station to secure your coach to Cascade, Tess. Enjoy your ride on the rails! Life's a journey to be lived with joy and exuberance."

Exuberance. When was the last time she'd known anything approaching that? As Mr. Penrose had predicted, the railway agent handed her a new ticket, grinning profusely. "Here you are, Mrs. Bennett! What an extraordinary stroke of luck that the movers and shakers of Colorado Springs were aboard in your hour of need!"

Tess glanced toward the door, but her two new friends had already gone. "Just two kindhearted souls helping a damsel in distress."

"Those two *souls* are none other than the Penrose and Tutt who've made millions in the gold mines," he replied in a conspiratorial whisper. "Spec's Broadmoor Hotel and other undertakings have made Colorado Springs *the* place for the wealthy to flock."

Tess accepted her ticket with a quiet smile. "Thank you for getting my ticket changed," she murmured as she rose from her chair. "Where would we be without the grace of God and the kindness of strangers?"

Back in her private Pullman, Tess pondered her reflection in the gilt-framed mirror. Was she really a woman any man would want? Even if she had only the black clothing on her back? True enough, Reed Mahaffey sought her attentions, but today, two total strangers had reaffirmed her allure without knowing a thing about her or her bank accounts.

And they know Santa! And they think I'm perfect for the position he's advertised.

Tess grinned, loving the roses in her cheeks, because she'd despaired of ever blooming again. She slipped the newspaper page from her dress pocket and reread the ad with more enlightened eyes: *A sweet future indeed for an Applicant who's both Naughty and Nice—and who believes in Magic!*

She certainly believed in magic now. A childlike excitement made her glow all over. As Tess Carnegy Bennett, she'd been reared to be the epitome of *nice,* under the most pressing of circumstances. So . . . just how naughty was *Naughty?*

Her giggle filled the opulent private car. She couldn't wait to find out!

3

"Daphne, you *naughty* girl! Leaving Edgar bound to the bedposts—legs and arms stretched across the bed in such an indecent pose!"

"You don't fool me for a moment, Blythe," came the saucy reply. "You're the one who rolled a sock into her elf costume—like a big ole cock!—and threatened to go to our Denver charity event that way unless Eddie—"

A flying pillow cut Daphne's retort short.

As Johnny Gazara smoothed the edge of a green, holly-shaped piece of glass, he glanced through the high transom window at the entry to Edgar Penney's master suite. Damn. How was a man supposed to work while two blond nymphs in black garter belts cavorted around their employer, who lay spread-eagle on the rumpled bed? Edgar Penney sported a huge erection as he laughed at their antics.

Not that Johnny was complaining: The owner of the Penney Candy Company paid him well above the rate mosaicists received in Paris or New York. And the childlike, reclusive man always suggested just one more mural, one more frieze, which he envisioned in glimmering shades of ceramic and glass, every time Johnny finished a project.

Nearly a year Johnny had worked here, enjoying the sumptuous guest quarters and the creativity Penney's designs demanded—not to mention the company of Edgar and his two comely companions. And yet . . . his heart yearned for life outside this snowbound little pocket of the Rockies, where cathedrals and grand hotels might commission him to create truly notable works of art.

The trouble with this imaginative house? It was mostly underground, hidden away from harsh winters and connected to the Penney Candy Factory, which turned a mind-boggling profit. Edgar Penney, the ageless entrepreneur behind confections known around the world, had built a playground here for his lovelies and occasional favored guests, but he himself rarely set foot in the real world.

The other problem with this place? Johnny could look, but he couldn't touch. Blythe and Daphne belonged to Edgar, and while they might tease him with their wayward games, Johnny went to bed alone. Long after the girls' laughter and Penney's cries of ecstasy fell silent each night, Johnny ached for a woman of his own.

A real man would've left months ago, his conscience chided when he rose in the wee hours to smoke. *So what's keeping you here? You could earn a fine living on those high-and-mighty masterpieces you daydream about.*

Or were those cathedral ceilings and hotel murals only figments of his wistful imagination? As ephemeral as the curls of minty-sweet smoke from his custom-carved pipe? This gift from Edgar Penney, given when Johnny had covered the factory's main wall with elaborate scenes from Candy Cane Lane, matched Edgar's pipe and symbolized their free spirits—as well as the invisible chains that bound them all here. Only after several long, loose conversations in which he and Penney had brainstormed incredible new confections and fantasies in glass did Edgar admit their custom blend of pipe tobacco was laced with opium.

Johnny could lay it aside anytime. Walk away to another job, another life.

But would the ideas go with you? What if it's this magical place—and the playful man behind it—that inspires your best imaginings?

A cacophony of bells, like those that jingled on sleighs and tolled in belfries and clanged around cows' necks—and the ones that called a farmer to his dinner—announced a visitor. Edgar raised his head from the mattress. Daphne and Blythe froze in place, one straddling Penney's hips as the other spread her legs above his face. Again the doorbell chimed like a choir of handbells gone awry, yet no one in the bedroom moved.

"Johnny, I must ask you to see who's here," Edgar pleaded mischievously. "The girls are nearly naked, and I . . . Well, you can tell our guest I'm all tied up at the moment!"

Gazara sighed. Carefully he laid aside the fragile holly leaves and their ruby-red berries, pieces of the stained-glass garland that would eventually stretch around every wall of Penney's suite. Down the ladder he went, then hurried between exotic mosaic dancers enacting the "Dance of the Sugarplum Fairy" on the hallway walls, to ascend the passageway that entered the vestibule at the opposite end of the house. Chances were good their guest would've given up and left—which was probably Penney's intent when he'd designed his rambling mansion beneath a mountain, leaving only the front door at ground level.

Johnny swung open the massive door, squinting in the bright daylight. "Yes?"

"Telegram for Mr. Penney." The local postman, a scarf wound up to his eyeballs, peered through his fogged eyeglasses. "Two of 'em, actually, but with that storm yesterday, nobody set foot in the elements."

They'd had a storm? Johnny noted the dramatic drifts and tall pines with icicles that glistened like ice daggers. "Thank you, sir. I'll take these to—"

"True what they say, 'bout Penney havin' squinty little eyes that can't tolerate the sun?"

Johnny paused over another local rumor. Edgar Penney had large, dreamlike eyes that radiated warmth like a cup of cocoa. "Nope." He took the envelopes, tipped the curious postman from a box on the table, and then closed the doors.

As he returned to the master suite, Johnny became curious: Edgar regularly received orders for candy but rarely got personal messages. On the oversize bed, Blythe was riding Edgar's hips, her head thrown back as she approached climax, while her friend straddled his face. Penney had his hands full of Daphne's pretty ass, so he couldn't open these telegrams right now. They were unsealed, too ... flaps loosely tucked. So, since no one would be the wiser, Johnny peeked.

The first note, dated this morning, told Edgar to watch for a pretty little widow named Tess to arrive shortly. The sender insisted Tess was exactly the kind of Penney Candy girl he was looking for.

Johnny tingled all over as he opened the other telegram, which had come from Tess herself. *Don't you dare hire anyone but Tess Bennett! I'll be in Cascade shortly and you'll see why!*

He stifled a laugh. Weeks had passed since Edgar had run his ad, and this lone applicant sounded pushy and full of herself and—

Tessssss, his mind rhapsodized. *Rhymes with yesssssssss!*

Johnny hardened against the seam of his pants. What were the chances *he* could woo this new elf, if indeed she met the Penney Candy girl criteria—or hell, even if she didn't! Mrs. Bennett surely had other worthwhile qualifications, even if she wasn't cute, petite, and a saucy blonde!

He glanced again at the first message: none other than

Spencer Penrose was endorsing this woman. The multimillion-
aire of Cripple Creek's gold mines was known for his way with
the ladies, and as one of Penney Candy's largest customers,
Penrose knew quite well what Edgar Penney looked for in an
assistant.

Johnny's heart fluttered. He closed his eyes. How would the
man buried beneath two blondes possibly pleasure a third one?
While they needed another elf to hand out candy at their up-
coming charity events, her presence would change *everything*.
How would Daphne and Blythe respond to yet another pretty
blonde vying for Edgar's attentions? And how would an un-
knowing applicant react, once she discovered their unconven-
tional living conditions?

"Gazara! What could possibly be so grave and complicated
that you've assumed such a serious expression? Or are you
praying?"

Johnny jumped and his eyes flew open. What the hell could
he say? Edgar lounged against the doorway, flushed and naked,
his gaze fixed on the telegrams.

"Sorry, I . . ." He handed over the notes. "It wasn't my place
to open your mail."

"We've received responses to my ad, have we not?" His face
glowed pink from sconces Johnny had fashioned as ruby glass
poinsettias. "I *knew* the right eyes would eventually see—and a
special heart respond to—my plea for another—"

The chaotic chiming of the doorbells made their eyebrows
rise.

Edgar's eyes shone like hot coffee. "You don't suppose that
could be—"

"Tess. *Yes!*" Johnny's heart pounded. "You're not dressed
for a guest, so I'll let her in. But don't expect me back for a
while, Edgar! Any decent woman would have second thoughts
when she sees . . ." As he gestured toward the four-poster bed,
where Blythe and Daphne sprawled across the wrecked sheets,

he was already hurrying along the hallway. What *luck!* Fastidious Mr. Penney wouldn't greet anyone until he'd bathed and dressed in fresh clothing, and he would insist his two lovers do the same. Or would he instruct the girls to remain in their rooms while he interviewed this applicant?

Please, God, make her take this job. And make her take me, too. Johnny trotted up the winding hallway, past his work—ballerinas in mother-of-pearl tutus, their arms forming heart-shaped arches beneath a ceiling that glistened with snowflakes and sugarplums dusted with tiny facets of glass. It was all over-done, with details only he and Edgar fully appreciated, yet this ostentatious home reflected its owner perfectly.

Mrs. Bennett's reaction to this décor would be the best gauge of her suitability. If she stared—or worse yet, frowned—she'd be gone. Edgar suffered no naysayers or employees of limited imagination. As Johnny reached the final rise toward the foyer, the doorbell chimed again. Bells of all sizes and tones clanged in the vaulted ceiling above him as he entered the mirrored vestibule that glowed with his own stained-glass designs.

Be still, my heart! He steadied himself with a deep breath. Was he smiling like a lovesick fool? Did he seem too needy? He'd gone such a long time without a woman; his desperation might announce itself in embarrassing ways. . . .

But if she balks at what she sees, it's better if she turns tail. Edgar's candy castle is no place for the faint of heart.

Johnny paused with his hand on the knob. If the postman had come back with another nosy question, he'd feel like a top-notch fool, wouldn't he? As the various bells died above him, he squared his shoulders. When he swung open the door, snowflakes whirled around a figure clad in black from top to toe.

The bluest eyes he'd ever seen widened at the sight of him. A black hood framed the cutest little peaches-and-cream face, the most dazzling smile.

Johnny groaned. In spite of his best intentions, his manhood saluted, and he was grateful for the snow glare that blinded her to his predicament. "Tess? Er . . . Mrs. Bennett?" he corrected in a voice that sounded painfully adolescent.

"*Santa?*" Her drawl whispered of magnolia blossoms caressed by a spring breeze.

Oh, God. He was in worse trouble than he'd feared.

4

Tess gripped her cloak, wishing she'd directed the coach driver to a dress shop instead of coming here directly from the station. When Mr. Tutt had noted her lack of luggage, he'd quietly suggested a seamstress in Colorado Springs who would send him the bill, but Tess was too proud—in too damn much of a hurry—to accept Charley's help.

And now she stood before the devil himself, olive-skinned with midnight hair and lashes, wearing a white silk shirt unbuttoned to such an indecent length she saw the curls on his broad chest. A hot yearning welled up and came out as a sigh.

His smile widened—as well it might! Hadn't she just announced she was lonely and desperate and *willing?* And then she'd called him Santa! How stupid was that? "Yes, I'm Mrs. Bennett—Tess—here to answer your advertisement. And . . . well, I had no idea what else to call you. *Sir.*"

Oh, his sly smile hid secrets. Tess stood absolutely still, determined to not lower her gaze, but the wind made her shiver.

Her inquisitor softened. "Please, come in! How rude of me to keep you waiting in this cold!" He took her arm, guiding her into a vestibule that sparkled like the inside of a queen's jewel box. "The house is underground, to discourage spies and busy-bodies, so we have no idea when it snows or—"

The house is underground. For a heart-stopping moment, Tess imagined herself in Henry's place, boxed and buried where the sun would never shine. It was a morose thought, the stuff of her nightmares after her husband and Claire had died, but it was *not* what she expected after reading that whimsical adver-tisement. Nor did the high-ceilinged entryway, with its sky-light and mirrors framed in faceted stained-glass gemstones, hint at anything so funereal.

"We hope you'll find Mr. Penney's home as delightful a place to live and work as we have," her greeter continued. He wasn't releasing her arm; instead, he rubbed her hands between his larger ones to warm them. "We've been looking forward to your arrival, dear lady."

He would think her dense if she didn't reply, yet Tess's head had already filled with more questions than answers, and she didn't even know this brazenly handsome fellow's name. "So . . . you're not the man who ran the ad in the *Rocky Mountain News,* asking for—"

"But I'm the man who ran the ad to the *News* office," he in-terrupted playfully. His smile flashed as he raised her knuckles to his lips. "Johnny Gazara. *So* nice to meet you, Tess," he purred. "And while I'm not directly associated with Edgar Penney's candy company, I've been decorating his home and factory for several months now. So if you have questions—any questions at all . . ."

Why is a dangerously attractive man like you becoming tongue-tied over a waif like me? sprang to mind, but Tess kept quiet. Mama had often remarked that while beauty might only be skin-deep, it was most men's strongest weakness.

And if this rake was hoping to be her mentor and close per-sonal friend, in a house that sounded decidedly strange, she wasn't sure how much she should ask him. Or reveal. It seemed that ever since she'd run away from home, men with alluring smiles had appeared to assist her. It was only a matter of time before one of them turned out to be the Big Bad Wolf—wasn't it?

Tess looked around the colorful vestibule to assess her situation. It would be a shame to leave now, after traveling so far on her high hopes of finding joy again . . . and it would be no easy feat to get a stagecoach, out here in this drifted hinterland. She'd delighted in looking at the deepest snow she'd ever seen while they'd rolled along a road that glistened with fine, powdery diamonds, swirls of sparkling white against a sky the color of morning glories. But it was another thing altogether to navigate this snowy mountain town on foot, wearing clothing more suited to Memphis.

Not that the man holding her hands seemed inclined to let go. He cocked his head slightly, still smiling in that secretive way. Could he hear how her pulse thrummed? If he could feel her rising excitement . . . Was he about to kiss her, or had it been so long she was misconstruing his cues?

Tess glanced away, pretending to admire the play of stained-glass colors in the sunbeam from the skylight. What if this whole adventure had been a bad idea from the start? Why had she picked up that newspaper, anyway, when Warren Coates had arranged an itinerary that was safer for a woman alone? Would she never listen to that inner voice that warned her to behave like a lady? To follow the rules for her own good?

"Have I said something to upset you, dear Tess?"

Everything you do upsets me. In the best possible way. She met his shining black eyes again. Damn. Johnny Gazara, a man as rakish as his name, stooped to meet her gaze with his onyx eyes.

He expected an answer. He expected a kiss. And then he expected a *yes*.

Tess sucked air, struck dumb by this man's intensity. "You say *you* have decorated this fabulous room, Mr.—"

"Please, call me Johnny. And, yes, I did!" He bowed, obviously pleased with his work and her response to it.

He'd regained control of his voice now, and his rich baritone wrapped itself around the need inside her . . . the need to hear such a masculine voice murmuring in her ear while his fine artist's hands did unthinkable things to her bare body. Tess inhaled deeply, hoping to clear her head, but his scent . . . the rich aroma of mint tobacco . . . harkened back to afternoons in Papa's study, where she'd felt so cherished and secure. So *loved*.

Her eyes drifted shut, even though Gazara knew exactly how to play her to his advantage. Her lips parted to meet his. Johnny's sigh was so soft and his breath so warm as he kissed her, framing her face with hands that barely skimmed her skin. It was an eager yet thorough exploration of her mouth that promised far more.

Just that fast she became his captive.

Tess rose to meet him, her arms encircling his neck as her senses reeled and her body came to life again after too many months of not having a man. Sweet and eager, Johnny tasted. When his tongue darted between her teeth, Tess's giggle echoed in the vestibule.

"And now that Mr. Gazara has welcomed you," a male voice resonated around them, "he'll be returning to his work."

Tess jerked away. Damn it, why did Johnny wear such a triumphant smile? She barely knew him, and already he'd compromised her—presumably in front of the man she'd come to work for!

"I'm delighted to meet you, Tess," he went on. "We heard of your arrival only moments ago, or I would've fetched you at the station. Edgar Penney at your service, my dear."

In the floor-to-ceiling mirrors, his reflection became a caricature caught in a kaleidoscope: A man dressed in a red, ermine-trimmed cloak and shiny black boots stepped briskly in front of her, his wrap swirling about his red trousers. Beneath his matching hat, his boyish grin widened as he gazed eagerly at her, holding her spellbound with his sparkling brown eyes. He caught her hands and fervently kissed her knuckles. Before Tess knew what was happening, he unfastened her cloak to sweep it back from her face and off her shoulders.

"Oh, my," he breathed. He glanced at Johnny Gazara. "Won't she look fetching in an elf suit?"

"She'd look fetching without one," Gazara muttered.

Edgar Penney assessed her with a lingering look, turning her face slightly, one side to the other, then stepping back to observe how her waist nipped in above her hips. He stared for a moment, as though he were looking *through* her black dress and her bloomers and corset. "I'm sorry for your loss, Mrs. Bennett. My mission is to put a smile on that arresting face and a song in your heart while you're here with us."

Tess's cheeks went hot. "I . . . My telegram must've sounded arrogant or cocky—"

"Around here, *cocky* is the norm." Penney's fingers followed the rise of her cheekbones to her ears.

"And I didn't mean to imply . . . for all I know you've hired an assistant, because the newspaper was dated—"

"And where did you see that paper, dear Tess?"

The room echoed with a silence she didn't know how to interpret. But then, what *had* made sense since the moment she'd met these two men? Johnny Gazara stood staunchly beside this dashing Santa, refusing to relinquish first rights to her, while Mr. Penney lifted her chin with his finger. "In the train station. In Memphis, sir."

"Memphis! That explains your bewitching accent." He grinned at Gazara again. "Who could've imagined my advertisement would make its way from the Rockies to the Mississippi? And then attract this Southern belle—precisely the right

Penney Candy girl—to our door? Magic, I tell you! Never stop believing in magic!"

Tess held her breath. What might Mr. Penney do next? No gentleman would take such liberties with a woman he'd met mere seconds ago, and yet he'd proclaimed her perfect—precisely right. And this after catching her in another man's embrace. "It is magic," she whispered. "And if ever I needed a visit from Saint Nicholas, it would be now."

Edgar Penney's eyes melted like chocolate. As though he, too, had suffered her trials this year, he wrapped his arms around her, holding her so close his exquisite ermine collar tickled her face as he breathed. He smelled clean and fresh, and his smooth-shaven cheek felt heavenly against hers. She sensed that in the silence of this memorable moment, important matters were being considered and problems were being solved . . . perhaps by this man's magic.

"You've come to the right place, Tess," he murmured. "Your life's about to take a wild turn—for the better. What we make here is joy! The candy is merely a token of that."

Tess longed to believe him. But what if this fellow turned out to be a shyster? A man who lured unassuming women to this remote outpost to—

She shook her head to free it from this unspeakable idea.

"Are you all right, dear heart?" Penney's fingertip teased the rim of her ear. "You've had a long journey, and it's rude of me to keep you standing here without explaining things. You see, I'm Edgar Penney. Each December, my Penney Candy girls hand out sweets to orphans at our charity events, where local merchants place their seasonal orders and our wealthier guests donate to the children's cause. Do you think you could do that for me?"

Just keep talking so I can watch your mouth. Tess blinked at this blatant thought. Moments ago she'd been losing herself in Johnny Gazara's kiss, and now she was allowing another man to hold her while Johnny watched. What had happened to the model wife and mother she'd been for so many years? It was as though Mrs. Henry Bennett had blown away with the powdery snow.

Then her eyes widened. "You mean, *the* Penney Candy? Known around the world for its vivid colors and incredibly intense flavors?"

"The very one."

"But you can't be old enough to . . . I mean . . ." Tess flushed at her rude remark. "The man on the packages leads one to believe you've been around, well, almost as long as Santa himself!"

"I took over the business from my grandfather. Generations have enjoyed our candy, and I didn't want to lose our customers' trust by changing our image." When Edgar removed his close-fitting red hat, his shimmering brown hair framed his face like a windswept mane. And indeed, he seemed the lionish sort, all high cheekbones and angular facial planes. "Shall we continue this interview while I show you the candy factory?"

"Oh, yes, I'd like that!"

"Excellent!" He gave Johnny a purposeful look. "Tell Blythe and Daphne I wish to remain uninterrupted during our tour. They'll meet Tess in due time."

Why did Gazara look like he'd bitten a lemon? Was he peeved about being upstaged? "Yes, of course, Edgar," he muttered. "We'll not wait for you at dinner, then."

"Please ask Hortense to freshen the room adjoining mine for our guest," her host continued breezily, "and, if you would be so kind, please take Mrs. Bennett's trunks there so she may unpack after our tour."

The vestibule grew quiet as both men looked for luggage. Johnny turned toward the door, thinking her personal effects were still outside.

"I have no trunks," Tess confessed. She held Edgar's penetrating gaze while she thought up a logical reason for this. But there was nothing logical about anything she'd done since Reed Mahaffey had come to the house too early, was there?

"I left home on the spur of a desperate moment." She sighed. No sense in lying, but no good reason to reveal every detail, either. "My husband and little girl died from yellow fever last summer. I couldn't spend December in the home where they had delighted in trimming the tree and shaking the presents. Matter of fact," she added sadly, "when I realized I had no one to buy gifts for, I couldn't stay in Memphis a moment longer. I . . . I didn't mean to burden you with my tale of woe."

"Tess, I'm sorry." Johnny squeezed her shoulder, his brow furrowed with sympathy. "It's good you didn't put yourself through the holiday alone."

"I repeat: It's my mission to put the roses back in your cheeks and to help you celebrate the season again." Edgar smiled warmly. "You're the perfect elf for handing out treats to our orphans! They'll sense your compassion—a kindred spirit. And you, in turn, will rediscover the joy of giving."

Her eyes filled with tears, damn it. She hadn't intended to invoke their pity. While she had sidestepped the topic of Mahaffey's one-sided courtship, she hadn't exactly lied. Gifts for her staff didn't count, the way presents for Henry and Claire had. . . .

And what could she possibly tell the Delaneys about where she'd gone and what she'd done? They would worry about her, no matter how Warren Coates assured them she was safe. But it was too late to be concerned about that, wasn't it?

Edgar Penney fixed her in his brown-eyed gaze as he offered his elbow. "Shall we go? I have so much to show you, my dear!"

5

"Would you look at him? Showing off the factory with such a grandiose air—as though he might bequeath it to her!" Johnny glared through the narrow band of windows that served as a supervision post in Edgar's suite. On either side of him, Blythe and Daphne watched Edgar and Tess as well. The conveyors clacked along, bearing specialty chocolates, Pinwheel Pops, and every sort of sweet imaginable as factory workers sorted and sacked, yet he had eyes only for the couple in red and black.

"No different from the way he escorted me around when I answered his ad," Blythe replied in a nostalgic tone. "Ten years it's been. I was as awed by him then as I am now. As amazed by his magic as Tess Bennett is."

"Same for me, five years ago," Daphne chimed in. "Edgar Penney has an ageless, childlike appeal about him. My own appearance changes with the years, yet he seems no different from the day I came here."

Johnny rolled his eyes. "And what we're watching doesn't bother you? Anyone can see he's more than smitten with Mrs. Bennett!"

"Is that a green streak in your voice, Johnny?" The flaxen curls at Daphne's temples quivered with her suppressed laughter. "Matter of fact, he intends to leave his factory to Blythe and me because he has no heirs—and because we'll carry on his traditions with the orphans."

"How do you feel about sharing your inheritance with another woman?" Johnny snapped. "Not to mention how *cozy* this bedroom will be with *three* of you pleasuring him! He's putting Tess in the adjoining room, you know."

Blythe, the older and more gracious of the two Penney Candy girls, placed her hands on his shoulders. "Johnny," she murmured, "it's not like you to sound so critical. We certainly can't complain about our pay or the living conditions."

"Speak for yourselves," he spouted. "You're not living like a monk in a whorehouse!"

"*Really!*" Daphne's lips pursed in a pretty pout. "I never dreamed you considered Blythe and me—"

"That's not what I meant. I'm sorry." Johnny inhaled to steady his temper, yet that only made him more aware of the lemon verbena soap she and Blythe had bathed with. Thoughts of them splashing in Edgar's big tub together only irritated him more, because he couldn't recall how Tess Bennett smelled. But her kiss was absolute heaven.

"You have no idea what it's like to live with two beautiful women who parade around half naked—or romp with Ed—while I must keep my hands and my . . . *urges* to myself," he explained. "It damn near kills me some days. I had to cut seven extra holly leaves yesterday because you two were playing hide-and-seek with him while I worked."

"But we love having you here, Johnny. You could play with us," Blythe replied. Her golden hair fell in loose waves around her shoulders, still damp from her bath. "While Edgar takes wonderful care of us, I feel better knowing there's another man in the house, you know? It's such a rambling place we'd not be aware of an intruder until it was too late."

"An intruder?" Daphne pulled her filmy white robe more closely around her shoulders. "Who would ever think of—"

"People realize how wealthy Edgar Penney is," the other blonde pointed out. "But I'm not really afraid of strangers getting inside, for he's devised ingenious safeguards. What I *meant* was that Johnny's become such a part of our family that we'd miss him if he were to go. He's a rock of reality in this world that runs on Edgar's make-believe and magic."

"Thank you, Blythe."

"Go? Where would you go, Johnny?" Daphne draped an arm around his shoulders, which meant one delectable breast brushed his chest. Her eyes didn't quite focus when she looked at him.

Johnny sighed. These lovelies had caught him in a conversational trap, and he'd never intended to offend or upset them. He'd never considered them whores, either. They'd escaped difficult lives to accept Edgar Penney's job and generosity. Not their fault that Ed took his pleasure as seriously as he did his business. What woman would refuse such a sweet deal?

Will Tess see this place for what it is? A playhouse for adults who indulge their fantasies? A playpen for pretty blondes who . . .

He glanced through the window again, down into the vast expanse of the factory, where a man in red had his arm around a blonde in black. It looked far too intimate already. "I'm concerned that Mrs. Bennett will be lured into this candy-striped cave before she realizes the consequences," he said sadly. "Edgar will catch her with his flattery and keep her with his opium. Just like he has the rest of us."

Two pairs of blue eyes widened. Two pretty blond heads tilted at coquettish angles as Daphne and Blythe considered what he'd said.

Blythe let out a sad-but-wise sigh. "I've always known about Edgar's addiction, but I've been a willing victim, Johnny." Her grin quirked. "Nobody's making me stay. I've banked plenty of money to live in the real world, if I cared to."

"Oh, don't leave me!" Daphne whimpered. "I'm so happy here, and . . . and where would I go? This will always be home to me, Blythe, so I want *you* to stay, too. And you, Johnny. Please? *Please?*"

The younger blonde had always been more susceptible to quicksilver moods, and her very round, very wide eyes suggested she'd been hitting the hookah. Daphne had been abandoned by a man who'd beaten her nearly to death, so Johnny understood why she wanted to stay here with Penney, out of circulation: She probably feared that "intruder" would be the beast from whom Ed had rescued her.

And what was Tess Bennett's story? There was more to her tale than a deceased husband and daughter—although a double dose of death might drive any woman to desperation. Her telegram had suggested a strong, playful spirit, yet still he saw those sad blue eyes peering out from beneath her black cloak. His heart swelled with the need to protect her. To honor her.

Who are you kidding? Before Penney showed up, you were seducing her.

Yes, there was that. Yet Tess appealed to him in a deeper, more sacred way. Any woman who'd left home with only the clothes on her back to answer an advertisement that took her far from the life she'd known had a backbone. She deserved better than to become one of Penney's playthings. She should have another family. People to love, who loved her in return.

Stirred by the intensity of this emotion, Johnny tightened all over. He suddenly wanted to be the man who made up for the husband and child Tess had lost—the friend, the lover, who saved her from growing old as a Penney Candy girl, only to be eclipsed when Edgar brought in yet another perky, petite blonde.

And where is THIS coming from? You've sworn to never let another woman wrap her strings around you like a noose.

Daphne still leaned on him, pleading with Blythe. In her high, childish whine, he heard the fate he could not allow Tess Bennett to know; he heard the call to get *out* of this house and become an artist who lived up to his abilities. His *calling.*

Johnny trembled at the thought. And for once it felt like an adventure—a quest to follow his star rather than a random twist of fate. Tess would inspire him to seek out the cathedrals and theaters where his stained-glass creations would capture the imaginations of more than Edgar Penney and his girls.

After all, how many people would ever *see* the artwork he'd lavished upon the walls of this recluse's hideaway? How many months of his life had he devoted to Ed's whims, when he could've been creating art that *mattered?*

Once more he observed the couple strolling the aisles of the busy candy factory. His heart thumped harder as he realized what he must do. *Tonight.*

6

Tess gazed around the beautiful room Edgar's housekeeper had freshened for her. The walls were covered in pink swirled paper that reminded her of cotton candy. A bed with a white canopy and counterpane took her back to her childhood; she could forget about that lonely home in Memphis, where Margaret and George clucked over her every crying spell. Here in this tucked-away haven—attached to the Penney Candy Factory!—she could feel like a girl again, yet soon she'd brighten the lives of hundreds of children who had no families. With a smile and a candy-stuffed stocking, she could bring them the spirit of Christmas. That sounded so much better than moping at home, trying to elude Reed Mahaffey.

Tess threw herself happily onto the bed. She felt tired from her journey, yet renewed. Eager to begin her work with the magical man who'd greeted her as Santa, whose voice and gentle manner encouraged her to be open to childlike wonderment again. *Awe* and *amazement* didn't come close to describing what her tour of Edgar's factory had inspired in her.

The man was a genius. Not only had he transformed his grandfather's floundering, outdated business into the world's best-known candy factory, he kept his employees happy on the job. By providing a pleasant, colorful workplace—enhanced greatly by Johnny Gazara's stained-glass designs—Edgar Penney had inspired the utmost loyalty in his factory workers, not to mention the two Penney Candy girls who had made his charity events more successful with each Christmas season.

Tess opened the drawer of the white nightstand. Magic again! Hortense had provided her a nightgown, and through the bathroom door she saw jars of bath salts and fluffy towels. A soak in a tub of hot, bubbly water sounded so heavenly. . . .

As she draped her black dress over a chair, Tess saw how out of place it looked in this room untouched by loneliness or grief. *Come tomorrow, I'll no longer wear mourning.* She smiled as she twisted the spigots and tossed in some scented salts. As she sank into the warm, lemon-scented bubbles, her head lolled blissfully against the rim of the tub. She would close her eyes for only a moment. . . .

As the water rose around her body, her cares floated away. She recalled phrases from Edgar's conversation, and then it was that dark-haired rogue she saw in her mind's eye—the one who'd tricked her into kissing him. She barely knew his name. Her body, however, had no such qualms: Her belly tightened with anticipation as she thought about what she secretly wanted Johnny Gazara to do to her.

She could picture him now, running his hand along her leg under the bathwater. Oh, how he made her quiver when his fingertips caressed her inner thighs but went no farther.

"Please . . . please," she murmured, showing him where she longed for his touch. Her legs parted so he couldn't possibly miss the hint—how brazen Johnny made her feel when he gazed at her with those obsidian eyes. And the nerve of him, to tease the sensitive skin of her abdomen on the way to tweaking her nipples! Her breasts swelled, aching for his touch, and as he cupped one and then the other, a wanton sigh escaped her.

"Johnny," she murmured. And, since this was her fantasy, he behaved exactly as she wanted him to.

"Yes, my Tess? How may I please you?" he asked in that low, molten voice. "I've waited all day . . . could barely restrain myself while Edgar escorted you around the factory with his arm around your shoulder. Was he fondling you? Like this?"

Tess sucked air at such naughtiness: Johnny was behind her now, reaching over her shoulders to knead her breasts as she squirmed with the pleasure of it.

"Did he touch you this way?" Johnny repeated, closer to her ear.

She moaned as he sent jolts of electricity through her body . . . which all landed between her legs, where she longed to be filled with this man. "No, Edgar was behaving himself—which is why I like you better, Johnny."

She giggled. Never had she admitted such a thing to a man. Nor had she let on to Henry that she'd imagined other men taking such liberties with her. Faithful, devoted wives had no such thoughts!

"May I play with the curls where your thighs come together?" he whispered. His mouth was so close to her ear she felt him forming every alluring word.

"Only if you don't stop there," she replied. "Put your finger inside me. Run it around the rim of my hot little hole and make me beg for you!"

His low laughter assured her that such an unladylike suggestion didn't offend him in the least. As he caressed her midsection, the rounded sides of her belly and the curve of her hip, Tess's mouth dropped open. Sheer need made her hips wiggle.

"I'm going to rub your mound . . . squeeze it lightly, to accustom you to my touch," he murmured. "No screaming or crying out, now. Edgar's on the other side of this wall. If he thinks you're pleasuring yourself, he'll be in here to help."

"Can't have that," she murmured through a fog of desire. It pooled inside her, sliding lower with his hand until his fingers were firmly tucked around her fleshy pillow of coarse curls.

Tess bit back a cry of utter need. How fabulous it felt, to tell a man what she wanted and to have him speak so freely of what he'd do to her. As her hips moved in his hand's rhythm, she felt hot inner spirals intensify toward a climax—a sensation like she'd never felt before.

"Inside," she whispered. "Please, oh *please*, dip inside my cunt! Rub me until I can't stand it anymore!"

Where had *that* come from? Never in her life had she uttered such a foul word. Where had she even heard it? Johnny's ragged sigh told her it affected him in a fierce sort of way—and that she'd answer to him before long. With the first stroke of his long finger in her cleft, Tess convulsed. He held her against the back of the tub with his other arm as that wayward finger tormented her inflamed flesh.

She panted his name—anything to keep her mind grounded while her body tried to fly. Tess writhed shamelessly against his hand, driven toward a destination she couldn't name, yet Johnny seemed eager to take her there. In and out went his relentless middle finger, and then another digit joined it, gently squeezing her sensitive little button between them.

Tess grimaced. Told herself not to scream, yet she couldn't keep her hips still. She pressed Johnny's hand harder to satisfy her need, finding just the right spots to take her where her body wanted to go. With a whimper and a gasp, she spasmed. Couldn't stop—drove his hand deeper inside as her body tightened . . . tightened . . . and there was nothing to do but cry out with—

Johnny swallowed her outburst with a passionate kiss, even as his hand refused to stop driving her to madness. On and on it surged, making her wriggle and splash and buck until she became one quivering, mindless, pleasure-seeking core, writhing in the water.

Finally she let out an ecstatic sigh and went limp all over. She wanted to float in this warm water as she regained herself and some semblance of sanity. Damned if he didn't tease her nub again, chuckling when she jerked.

"My God . . . such a passionate woman you are, Tess," he murmured, sounding awestruck. "I hope you'll pleasure me, too, sweet lady. My cock's throbbing so hard I had to let it out of my pants."

The image made her go hot all over. Maybe—*maybe*—her body would recover enough to accommodate him, even though she wanted to drift into a sweet sleep like she hadn't known for months.

"Let's dry you off and get you to bed," her lover whispered. "You won't want to wake up in this water when it goes cold. I'll get you a towel."

When his arms slipped away from her body, Tess realized the bathwater was already cooling. She grinned. Johnny Gazara kicked up as much heat as she'd imagined from the moment he'd stolen that first kiss. Or had *she* initiated that sudden, unthinkable breach of propriety—right there in her potential employer's foyer?

Not that it mattered. She was going to relax in the water a bit longer, to relive that excruciating excitement her fantasy man had introduced her to. . . .

"Stand up, love. Let me dry your exquisite body."

Her hands found the rim of the tub. She rocked slowly forward. . . .

Open your eyes or you'll lose your balance. Do you want to flounder like a fish, or worse, fall and hurt yourself? Everyone will come running and find you naked.

Her eyelids fluttered open. Reluctantly, she brought herself out of fantasy's trance.

The Johnny Gazara standing beside the tub with a fluffy white towel was very, very real. And very aroused: His manhood jutted from his fly to gaze at her with that single eye, just inches from her face. He might as well have splashed her with cold water, the way goose bumps suddenly covered her body. That had been no *daydream!* Johnny had so deftly followed her script while she whispered her desires; he'd made it *real.* And now he expected attention in return!

She suddenly remembered that no decent woman would tolerate such behavior. "How'd you get in here?" she demanded in a hoarse whisper. "And who gave you permission to take such liberties while I was—"

"Your tub was running over." He gestured toward a pile of wet towels he'd mopped the floor with. "You fell asleep before you turned off the water, and once you begged for my attention—telling me what to do to you—well, who was I to deny a lady's delightfully decadent requests?"

Delightfully decadent. Was that anything like *naughty?* Growing up a sheltered young lady and marrying early had prevented much temptation from crossing her path. It was a novelty to sit in a bathtub with a devilish man's erection pointed at her. She had the sudden urge to take it into her mouth.

Did proper women do that? She'd never considered such a thing with Henry, yet at this moment it seemed . . . decadent. Most likely delightful, too—especially for Johnny.

The tautness of his face and stance drove her to boldness again. "You're probably wondering if I'll reciprocate your favors." It came out in a husky voice she didn't recognize as her own.

"No doubt in my mind you will, Tess," he rasped, his eyes closing in anticipation. "Since the moment we met, I've wanted to . . . oh, Jesus, woman . . ."

Tess smiled—very carefully, as she'd taken the tip of him

into her mouth. Johnny sucked air between his clenched teeth as one hand went to her cheek and the other steadied that proud cock. She drew her lips up over the ridge and then found that enticing little hole with the tip of her tongue.

Johnny moaned. "Just once more—take me into your sweet, hot mouth and draw your lips slowly up my shaft . . . yes, oh, God, yessss. Tessss . . ."

He was quivering, totally at her mercy, with his head thrown back and his hips thrust forward. She carefully took in inch by warm inch of a male member that seemed a lot larger than what Henry had put inside her, down there . . . all of it done in the dark and without much ado. She marveled at the springiness of the black hair, the taut heat of his egg-shaped testicles. As she traced the deep pink skin back up the length of him and felt the pulse in his veins, her own heartbeat hammered. She felt slick between her legs again. What were these crazy sensations?

"You can't torment me this way or I'll shoot all over you," Johnny whispered. Again he held up the towel, entreating her with a look that made her melt. "What a shame to come too soon, after waiting so long for a woman to love."

She cocked her head. "You live here with Blythe and Daphne, and you do without?" she challenged. "I met them only briefly, but—"

"Edgar decreed, my first day here, that I could look but never touch. Had he caught me in this position with either of them, I'd have been long gone."

"So why are you here with *me?* Surely the same rule applies."

"Not if I stake my claim before he lures you into his web, sweetheart." He lowered his face to hers. "It's a fine life here, don't get me wrong—and you're the perfect Penney Candy girl, Tess—but how the hell's he supposed to pleasure *three* of you? And why should I stand for that? Enough's enough!"

Edgar Penney—the man in the Santa suit who gave out candy and major donations to orphans—had both of those blondes as his lovers? And he'd ordered Johnny Gazara to keep his warm, tender hands to himself? Tess stood up, gauging this man's reaction to her body. While he rubbed her dry, he devoured her with his gaze, kissing the skin where the towel had been. "So . . . this is really about staking a claim rather than any attraction you feel for me?" she speculated.

His face fell. "Oh, Tess, that sounded horribly crude, didn't it? I never intended to make you feel that way, but once you become Edgar's lover, he has a way of . . . keeping you under his spell." He grasped her shoulders to make his point. "Blythe and Daphne realize he diffuses opium into the air, scented with peppermint. But he provides everything they need—more than they could possibly want—so they say they don't care about how he . . . holds them hostage. Well, I care plenty. And I don't want you falling into that trap!"

"Opium?" This situation sounded more bizarre—more ominous—with every word Johnny Gazara uttered. Was he making it up to dissuade her from taking the job? Too late— she'd already accepted Edgar's offer! "All I know about opium is that it's what laudanum's made from and that addicts spend their time in dens promising their providers *anything* to ensure their supply doesn't run out."

"*Not* the future we have in mind for you."

She considered this as he briskly rubbed the towel over her damp body. "How does he manage the candy business in such a state? And how do Blythe and Daphne appear in public—to give little children candy—if they're constantly under the influence of . . ." Tess sobered. "Is that why my room smells like peppermint? I thought the aroma had drifted in from the candy factory."

"I've never seen them pie-eyed in public, but they spend *most* of their time here, in the off-season, helping Ed with various phases of his business. Needless to say, they're rarely without a smile," he added wryly. "He keeps the dosage light enough to maintain their loyalty without overdosing them. You'll notice that most days, everything here is carefree and happy. Playful."

He caught the towel behind her, to hold her bare body against his. "I'm sorry I brought it up," he whispered. "We were having such a fine time. But I thought you should know a secret about Penney Candy before you stay too long to escape that fate."

Is that the poppy talking, or Johnny? He doesn't fit the image of an addict, but what do you know about such things? You just met him!

Tess hesitated. Should she trust him? Johnny had taken advantage of her randy mental adventures while she was nearly asleep. He looked so earnest—but then, didn't any man who held a naked woman?

Truth be told, sex had never held much fascination. It had occurred at Henry's whim, and Mama had implied she wasn't *supposed* to enjoy it as much as he did. Indeed, her husband had handled sex much as he had his business affairs: quickly and efficiently, so he could be on to his next task.

Yet right now, even as Johnny Gazara informed her of the potential pitfalls of this place, he had already met her secret needs without having to ask about them. And right now, that seemed reason enough to give him the benefit of the doubt. Maybe it was the incense of peppermint in the air, but Tess had never felt more alive. More daring. More *playful*. And wasn't that a fine alternative to her mood when she'd escaped the house in Memphis and Reed Mahaffey's manipulation?

"What do you want for Christmas, Johnny?" she murmured, running a fingertip through the ebony hairs on his chest. It was a question from out of the blue, but a man revealed a lot about himself when he spoke of giving and receiving.

"If I'm lucky, she's right here in my hands." He cupped her breasts as though they were exquisite treasures. "You've inspired me to finish my projects here and move on."

Disappointment punched her in the stomach.

"And I'll take you along," he continued in a voice rising with excitement. "You can carry out your Christmas assignments here, and then we can leave together. It's preposterous to think of such things so soon, but—"

"No more preposterous than hopping the train to Cascade, Colorado," she mused. Why did her heart flutter like birds' wings at the thought of going away with this man? She'd met him only a few hours ago!

"When I saw your sweet, sad face peering out of your cloak, something inside me came *alive* again, and—" Johnny nipped his lip. "I sound addled from the opium myself, don't I? But you've inspired me to take my art to a higher level. I mean, how many more murals does Penney need? And who else will ever see them?"

Never had a man bared his soul to her. Never had Henry shared whatever passion he'd felt for his work.

That was it, wasn't it? Johnny Gazara flushed with a *passion* that stirred her as much as his physical presence . . . not to mention the way his dark eyes worshipped her as he spoke in a tone approaching reverence. His stained-glass creations glowed with a talent that came from within, while Henry had bought and sold cotton others had raised. Bennett and Mahaffey specialized in shrewdness and market savvy, but this man turned pieces of glass and ceramic into scenes that had made her gape in awe during her tour with Edgar Penney.

Johnny's gaze intensified. He'd stopped talking to recapture her attention. "I'm babbling," he said with a shake of his head. "Been so long since I had someone I could really talk to and . . . well, what do *you* want for Christmas, Tess?"

Her heart rose into her throat. Johnny Gazara had remained

144 / Melissa MacNeal

remarkably patient, considering his aroused state . . . and his wand looked ready to make a kind of magic she hadn't anticipated when she'd read that newspaper ad. Turnabout was fair play, but their talk took on a different tone when she had to answer her own question. "I want a home where love lives again," she whispered.

Had she said too much? Tess watched for a reaction that suggested Johnny would flee the first chance he got. She could never have said such a thing to Reed Mahaffey: He would claim he was *so* willing to give her exactly what she'd asked for, but his concepts of *love* and *home* would never in a million years mesh with hers.

Johnny, on the other hand, looked awestruck. His Adam's apple bobbed when he swallowed. He gazed at her with glistening eyes as though she couldn't possibly be real. "Tess," he whispered. "Oh, Tess . . . I can't recall the last time I felt at home. But I'd like to get there for Christmas. Home for Christmas . . . with you."

A tear spilled down her cheek. Tess twined her arms around Johnny's neck as he pulled her against his warm, solid body. For several moments they stood, breathing together, awash in these fresh new feelings. With a contented sigh, Tess kissed his neck. Johnny's lips found hers and the kiss deepened without feeling hurried. He cradled her head in his hands to lavish his affection on her, even as she felt the hard ridge of him riding her bare thigh. On and on their lips caressed, silk to silk, as their tongues teased in an elaborate dance. Tess's towel had fallen, but she was becoming very warm . . . very aware of Johnny's heat.

"Make love to me," she pleaded softly. "I've never asked a man for that—at least not when I was fully conscious."

Johnny chuckled. "I'm damn glad you did, because the *waiting* is about to kill me. You'll never have to ask me again, Tess."

He scooped her into his arms as though she were a child, his dark eyes burning into hers. Tess clung to him, her heart racing. This was not the sort of behavior she engaged in. She was a wife and a mother—a widow. Part owner of Bennett and Mahaffey. A pillar in her church back home.

But she was about to become a *lover,* in ways she'd never before imagined.

7

_____

Johnny's hands trembled as he lit the candles on the night-stand. Tess Bennett was by no means the first delectable woman he'd ever bedded, yet she had an openness, a sweetness, that called out to him. *I want a home where love lives again.* Her words sent an electrical surge of *Yessss* through him, even though it was too soon to be getting so entangled. He knew so little about her . . .

But she'd responded to his touch, even when she was drifting in a dream. She'd seen *him* in her fantasy . . . and she'd let down her proverbial hair, using bold language and directives. Tess had crossed every boundary she'd known as a proper wife and mother, yet there was no guilt or apology. No shrinking away from what she wanted.

She'd also been deprived of the kind of loving that made her pulse race off the map, into her body's uncharted territories. And didn't he long to be her scout, her guide into passionate lands they could discover together? Didn't his heart cry out to spend Christmas at *home*, with *her*? Wherever that may be.

Tess lay demurely on the canopy bed. Her blue eyes brightened in the candlelight as she watched his every move. Her golden hair had fallen loose to swirl on the pillow, tempting his fingers to play in its softness. And her bare body . . . now, *there* was a playground no man could resist. Yet he sensed Tess had allowed him liberties no one else—not even her husband—had taken.

Johnny wanted to show her something new that would make the most of her sensitivity, something that would ensure his place in her heart as well as in her body's memory of physical ecstasy.

"You have on too many clothes," she murmured. "You've seen me naked in all manner of positions—a slave to your torment. So it's only fair for me to gawk at *you* now!"

She giggled and Johnny held a finger to his lips, nodding toward the wall that adjoined Edgar's bedroom. "When you see me in the altogether, don't scream and run off," he teased. "Three others would make the most of your naked, aroused state—in nooks of this house where you'd never find your way out."

Tess nipped her lush lower lip. God, she looked so innocent yet so . . . knowing.

"Silence must be our code," he continued as he unbuttoned his shirt. "We can't make any noise now, and we can't act as though any of this has happened between us."

She nodded again, even as her eyes followed his fingers down the front of his shirt. How he loved the way her lips parted and her eyes widened as he bared his shoulders and chest. Tess reached out and he stepped closer to the bed, reveling in the airy stroke of her fingertips through his hair.

"Forced silence makes the loving more intense, you know," he murmured in a strained voice. "Think of it as immersing ourselves in sensations we can compare later, if you—" Johnny sucked air when she playfully gripped his erection. Damn her, she was giggling soundlessly. Doing this to force *his* silence and

show him how difficult it would be for them to remain undetected.

Or was this a fallacy? Maybe Edgar was already aware of
their games in the bathroom. After all, Penney had caught them
kissing in the vestibule. The candy maker's *magic* might've included ways of spying, from the first, that Johnny had no idea
about, to confirm that he wasn't double dipping with Daphne
and Blythe.

But this was no time for such concerns to come between him
and this lush, loving woman. *Tess . . . yesssssssss.* He kicked off
his pants and eased onto the bed with her, testing the groan of
the mattress ropes. When he rose to his knees, straddling her,
Tess opened her arms.

Such a sweet, sweet kiss, lying against her soft breasts and
belly, skin to skin. It was all he could do not to plunge into the
slit that begged him for attention: Tess's hips undulated beneath
him as she surrendered to his lips with that adventurous vulnerability he'd already fallen for.

How long since she'd held a man? Johnny sensed Tess had
been a faithful wife, and the way she welcomed him, as a lover
she'd met mere hours ago, inspired him: He would make this a
rendezvous she'd never forget, no matter what happened with
Edgar.

"Lie absolutely still, no matter what. Agreed?" he whispered as he nuzzled her soft hair.

"Only if you agree to the same thing when it's my turn to
torment *you,*" she purred. Her chuckle sent a delicious jolt of
need through him. "Turnabout's fair play. All's fair in love and
war."

She had him there. Tess had him trapped between her thighs,
too, positioned to enter with just a lift of her hips and his surge
forward. Johnny forced himself to his knees again, turning to
face her feet. Her gasp confirmed his suspicions: She wasn't accustomed to having a man look at her most intimate parts.

"God, Tess," he rasped, fingering the deep pink folds. The lemon scent of her bathwater lingered there, with the alluring fragrance from deep within her molten body, so responsive . . . so open to him from this angle.

The first touch of his tongue made her squirm, but not from trying to get away. Her thighs quivered and she grasped his hips as he leaned lower. When he looked between his legs, Johnny saw the ecstasy—the yearning—on her face. "Absolutely still, remember?"

Tess nodded and braced her legs in this open position, her slit and its blond curls fully displayed. He dipped down for another sip, telling himself he should proceed slowly to enhance their mutual enjoyment—but what a futile idea. She tasted warm and sweet, and with the first insertion of his tongue, Johnny knew this woman had total, effortless control over him. He would be a fool for her, too eager and needy to hold back.

As he licked from the top of her slit to the bottom, running his tongue between the folds, her body strained to remain motionless. He gently inserted a digit from each hand to hold her open, stroking her flesh with his fingertips as he circled her sensitive little nub with his tongue.

Her gasp filled the room, filled his heart: Tess responded to every nuance, shying away from nothing. If he wasn't careful, they'd both be screaming. Johnny hated to stop, but his cock was throbbing to be where his tongue had blazed a warm, willing trail.

As though she knew he was about to switch positions, Tess caught him gently in her grip to knead him as though she were milking a cow. Johnny's eyes flew open. Had she been reaching for him because his cock dangled above her face, or did she mean to make him take his own torment, indeed? He paused as her fingers kneaded his member, gently yet with an insistence that had him ready to fire off a first round.

"You moved!" he accused through clenched teeth.

"So did you."

"But we agreed—"

"You suggested and I went along—for as long as I could stand it," she replied breathlessly. "No fair driving me up to the ceiling with that naughty tongue of yours if I can't take you with me."

Johnny grinned in spite of the way fire spiraled inside him. "Let me turn around. I want to watch your face when—"

"That's more like it. While this is an intriguing view, I much prefer your eyes and nose and . . . lips."

Such Southern gentility, expressed in that understated drawl, drew him even deeper into this entanglement. Johnny swung around, thinking how he might draw out their play yet distance himself a bit.

"Stick that thing inside me and love me like you *mean* it," she said in a guttural whisper. "I don't care what happens in a few days, or a few weeks. Right now I need a man who can't hold back—can't resist me on an animal level, regardless of the rules that define relationships."

She'd said several mouthfuls, but this was no time to analyze it all. How could any man resist such an exquisite woman? Had her husband acted so detached she felt excluded from what should have been their most intimate moments? Johnny had never been married, but he'd had a long-term lover. He couldn't imagine his woman feeling more like the cold, wet spot on the sheets than like the impassioned partner who'd helped create it. "Tess, I hope—"

"Well, I *need*," she rasped, wrapping her legs around his hips. "And I *want!*"

Johnny slid inside her, grimacing at the hot, tight pleasure of her inner grip. He angled his hips to delve deeper. Tess's thighs tightened, urging him to rock and stroke even as he valiantly held back to prolong their first coming together. She panted his name, and his body overruled any implications of her plea.

Could Tess separate herself afterward? Or would she cling,

equating his surge of passion to a promise that he'd be with her forever?

And what if she gets pregnant? It's been so long. She caught you unprepared—

Too late for reason. Johnny slipped into that state of arousal that knew only *forward* and sought that state of pleasure expressible only on an innate, physical plane. Tess embraced his entire body with hers, writhing to meet his thrusts. Her eyes closed and her lips parted, painting the loveliest portrait of passion he'd ever seen as the candles flickered beside their heads. No matter what came afterward, this moment would etch itself indelibly on his soul.

"Tess, if there's a baby—"

"I'll have someone to love again."

"Or if this doesn't work out—"

"It's still the best damn thing that's ever happened to me," she breathed against his ear. "Don't make sense of it, Johnny. Make me a woman who knows the pleasure she's capable of giving—and receiving."

He closed his eyes to concentrate on her, for the few remaining moments his brain could engage. He arched inside her, to stroke Tess's most-buried treasure with his hard tip. She clenched her teeth as she reached toward a pinnacle he knew she'd never before approached. And as Johnny realized how this sweet woman honored him with the entrusting of her body and soul, he lost control. His mind shattered as he gave in to uncontrollable spasms of heat and pleasure that nearly made him pass out. He couldn't recall ever responding so intensely, for so many surges.

And then he couldn't recall anything at all. He simply collapsed.

Tess buried her face in the crook of Johnny's neck as the convulsions overtook her. She held him hard, afraid she'd lose her grip on reality if she let go, even as his shuddering body drove her on. What *was* this madness? This wild, giddy quivering in her nether regions? Was this how *passion* felt?

She wondered if Johnny had sensed her inexperience—had wished, perhaps, he hadn't responded to her lurid suggestions. Yet his breathing sounded as rapid and shallow as hers. And judging from the grimace and gasp that had escaped him just before he plunged, he'd enjoyed these sensations—his climax— far more than Henry had ever seemed to. And *she* had made this possible!

Tess took inventory of this sensual moment: the solid weight of Johnny's body, which fit against her so perfectly . . . the warm velvet of his skin . . . the tangy scent surrounding their sated bodies . . . the slick wetness oozing down her thighs even as his manhood remained rigid inside her . . . the salt of his damp hairline when she kissed him. His murmured questions came back to her: What if there was a baby? What if this had been a big mistake, getting involved too soon?

Yet a sense of peace prevailed. She hoped this moment would last forever—at least in her mind—because even if she never again made love to Johnny Gazara, he'd shown her what she'd been missing.

A shadow stirred near the door: Edgar Penney had peered in and had then disappeared. She felt more concern for Johnny's fate than her own. She could return to Memphis, but she had no idea if the lover in her arms had other options. She knew so damn little about either man, yet she rested, content. Whatever happened, happened.

And wasn't *that* a Christmas miracle? Not so long ago, she'd have tied herself in knots with worry. Guilt. Yet now, she saw no need to tell Johnny their employer had caught them. Why ruin the most fabulous experience of her life?

He rolled to one side of her, remaining in her embrace. How soft his hair felt against her skin . . . how pleasantly rough the masculine shadow along his jaw. "Thank you," she prayed against his neck.

"Believe me, Tess," he whispered. "You were so damn wonderful."

She hugged him harder. "You don't have to tell me—"

"Oh, but I do." Johnny rose on one elbow to support his head in his hand. His eyes glimmered in the candles' glow. "Don't take this wrong, all right? I . . . lived with a woman for a long while before I came here. And I *never* shared what you and I are recovering from. Incredible. Absolutely, undeniably the best sex I've ever had."

Tess closed her eyes. "If you're just saying that to encourage me, I don't want to know."

He chuckled ruefully. "I would never lie to you about such a thing."

Strangely unruffled by his mention of a former lover, Tess ran a finger up the hollow of his spine. "Why'd you leave her? Not that it's my business to—"

"Francine DuPont was a great patron of the arts—as well she could afford to be," he replied in a faraway voice. "She hired me to create stained-glass murals in her town home in Denver. Enticed me into her bed with pretty promises of introducing me to other socialites who'd commission my work."

Tess's eyebrows rose. "And?"

A mirthless laugh escaped him. "Her husband returned unannounced from his diplomatic post abroad, so I left without so much as my clothing—not to mention going unpaid for most of my work."

She couldn't find it in her heart to chide him for getting involved with a married woman. Odd, how her standards faded away in Johnny's presence.

"Francine had claimed she was a widow—had hidden away all evidence of a man in her life to maintain her ruse while I worked for her." He cleared his throat sheepishly. "She knew all along that Mr. DuPont would return, of course. Which is why I vowed to never, *ever* involve myself with a wealthy woman again. Bitches, all of them! She took advantage of my talent and generous nature, knowing I had no source of income, save myself."

Tess's heart stopped. While she truly was a widow, she'd not revealed her circumstances to Edgar or Johnny. Would either of them guess she'd fled a man who wanted her money, as Spec Penrose had on the train?

A worm of regret wiggled inside her, but she wouldn't—couldn't—let on about the lucrative business that was now half hers. No need for anyone in this little Colorado outpost to know about the life she'd run from. And no one in Memphis had any way to find her.

When Johnny's lips sought hers, she melted against him. She would fully experience the pleasure of the present, without letting her past dampen it. Daphne and Blythe were to coach her tomorrow morning, before their first charity event in Cripple Creek. This rebirth—this fresh start—would be every bit as profound as making love to Johnny Gazara, and there would be no looking back. Once she donned her elf costume to give candy to eager little orphans, Tess Bennett, the lonely woman from the mansion in Memphis, would no longer exist, would she?

8

"Oh, looky! Candy canes with green and purple stripes!"

"Do they *taste* green and purple? Or do they set your mouth on fire, like the Dragon Candy? That's *my* favorite!"

"My stockin's so full it's gonna spill out! Thanks, Elfie!"

Tess smiled at the children who'd gathered around her in the hotel's decorated ballroom. Their pinched faces brightened as they discovered the treats in their felt stockings, and she found herself drawn to every one of them, tucking flyaway curls behind ears and looking deeply into their wide eyes. Who could've guessed they would touch her heart this way? Did one of the girls have Claire's shy, dimpled smile? Or did she only imagine her daughter's features because she so badly *wanted* to see her?

"How's it going, Tess?" Blythe, also decked out in her form-fitting suit of short green overalls with a white shirt and candy-striped tights, tossed back the pom-pom of her red fur hat. "You're a natural for this job!"

Tess shrugged, excruciatingly happy. "So many children without families. What a fine thing Edgar does, handing out these gifts."

"He's a kid at heart. Was an orphan himself, you know, until a kindly old couple adopted him to help with making candy in their kitchen. That's how it all started." Blythe smiled brightly as a new bunch of children entered the ballroom, their eyes aglow with anticipation. "If today's orders are any indication, the season's going to be the best ever for Penney Candy. See those merchants and mine owners crowding Daphne's desk to place their orders? I'd better go help her."

Well-heeled gentlemen in vested suits were lined up at the table draped in a candy-striped tablecloth, grinning at the other Penney Candy elf. As Daphne enticed them with her display of colorful, imaginative candies, what man *wouldn't* increase his order? They were dealing with a flirtatious blue-eyed blonde whose clothing fit her like a second skin. Edgar Penney might be an eccentric recluse, but he knew how to market his product to male merchants.

"Say, lady, can ya gimme two of those stockings?"

Tess turned, thinking how she should phrase her polite but firm refusal—until she saw the little boy's twisted leg and the crutch that supported him. He could've been a carrot-top Tiny Tim stepping out of the Dickens Christmas story. He gestured toward the wall where more children sat, eagerly awaiting their turns to come forward.

"My sister Gracie, she'll get trampled if she walks over here," he explained in a winsome voice. He was probably ten but seemed much older. "Last year a kid yanked her stocking out of her hand, but I'll whack 'em with my crutch if somebody grabs it from *me!*"

Tess's heart rose into her throat. What a brave little boy—and what a loving brother. "Shall we go together? I'd like to wish Gracie a Merry Christmas," she answered in a quavery voice.

He led Tess by the hand, and then she knelt before a red-headed girl who looked like a doll in her wicker wheelchair . . .

a doll with only one shoe protruding from her skirt. How could it be that both brother and sister had malformed legs? How long had they lived at the orphanage? It seemed unlikely anyone would adopt such a pair. . . .

Gracie flashed a gap-toothed grin. Coppery curls bounced around her face as she peered at her bright, shiny candy. "You weally are one of Santa's elves, huh?" she queried.

"I am!" Tess tweaked her freckled nose. "And Santa knows you've been very, very good this year."

"Good enough that he'll bwing me and Stefan a mama? We pway weally hard, but we been waiting . . . and waiting."

Tess could barely look this angel, Gracie, in the eye. Stefan stood beside his sister, awaiting Tess's response as though his young life depended on it. How could she possibly answer such a heart-rending request? "I-I'll remind him, honey," she murmured.

Stefan shrugged. He'd heard that before. "Lotta kids are askin' Santa for moms, I guess," he said, glancing toward the children who headed toward the door. "But thanks for the stockings. And if ya see that Mr. Penney who's on the package, tell him he makes the best dang candy!"

"I'll do that, Stefan."

Heart thudding, she watched the children line up by the ballroom door and waved at Gracie and her brother when they turned to smile at her.

"See ya next Chwistmas!" the little girl sang out, waving a pink and green Pinwheel Pop.

Why did that thought claw at her soul? How many of these events had those two children attended, yet still they asked Santa for a mother? Such hope in their hearts . . .

A movement by the huge Christmas tree caught her eye, and Tess smiled at Johnny Gazara. He'd driven them into Cripple Creek today, to the Imperial Hotel, as Edgar rarely attended these events. The more Tess heard about Edgar Penney's idiosyncrasies, the more she marveled at the man's ability to delight millions with his candy creations while turning an astounding profit.

But money was the last thing on her mind when she looked at Johnny. Again he wore a white shirt that set off his olive complexion, and his hair framed his face like wings of midnight. "The children adore you!" he exclaimed as he grabbed her hands. "Is it any wonder? You're not much taller than they are, and you look so much like an elf—well, except for *these*." When he gawked at her breasts, his wolfish expression made her giggle.

"What a day," she replied wistfully. "I had no idea I'd be so drawn to these orphans. Just the thought of them spending Christmas in an institution, without families, well..." She looked away, blinking rapidly.

Johnny gently thumbed her tears. "That's why Daphne and Blythe pressed Edgar to hire another Penney Candy girl. The hardest part is seeing the same little faces, year after year, as their eyes grow hopeless and their voices lose their music."

Tess nodded. She felt silly, crying this way. She couldn't solve all the problems of the world no matter how badly she wanted to.

"If you'll come to my room tonight," he whispered, "I'll restore your sense of fun and frolic. I know a game to get you back into the Christmas spirit. Naked."

"A game?" She'd never considered sex as play. "If it'll remind me of these children, I won't guarantee you—"

"Tess? Tess Bennett, is that *you* in that elf costume?"

She dropped Johnny's hands, turning to see who'd called to her. The children had gone and the merchants were leaving, too, so there was no mistaking the two mustachioed, vested men who approached with wide grins. "Spec! And Charley!" She hurried toward them, suddenly more aware of how her costume accentuated body parts she'd always camouflaged.

"Thank you so much for looking after me on the train. And for your message to Mr. Penney."

"It was the least we could do, my dear." Spencer Penrose bowed slightly. "And didn't I promise you'd be the perfect Penney Candy girl?"

"Well, no. You were too busy teasing me!"

"And talking you out of those widow's weeds, thank God," Charley chimed in. "Begging your pardon, my dear, but you look much prettier in red and green than you did in black."

"Especially red and green that *clings,* so it wiggles when you do!"

Tess's cheeks flared. It wasn't good policy to reprimand guests who'd probably ordered hundreds of dollars of Penney Candy, and yet . . . "I . . . I suppose that was intended as a compliment—"

"Please excuse Mr. Penrose's breach of etiquette," Charley Tutt interrupted with a stern glance at his companion. "He's so overwhelmed by the improvement in your spirits—your generosity and kindness toward the orphans—that he lost track of his tongue."

"Please forgive me, Tess," Spec implored as he reached for her hands. "That *was* a crude remark. What might I do to make it up to you?"

"I think we'd best move on, gentlemen. Mr. Penney doesn't tolerate such behavior around his female employees." Johnny Gazara stepped up beside her to gaze pointedly at the two men. "Thank you so much for participating in our charity event today."

The pair in tweeds and ties gave Johnny a looking-over, but then they nodded and walked toward the door. Tess felt even more uncomfortable now. Johnny had been protecting her honor, yet she hadn't really felt offended by Spec's suggestive remark. After all, Blythe and Daphne wore the same costume, and neither of them seemed ill at ease.

"And how do you know Penrose and Tutt?" Johnny demanded.

Tess almost told him it was none of his damned business. Or did that edge to his question imply he was seriously interested in her? Watching out for her in public? "I met them on the train. They were kind enough to get my connections changed so I would arrive in Cascade rather than Denver," she replied evenly. "Is that jealousy I hear, Johnny? *Envy*, because—from what I've been told—they own a great deal of Colorado Springs and Cripple Creek, between them?"

His mouth clapped shut. His eyes shone like hot obsidian.

Tess knew an advantage when she held one. "I thought it very kind of Mr. Tutt, when he saw that I had no luggage, to offer assistance and the name of a seamstress," she remarked with a purposeful smile. "And if Spec's behavior seems inappropriate, well, he at least hasn't hidden in my bathroom to catch me napping naked. *Has* he?"

She pivoted on the heel of one pointy-toed elfin slipper, to help Blythe and Daphne gather the remaining candy and stockings. Then she turned to address Johnny again, hoping she wasn't overplaying her ace. "*Do* I wiggle in these clingy clothes, Mr. Gazara? If I deserved Spec's lewd remark, perhaps it's *I* who should mend her ways."

His slow, wicked grin spoke volumes. "Don't change a thing for me, Tess. But if you'd like more ... personalized advice, come find me tonight. We'll see who's naughty—and who's nice."

9

"It's a game Ed and I devised as an adult novelty. Something for a generation already loyal to Penney Candy, yet . . . hungry for a fresh adventure." Curiosity fired Tess's lovely blue eyes as he opened a red satin box. Down the hall, Penney's suite reeked of peppermint—Edgar relived the triumphs of each charity event with his girls, over a hookah—so this tryst would go undetected as long as Tess returned to her room soon afterward.

She picked out a gold-wrapped cube. "What's the *N* stand for?" she asked as she held it to her nose. "Oh, my . . . rich, wicked chocolate!"

"Not for the kiddies!" Johnny teased as he joined her on the side of the bed. "'Naughty or Nice' is Santa's way of rewarding adults for being very good—or very, very bad."

She laughed, thank goodness. He'd overstepped this afternoon and she'd nailed his envy for what it was: distrust of anyone who, like Francine DuPont, could satisfy every whim with money. When Tess paused with her fingernail at the edge of the wrapper, he held his breath.

"And which are you, Johnny? Naughty or nice?"

His lips quirked. *"Yes,"* he teased. "Whatever you wish me to be, Tess. Open that carefully, read what's written inside the wrapper, and then we'll see what comes up."

"You don't fool me for a second," she whispered. "You've been up since before I found your room. You got perturbed with Spec Penrose for suggesting—Oh, my stars!"

"Read it to me," he murmured against the nape of her graceful neck.

Tess cleared her throat as though she'd gotten a chunk of candy caught in it. "It says, 'face away from your partner, lean over, and . . . and hold yourself open for inspection.' What kind of game *is* this?"

Johnny chuckled and kissed her. "If you feel naughty, you may follow through. Or if I feel nice, I can let you enjoy your chocolate while I unwrap a piece. No right or wrong way to play. We make it up as we go along."

She popped the chocolate into her mouth. Her eyes closed and she sighed languidly. "I don't know what's in this—"

"Very potent liqueur. Flavors vary from one piece to the next."

"But things would get naughty even in a roomful of starchy old church ladies if you passed around that red box."

"That's the idea. But we've no need for church ladies right now." Johnny chose a fat candy with a green wrapper and twisted its ends loose. "It's just you, me, and this nice box of naughty treats. So now that you understand the game, I'll go first."

He popped the hard candy into his mouth and cracked the shell, so the buttery rum liqueur oozed over his tongue. As he smoothed the wrapper, he chortled. "Oh, Tess, you'll like this one: 'As your partner lies naked, spread-eagle, test for ticklish spots.'"

She laughed, and then clapped her hand over her mouth. "Are you the partner, or am I?"

"You choose. I live to make you happy, my dear."

Coyly she slipped her green velvet straps over her shoulders. "Do Blythe and Daphne wear these clingy outfits in public or only to the Penney Candy events? The children love to mingle with elves, while the merchants lay down a *lot* of cash as they ogle these costumes."

"Edgar wants everyone to have a good time."

She slid off the bed's edge, yanked down her striped tights, and then leaned over, as her piece of chocolate had suggested. "I'm not ticklish here," she informed him as she pointed to her pussy. "So don't bother sticking your cock up it to find out." She stuck out her tongue with her face upside down between her lovely legs, looking naughty, indeed.

Johnny stifled a laugh. "That leaves me plenty of other places to test," he said as he shrugged out of his shirt. "So I'll leave your hot, needy little cunt to fend for herself. Or . . ."

He quickly inserted a finger to tease the rim of her tight little hole. "You said nothing about what I was doing with my hands."

"Naughty! You are *so* bad, Johnny!"

"So here's where I make things up as we go along." He reached under her tight shirt to cup her breasts, rubbing her bared bottom against his crotch. He *had* been ready for her, hours ago, and watching her lean over had taken him over the edge. Tess giggled, provoking him to gyrate and moan. "Change your mind yet, little girl?"

"*No,* but *you* will be the one going spread-eagle for inspection." She pivoted to tug him off the tall bed. "Feet to the floor, you! I'm taking down your pants, and then you're to spread your legs so all is fully revealed. Understand me?"

What could he say? Tess was pressed against him, her face in his, her voice brooking no argument. And his cock was responding. "You're speaking my language, loud and clear," he replied hoarsely. "So if you'll get out of my *fucking* way, I'll do as I'm told."

"You *fucking* well better," she growled back, and then her eyes widened. "I can't believe I said that word!"

"Must be the candy. Have some more!" Johnny grabbed a red wrapper from the box and deftly twisted off the paper to read its message. "Hop on for a wild ride. Finish what you've started, elf."

"It does *not* say that!"

"I say it does." He popped the chocolate into her open mouth. "And I'm saying if you jump my bones, and I grab your ass and hang on for dear life, we'll both explode."

She hopped and he caught her. The tights around her knees restricted her movement, and that added to the pleasure, didn't it? As Tess undulated against his hard cock, he thrilled to the way she responded to this sort of play—as much because she loved it as because the candy was lowering her inhibitions.

Then again, the way she moved so perfectly against him, positioning herself to accept his first thrust, told Johnny she had left any misgivings and disappointments about sex behind—all the way back in Memphis. And what a fine thing, that she allowed him to enjoy the newer, happier Tess Bennett now that she'd shed her widow's weeds.

"Stick that thing inside me," she demanded in a raw whisper.

"What thing? Call it a specific name, and tell me precisely where to put it."

She wrapped herself more tightly around him, her hips wiggling with need. "Fuck my cunt," she commanded him. "Ram your cock up inside it and don't stop until I'm calling out your name, bad boy."

With a groan, he obeyed, thrusting up inside her and holding on tight while she ground herself against him. Tess was rapidly approaching the point of no return. He could feel it in her clenching muscles, could hear the desperation in her moans.

"Hang on," he rasped. "I'll slip my arms under your knees, slide those tights up out of the way so you're hanging suspended, like—"

"Oh, Jesus . . . oh, Johnny, this angle is . . . well, I feel so open! So—" Her head dropped back, and as she arched against him, she was the picture of utter ecstasy.

Johnny slowed his thrusts to prolong the intense pleasure building between their straining, hot bodies. He focused on creating friction inside her, in all the right spots, and her immersion in their play—her body's response to his—made his heart sing.

"Don't stop," she whimpered, hunching and rubbing her clit against him. "I had no idea—have never felt these wild spirals of . . . oh, God . . . ohhh, gawwww—"

Johnny grimaced with his own impending release as Tess stifled her scream against his shoulder. He surged with her, astounded by the way her inner muscles gripped his cock and demanded their due. He lost all track of time and place . . . shot into that hot center of pleasure where his body and hers became one on the deepest, most primal level. He convulsed. Lost himself in her.

When he came back to his senses, he loosened his hold on her. Tess spasmed again, one last little shimmer of sensation, before she went limp in his embrace.

"My God," he murmured, kissing her neck. "I can't . . . It's never, *ever* been so intense for me, Tess. So gawd-awesome spectacular! I hope you—"

"Shhhh," she breathed, tickling the hairs on his nape. "Let's drift a bit. This wonderland we've made is a nice place, and I want to live here for a long while . . . with you."

Johnny closed his eyes with the sweetness of her sentiment. He felt the same, and it scared him to death. What did he know about Tess Bennett, really? She looked cute in her elf suit . . .

she gave heart and soul to those underprivileged kids ... she seemed so fearless.

But what was she running from? Or *who?*

As she slid from his arms, Johnny hugged her close. "Tess, I—"

"It was the best ever for me, too, Johnny," she blurted. "I've never felt this incredible in my entire life—and I'd better get back to my room before I say things that terrify us both."

He nodded mutely. Watched her tug her tights over her sweet little backside and then tiptoe out of his room after checking the hallway. Her wiggling finger-wave did funny things to his heart.

He was falling too damned hard, too damned fast. And for the first time ever, he felt deliriously, out-of-his-mind happy about that.

But who was she, really?

10

Dear Margaret and George,

I hope you've not been worried, as Warren said he'd inform you that I was safely on my way to an adventure he himself arranged for me. Well, I took a bit of a side trip. Would you believe it? For the first time in my life, I'm employed! Handing out candy to orphans as a Penney Candy elf. Sharing Christmas with children who are as lost and lonely as I—but not anymore.

Please don't feel you failed me. I simply couldn't face an entire afternoon of Reed's hovering and fawning over my money. I shall return sometime after the holidays.

Tess paused, nipping her lip. Would she return to Memphis alone? Probably best not to hint that she'd gotten in over her head with a man who worked far more potent magic than Edgar Penney.

She noted the candy canes in the company letterhead. The sweet tang of peppermint still lingered even though all had gone quiet in the master suite. When she'd peered through the stained-glass embellishments on Edgar's door, the sight of two scantily clad blondes on the rumpled bed with Edgar confirmed Johnny's initial warning: He hadn't wanted her to become just another hapless, helpless elf lying in that heap of entangled limbs. The large hookah in the corner, striped in red and white, validated Johnny's claim, too, making her wary of staying beyond the holidays. What was there for her to *do* after the Christmas season passed?

Tess sighed and resumed her writing.

> *Please close up the house and enjoy the Christmas season. After putting up with my moods these past months, you deserve a long vacation for your loyalty. And please believe I'm happy and well. When I return, I'll have a better idea about how to deal with Reed. Please don't tell him where I've gone.*

"Are you writing a novel, Tessie? Are we gonna be in your booky . . . with our nooky?"

Tess glanced across her room, which was dark except for the candle that burned on her small desk. From the doorway, Daphne's grin looked lopsided. Her hair hung in uneven rivulets around her pale face, some of it unpinned. She wore a rumpled white camisole and nothing else. As though unaware of where she was, the young blonde absently scratched the curls between her bare thighs and then sniffed her fingers.

"We missed you, Tessie," she continued in a childlike whine. "I was gonna come find you so you could celebrate with us, but Blythe said you might not . . . want to."

Tess hesitated. How did she answer that without further incriminating herself and Johnny? "And why would I not want to celebrate such a wonderful day?" she asked. Better to test Daphne's faculties than be tested herself. "Such dear little souls, those children were. It was good to bring them some Christmas cheer."

The young blonde rested her head against the doorjamb, grinning sleepily. "Blythe spent several years in that place where they came from today," she replied in a faraway voice. "That's how Eddie found her. Then they took me in and . . . loved me."

"They're very kindhearted. Both of them." Tess wondered if Daphne was dazed from the opium, telling such a tale. "How old are you, Daphne? I swear the rarified air out here makes everyone seem so young and—"

"Nineteen. I fibbed about my age when Eddie hired me." She chuckled vapidly. "But he loved me, anyway, after he found out. We're a happy little family here . . . but I'm babbling, aren't I? Time for bed. We go to Colorado Springs tomorrow, and I need my beauty rest!"

How much of that should she believe? Tess pondered Edgar Penney's penchant for blondes—young, biddable, and seemingly desperate blondes. Why had he run his most recent advertisement and then acted as though he'd designed it specifically to find *her*?

Or did he just *seem* to possess magical, mystical powers? Was his mystique a result of his after-hours habit, rather than any pull he had on unseen strings?

It was more than she cared to know right now. She owed Johnny a huge favor for warning her about the reality behind the pretty stained-glass panels he'd created here.

Tess wrote a few last lines, sealed the letter in an envelope, and put it beside her elf costume to mail in the morning. Better to be in bed, at least pretending to sleep, if Edgar came to check on her. As she slipped between the fresh sheets, she wondered if Johnny was already dreaming . . . of her?

"Oh, my! That's the biggest bouquet of roses I've ever seen!" Blythe exclaimed. She left the table where they were filling stockings to greet the deliveryman. "Are you in the right room, sir? We're preparing for the Penney Candy charity event—"

"You happen to be Tess Bennett?" the old fellow demanded. "Heavy as this is, I gotta set it down, 'fore I drops it."

Tess glanced up, her hand full of sparkly lollipops. "I'm Mrs. Bennett. But who'd be sending me roses?"

"That's what the note in the envelope'll tell ya, I'll wager. Afternoon to ya!" After he deftly plucked a red Licorice Lizard from the stocking in Tess's hand, the deliveryman headed for the doors across the large ballroom. "What with a piece of my favorite Penney Candy and the tip from the gent who sent those, I'm ready for Christmas, I can tell ya!"

"Who sent you flowers, Tess?" Daphne had recovered from her previous evening's activities, and her eyes shone bright with curiosity.

Who, indeed? Tess sent a questioning glance to Johnny, who carried more crates of candy in from their coach, but he seemed genuinely surprised—and maybe a little bemused—when he saw the enormous vase of perfect red roses. Surely Edgar hadn't sent her such a gift after only two days on the job. . . .

And what if it came from Reed? What if Warren Coates had to tell him where you'd gone, at the risk of being dismissed?

Heart pounding, Tess slipped a fingernail beneath the red wax seal. The note was brief, written in a meticulous male hand: *Again, my sincerest apologies for speaking out of turn, dear Tess. Gorgeous as these roses are, they wither in comparison to your lovely light. Welcome to my hotel!*

"Spencer Penrose," she breathed. She looked up to find

Daphne, Blythe, and Johnny admiring the huge bouquet of velvety, wine-red roses. At least two dozen of them filled the vase, and having them shipped in from the coast had cost a small fortune. "He's apologizing again for remarking about how my elf costume, uh, wiggles when I walk."

"It's *designed* to wiggle, silly!" Daphne playfully tugged at the hem of her short green overalls. "Who'd order so much of our candy if we were little old men in beards, wearing pointy hats and shoes?"

"Who indeed?" Johnny queried, watching her face with that edgy expression she now recognized as envy. "Penrose could buy and sell us all—including Edgar—if he chose to. There's more to this story than Mrs. Bennett's telling us."

"Johnny, really! Not every man has ulterior motives for sending such a gift." Blythe drew one exquisite long-stemmed rose from the vase. After she inhaled its delicate fragrance, she placed it playfully between her teeth and batted her eyes at him.

"That's right!" Daphne slung her arm around Tess's shoulders. "*Some* men send presents just because we girls deserve them. Just because they like to watch our eyes light up."

"Or watch your legs spread." Johnny's expression remained suspicious, almost hard, as his eyes lingered on the fit of Tess's tights and formfitting overalls. "We'd best fill the rest of these stockings. The urchins shall arrive soon."

Tess's heart withered. Mere hours ago, this man had rhapsodized about how their lovemaking had taken him to newfound heights, yet now his attitude scraped the bottom of the barrel—a barrel of sour pickles. All because of a bouquet of roses from a man who could afford anything he wanted? She rejoined Blythe and Daphne at their candy-covered table, but she'd lost her sparkle. It was for damn sure she'd go to her room alone after today's event. No sense in getting more involved with a man whose back got up every time someone flashed money, was there?

Her mood improved when the children arrived to gaze wide-eyed at their surroundings. The Broadmoor's ballroom had been transformed into a fairyland of twinkling Christmas trees and huge, glittery snowflakes that hung from the ceiling. A gingerbread cottage sat in one corner, where a kindly Saint Nicholas—who looked suspiciously like Edgar, hidden beneath a beard like white cotton candy—greeted the orphans and listened to their Christmas wishes after they'd received their candy from Tess and Daphne.

Blythe took orders from the local merchants in the bar area while uniformed waiters passed among them trays of pastries, cheeses, fruits, and flutes of champagne. A string quartet played carols, and the event came to a high point when Spencer Penrose arrived in a special sleigh fitted with wheels and pulled by a matched pair of sled dogs.

After he invited Tess, Daphne, and Blythe to ride around the huge room with him, tossing loose candy to their delighted young guests, he treated Johnny and the other men to imported cigars and brandy, which Blythe poured for them. By the time Daphne and Tess gave the children final hugs and the biggest candy canes she had ever seen, the adults were enjoying the event even more than the children.

As the last of those earnest little faces left the ballroom, Tess sighed deeply. So much poverty and yearning in the world, even here where the Cripple Creek gold mines had made overnight millionaires of several. Her heart ached for those little boys and girls who returned to an institution rather than a home.

When something tapped her shoulder, Tess turned to find Johnny Gazara smiling wryly, with an oversize candy cane in his hand. "I did it again, didn't I? Let my aversion to wealth spoil your day with these children." He brought his other hand from behind his back, offering her a familiar red satin box filled with wrapped candies. "I'm not a very lovable man sometimes.

Our little candy game won't make up for my moods, but maybe it'll make you smile."

Tess glanced at the shiny wrappers of red, green, and gold. She almost told him about being a wealthy man's widow, yet something warned her not to derail this moment of apology. "The Naughty or Nice game?" she asked quietly. "Right now I'm feeling confused and sorry instead, Johnny. You claim I'm the best ever, yet Francine DuPont still has her invisible claws in you. Why should I compete with your bitter memories of her?"

When he opened his mouth to protest, Tess turned away. While Blythe calculated the afternoon's orders, Daphne packed the remaining candy. The glorious, decorated trees, the elaborate cottage made of spicy, fragrant gingerbread, a sparkling sleigh and children eagerly speaking to Santa: These things had reminded her of Christmas mornings with Claire, more than she cared to admit. Even if her little girl would never again awaken to these trappings of happiness, Tess felt a sudden pang of homesickness.

Would Margaret and George go on holiday, as she'd asked them to? The house would echo with silence, yet she craved its familiarity. No one would be chatty or pie-eyed; she could walk to church or meet friends for luncheon without bundling up in furs to be trundled for miles through the drifted snow. A favorite crimson gown hung in the back of her armoire, and even if she didn't attend any holiday parties, Tess had a sudden yearning to wear her own clothes rather than this elf costume or the dresses Blythe and Daphne shared with her.

"I've work to do." She handed the scarlet box back to Johnny. Funny, how a phrase once so foreign to her sounded rather inviting now . . . a way to keep from thinking too much about what she was missing, during this adventure where Johnny's magic had fallen short today.

11

"This is absurd! Tess might return at any moment—from wherever the hell she ran off to—and you're *leaving?* For two weeks?" Reed Mahaffey's eyes flashed with disdain. "What are you not telling me?"

Margaret Delaney now realized why Tess had never liked this man: He behaved like a spoiled child. Little Claire, with her flights of fancy and ways of cajoling her daddy, had never spoken with such a *tone.* Margaret's hand closed over the note she'd stuffed into her apron pocket when the doorbell had rung repeatedly. No need for Mr. Mahaffey to see the details of Tess's adventure, nor the address on her letter.

"Mr. Coates assured me he'd seen to Tess's safety, and I have since received word from her that she's having the time of her life," the housekeeper replied staunchly. The *thump-thump* of a trunk on the carpeted stairway assured her George was on his way, should Mr. Mahaffey require firmer words.

"That's a lie and you know it. Tess was devoted to Henry, so lost without her daughter—"

"That *you* can take neither of their places in this home. Nor in Tess's heart," Margaret finished boldly. She subtly escorted him out the door, step by backward step. "So if you please, Mr. Mahaffey, we'll be on our way. Should you require assistance with settling your business affairs, Mr. Bennett's attorney can provide—"

"I cannot *believe* Tess ran off to parts unknown rather than settle down with me," he spouted. "You *know* I could provide the finer things she's become accustomed to—"

"*Things* have nothing to do with where she's gone, sir. I assure you."

He lowered his glittering eyes to the same level as hers. Then he grabbed the hand she kept in her pocket. "Don't play games with *me*, Mrs. Delaney!" he snarled. "I have every right to—"

"George!" she cried out, gripping the letter. Her heart pounded frantically. What a bully he was. "*George!* Please come speak with Mr. Mahaffey about—Unhand me, sir! It's none of your—" Her howl rang in the vestibule when Reed twisted her wrist to pry Tess's letter from her fingers.

"Let me see this—"

"Get out!" George ordered. In his agitation, he released the trunk handle and then had to grab the stairway railing when the heavy luggage nearly bowled him over.

As the trunk clattered down the last few steps to skid onto the foyer floor, Reed gleefully read the page he'd torn away from her. "The Penney Candy Factory? What the *hell* is Tess doing in Cascade, Colorado, handing out sweets to orphans?" he scoffed. "Good God, wasn't she on enough charity committees that she could've done that here?"

Fighting tears as she rubbed her throbbing wrist, Margaret nearly spat on him. "Are you happy now? Was it worth overpowering a woman your mother's age to find out—"

"Yes. It was." He tossed aside the torn letter. "You go ahead and take your little vacation, you and old George, for Tess won't require your services any longer."

The windows rattled with the force of the slamming door.

Margaret doubled over with the pain in her wrist, and when her husband wrapped his arm around her, she felt him trembling with rage and fear. "We . . . we might as well be on our way," she said between sobs. "If Mr. Mahaffey finds our Tess, she'll think we've betrayed her. I was such a fool to believe that awful man—"

"He won't get away with this," George snapped. "I'm informing the Memphis police of this incident, and I'll send a telegram to the candy factory. Much as he loves children, surely Mr. Penney will protect our Tess!"

At the chiming and jangling and tolling of the bells in his vestibule, Edgar Penney looked up from his ledger. The happy racket of his doorbell made him laugh—not just because it was such an outrageous chorus of sounds, but because it matched his triumphant mood: Candy sales at his charity events had tripled. He attributed this to Tess Bennett's presence, because it left his other two girls free to flirt with familiar merchants, who in turn noted the way Tess truly adored the orphans they supported at these events.

Spec Penrose had referred to her as a Madonna whose radiance warmed everyone she met. Edgar thought this might be an exaggeration, but there was no exaggerating the amount of specialty candy the Broadmoor's owner had ordered for use at his hotel. Not to mention the generous donation he'd made to the local orphanages.

As he ascended the winding hallway to the front door, however, Edgar sensed a different sort of urgency awaiting him. Indeed, the young messenger was panting as though he'd sprinted from the telegraph office. Edgar reached into the tip box and picked up a stuffed stocking left from the Broadmoor event. "You must've hurried," he remarked as the lad latched on to the candy.

"Mr. Campbell, he said it were important, seein' as how both of these messages come across the wire one right after t'other!" The kid's freckles glistened beneath the fringe of cinnamon hair sticking out of his hat. "He told me to wait for a reply."

"Good lad. Enjoy a Pinwheel Pop while I read." Edgar chuckled when the boy spun the turquoise, pink, and yellow sucker with his finger. The colors whirled like a kaleidoscope, and inside the hard candy coating, a core of fudge waited to be savored, smeared on the tongues and lips of those who nibbled their way around the coiled layers. Pinwheel Pops had been one of his earliest creations, and it remained a favorite.

But something more serious—potentially more exciting—demanded his attention now. Edgar first opened a message from a Reed Mahaffey, Esquire, who announced his impending arrival to escort Tess Bennett back to Memphis, where she belonged.

Edgar's lips twitched. Mr. Mahaffey had quite a surprise awaiting him, didn't he? As he slipped a finger beneath the wax seal of the second envelope, Edgar grinned at the delivery boy. The outer inch of the lollipop had disappeared, and he was crunching happily on a mouthful of candy-coated fudge while he spun the sucker again. "If I were to improve on that—new flavor combinations, perhaps—what would you suggest, my man?"

The kid's eyebrows shot up. "How 'bout a rainbow, where the seven colors blend into each other around the coils? And each color is a different flavor—like purple for grape and red for cherry, and then orange and lemon and lime?" he replied eagerly before nibbling another inch of the coil. "That sounds pretty complicated, though."

"It's ingenious! And what flavor would blue be?"

The boy stopped crunching to ponder this. "Nothing so ordinary as blueberry. It would have to sparkle like a sunlit sky, so you'd have to keep eating to get to the blue parts, to figure out just what it *does* taste like."

"What's your name, boy?" Edgar asked, reaching for paper and pen. "I might just be looking for a bright fellow like you to assist with my new creations."

His face glowed like a Christmas tree. "Patrick O'Grady, sir! I couldn't think of a finer—sweeter—place to work, Mr. Penney."

"Write your name and address, then." He noted the boy's quick, decisive strokes and well-formed letters. Teachable, that one. A worker, too, with an imagination that took nothing for granted.

Unfortunately, the second telegram wasn't nearly as inspiring as this conversation with Patrick: *If a Reed Mahaffey finds his way to your factory, Mr. Penney, we beg your protection for Miss Tess! He's a wolf in sheep's clothing with fangs lurking behind his pretty words. Tell Tess that Margaret and I are ever at her service. George Delaney.*

His eyebrows rose. The delectable Tess Bennett created a stir wherever she went, it seemed. He glanced at the messenger boy, whose eyes were closed as he chewed a huge mouthful of the crunchy fudge sucker. "No replies, Patrick. I thank you for waiting, and I'll contact you come first of the new year. Merry Christmas to you!"

"Merry Christmas to *you*—Santa!"

Edgar's heart skipped happily as the boy bounded up and over the drifts rather than taking the cleared walkway. He himself had once been so full of eager energy. And while he was doing extremely well, he . . . well, he had the world's largest candy factory to run. A reputation to maintain. And there was no hiding from such *responsibility*.

And he had a conflict simmering like a vat of syrup, too. Tess remained blissfully unaware of being its catalyst. The flame two men flew toward like moths.

Moths with their antennae between their legs, he mused.

Edgar ripped the telegrams into shreds. Best to let nature take its course, to see whether Johnny Gazara came out the victor or if this Mr. Mahaffey took home his prize. Survival of the fittest, as Mr. Darwin had theorized.

He headed back to his suite, where Blythe and Daphne would distract him from such serious matters. Given the unruly ways of Mother Nature here in Cascade, he had two, maybe three days before the train delivered Johnny's competition. By then, they'd be on their way to the charity event in Denver.

And may the best moth win!

12

Tess quickly realized that while the leisurely rich in Colorado Springs sported tweeds and ties, Denver's movers and shakers swaggered into the Brown Palace wearing tooled boots and wide-brimmed Western hats. These fellows, whether cattlemen or railroad barons, eyed her with unflinching adoration as they smoked their stogies and tossed back their whiskey.

"Little lady, you ever get tired of handin' out candy, I got a place for ya on my spread," one fellow intimated, not five minutes after he'd arrived. He glanced at a page he'd torn from a newspaper and then ogled her again. "This here pitcher, it's cute but it don't do ya justice, honey."

Tess gaped. Right there in the *Rocky Mountain News*, in a full-page advertisement listing their charity appearances, was a sketch of *her* wearing her elf costume! "Where'd you get this? I had no idea—"

"Oh, it's all over the West, I reckon," the rancher replied with a boozy chuckle. "Not the first time I've come to one of these here charity shindigs, but today I came to *attention*. If ya know what I mean."

"Tess is our newest Penney Candy girl," Johnny Gazara joined in, slipping an arm around her shoulders. "And, like Blythe and Daphne, she's lovely to look at, but she's not on the menu. If ya know what I mean."

The overblown cowboy sucked on his cigar, sizing up his competition . . . now her bodyguard, apparently. "And you would be . . . ?"

"Mr. Penney's representative, protecting his many interests." Johnny eyed her with a secretive grin. "I'm also the artist who draws his advertisements. Doing my part to sell Mr. Penney's confections as we promote his charitable contributions during this season that's all about love and joy."

"I'll just bet you are," the fellow muttered. When he spotted a cohort across the crowded room, he excused himself, leaving Tess to gaze at the newspaper page.

"I had no idea you could draw so—"

"I'm an artist, honey. I sketch out every stained-glass or mosaic design before I commit it to glass." His smile warmed as he gazed at her. "You, however, are a far more exciting subject than bags of candy. Sweeter, too—and I'm trying to make my way back into your good graces, if you'll—"

"*Needy*, are we?" she purred.

Across the room, the first group of children burst through the double doors to this large parlor. She felt their excitement as they spied the cookies hanging on the tall pine trees and smelled the mulled cider. Their cheeks were pink with the cold, and they seemed so precious, so hopeful, at this young age that a second set of parents would love them enough to take them home.

I want a home where love lives again.

Her earlier words haunted her as she looked from Johnny's dark eyes to the expectant faces of the children who crowded around Daphne for their stockings. "Better get to work," she murmured.

Immediately she felt better. Surrounded by those eager eyes and such appreciative grins, Tess lost herself in greeting yet another group of orphans who wouldn't have food and shelter were it not for the generosity of men like Edgar Penney. Here again she saw a little blonde so like her Claire she had to look away for a moment. When would this sadness end? When could she see slender, innocent little girls without feeling a chasm widen in her heart?

"Ha! I knew I'd find you, Tess. You're coming with me—*now*!" Before that familiar voice registered or her eyes could find him, a man grabbed a strap of her overalls and nearly yanked her off her feet. "Of all the disgraceful—What on God's earth are you trying to prove, having your likeness in the newspaper, dressed this way for all the world to see? Henry would be appalled!"

Terror galloped off with her pulse before she could catch it, before she could collect her thoughts to outmaneuver him. "Reed!" she gasped. "Let me go. I'm handing out—"

"I've already told *one* fellow to keep his hands to himself," Johnny warned as he rushed to her side. "So if you'll kindly—"

"I didn't come here to be *kind*," Reed jeered. "I'm claiming my runaway fiancée!"

Tess stopped breathing. With Johnny staring at Reed Mahaffey as though he might punch both his eyes out, she was in a dangerous place . . . and not just because both men were snarling like territorial dogs. What might Reed say that would reveal her real circumstances? Already he was lying, trying to control this situation by pushing her around rather than requesting her cooperation. He hadn't changed a whit. If anything, he'd grown more determined to force his wishes upon her.

"I am *not* your fiancée!" she replied, shrugging to free herself. This only tugged her green straps suggestively over her breasts, however—something neither man missed. "And this is *not* the place to have this conversation. The children are watching."

Indeed, the spacious hall had gone silent as all eyes focused on her, Reed, and Johnny Gazara—a dramatic, fascinating triangle. Except she didn't intend to remain between these two opposing sides for long.

Johnny smacked Reed's fingers away from her, glaring. "We shall remove ourselves from this party before we make a shambles of it. Daphne!" he called over to the blonde who watched them as though fixed to the floor. "Please proceed! Our young guests are eager for their gifts."

As he steered Tess toward a door at the rear of the room, however, Reed was having none of it. "You cannot tell *me*. Unhand her!" he demanded shrilly. "This is none of your affair."

"Oh, but Tess and I are involved in quite a nice affair, and we don't need *you* ruining it," Johnny replied in a dangerously low voice. As he guided her through the door, he remained between her and Reed. They entered a narrow service hallway the catering staff used, and then her raven-haired escort turned to confront her uninvited guest. "Who are you?" he demanded. "And what gives you the right to barge in and—"

"I have no reason to answer that until *you* do, sir," Reed retorted. "And as for your *affair* with Tess—"

"Oh, stop it! Both of you!" Tess stepped away from them, crossing her arms over breasts that felt lewdly loose. "Johnny Gazara, this is Reed Mahaffey, my deceased husband's partner. Reed, Mr. Gazara is employed by the Penney Candy Company—as I am—and your intrusion—"

"If there was ever a woman on God's earth who didn't need to work for money, it's you, Tess. We're gathering your things and going home."

Her cheeks tingled with heat. A blind woman couldn't miss the questions in Johnny's eyes as his obsidian gaze lingered on Reed's face.

Then he looked directly at her. "Please explain what you've just said, Mr. Mahaffey," he said quietly. "We circulate among many powerful, wealthy men as we accept their donations. *Most* of these gentlemen inquire about keeping company with our lovely Penney Candy girls, so I'm sure you'll understand my *hesitation*—my *concerns*—about letting her go with you, sir. Especially since she seems none too eager to see you."

Never had Johnny sounded more eloquent... or more damning. After all the ecstasy and dreams they had shared, in bed and during the long rides to these charity events, he was letting Reed explain this situation—giving Reed the benefit of the doubt. Her stomach knotted. Mahaffey would inflate the details to make *her* look disreputable: the runaway, deceptive, ungrateful widow who didn't have sense enough to know how good her life was.

I want a home where love lives again.

And she'd come here to chase that dream, hadn't she? What exactly had she done wrong?

The answer to that was damning yet undeniable: She'd fallen for Johnny and he'd surely fallen for her, too, so why was it *her* problem that she had money?

Because Reed wants it and Johnny despises it.

It was as simple yet as complicated as that, wasn't it?

"Mrs. Bennett is my late partner's widow," Reed repeated in a solicitous voice. "As the wife of the South's most successful cotton factor, she has enjoyed all the benefits—all the privileges and luxuries—that come with the wealth and power you've already spoken of, Mr. Gazara."

Johnny's eyes blazed with her apparent betrayal, even though discretion about her wealth had been her best defense against another man taking advantage of her. No sense in dodging the issue any longer, was there? She focused on her lover, refusing to cower. "Reed wants to marry me so he won't have to buy out Henry's share of the business."

"Tess, that's the most inappropriate, absurd—" Again Reed grabbed her to shake some sense into her.

And again she jerked away, while Johnny stepped between them. He shoved his competition to the wall. "Take the hint, pal! She wants nothing to do with you," he snarled. "Tess came all the way to Colorado to—"

"If you think I'll let her take up with the likes of *you*—"

Disgusted, Tess threw open the door to the reception room. "Gentlemen!" she called out. "We've got a brawl brewing out here!"

Within seconds, every man in the reception room had surged into the hallway: witnesses, as she saw them. "This man is trying to take me home—"

"Yeah, well, if the little lady ain't goin' home with me, she ain't goin' with nobody!"

"You're not from around these parts, are you, pretty boy? The lady's told you to—"

"Tess!" Reed protested when a burly businessman on each side of him lifted him from the floor. "What the hell's *this* about? You and I have business to discuss!"

She stood amid the suited Denver tycoons, feeling awkwardly underdressed and wishing she could just walk away from this fiasco. But running from Reed hadn't gotten her where she needed to go. "Escort this man to the train, please," she asked the Texan who'd first invited her home. Then she sighed wearily. "Get your affairs in order at the office, Reed. I want nothing more to do with you, and since you can't hear *me* saying that, Henry's lawyer will be contacting you. To dissolve the partnership."

His boyish face turned the color of raw beef. "You can't just dismiss me like *that*," he said with a sharp snap of his fingers. "Henry always said the business would be mine if—Any way you look at this, I'm entitled to my half—"

"I beg your pardon." Tess despised conflict, whether private or in the presence of men she didn't even know, but it was time to stand her ground. "Henry was the senior partner who took you under his wing. Doesn't take a business wizard to figure your share of Bennett and Mahaffey as the smaller of the two.

"And mark my words," she continued, sensing every gentleman present would enforce her threat, "if you come to my house again or lay another hand on me, you'll receive *nothing*, Reed. I saw through your schemes before we prayed over Henry's grave."

"You tell him, Tess!"

"Atta way, little lady. Come on, Mahaffey. You've got a train to catch."

13

The coach ride back to Cascade was painfully quiet. Edgar had elected to sit up with the driver, which left Tess to sit on the seat between Daphne and Blythe, who held their questions for later. Johnny slouched across from them, his arms crossed tightly as he stared out the window to avoid looking at her.

Tess regretted using her money to put Reed Mahaffey in his place, but it was a language he understood. Johnny Gazara understood it, too. How ironic that he'd left his former lover because she was well married and duplicitous—and today *she* had acted much the same, hadn't she? She had no husband coming home, but her dark-haired lover was leaving her because he associated moneyed women with desertion and betrayal, and she'd given him no reason to believe differently.

When they arrived at the candy factory, Johnny hopped down from the carriage to carry in the boxes of extra candy and their orders from the day's event. No whispered hints of meeting in his room, no exchange of heated glances or enticement to spend the next several hours with him. Tess's heart thudded. She stepped down first and then helped Daphne and Blythe to the snow-lined walkway.

188 / Melissa MacNeal

"Tessie, can we do anything to help?" Daphne whispered, glancing toward the carriage's boot, where Johnny talked tersely with their driver. "That was the most *awful* scene in the hotel hallway."

"Thank goodness Johnny sent that other fellow packing," Blythe remarked. "But now he's acting as if—"

"It was my doing that Reed left, after I delivered an ultimatum about dissolving my partnership with him. Then our Denver benefactors ushered him to the train station," Tess corrected. She sighed as the three of them started for the door. "Johnny found out about my money and watched me use it as a weapon—like his former lover did—so he wants nothing more to do with me."

"But it was self-defense against that . . . that self-serving bully!" Blythe protested. "I suspected you weren't telling us everything, but we all have our secrets. I . . . I hope you and Johnny can patch this up."

"If either of you leaves, well"—Daphne's face withered and she sniffled loudly—"it'll be so deadly dull around here, won't it, Blythe? Edgar treats us wonderfully, but . . . it's been so nice to have Johnny here making his stained-glass murals and to have *you* for a new friend, too, Tessie! After Christmas, the factory remains busy, but we Penney Candy girls . . ."

"We must make our own entertainment, that's for sure." Blythe sighed. "Maybe I can convince Johnny you deserve another chance, Tess. The moment you arrived, it was love at first sight for him. We *all* saw that. Only a *man* would mess up such magic."

That evening, Tess winced at the sound of shattering glass. In his studio, Johnny sorted sheets of colors into the open trunks around him. So engrossed in his packing he was, muttering that women were all lying bitches, he didn't notice her standing sadly in his doorway. When a large piece of shiny green glass landed in the trunk with a loud *whack!* a cry escaped her.

He looked up. The section of cranberry glass in his hands shimmered like bright blood. "Don't bother begging or trying Blythe's provocative ploys to make me stay, Tess. I should've left long ago."

Her brow furrowed with irritation. "So why didn't you?"

"Beats the hell out of *me!*" The sheet of red glass shattered atop the other pieces in the trunk. "Maybe it was Penney's peppermint incense fogging my mind. Or maybe I thought all these visions of sugarplums would provide a pleasant retreat from conniving women. But, no!" he exclaimed vehemently. "*You* had to come along, saying you were so alone. Pretending to be destitute, with only one black gown to your name!"

Tess stood straighter. She'd borrowed Blythe's most conservative dress for this conversation so she'd be appropriately covered, but *sex* was not going to happen no matter what she wore. Johnny was wallowing. And in his way, he sounded every bit as spoiled and self-centered as Reed Mahaffey, didn't he? Maybe it was best to state her case and be done with it.

"I *am* alone," she pointed out in a low voice. "And, as I told Reed, I have *no* interest in marrying him. And yes, I am a wealthy woman, Johnny, but my husband's money didn't protect him or our little girl from yellow fever. And now it's made me a target for fortune hunters."

Johnny's eyebrow rose like a raven's wing. "No danger of *me* chasing after your money, my dear. I've always worked for my living, and I'm proud of it!"

"As well you should be. Your work is glorious. Unlike anything I've ever seen."

"Well, enjoy it to your heart's content. *I* choose to move on." He tossed another sheet of red glass into an open trunk. "Time to return to reality. Time to end these trips down Candy Cane Lane and take on serious projects. At cathedrals and museums."

"Good for you! I sincerely hope you find what you're searching for." Tess refrained from sinking to his level, despite the despair that threatened to engulf her as he locked his big trunks. Where was that magic everyone else here believed in? It appeared she'd have to make her own, because everything she'd come to love these past few weeks was shattering like Gazara's glass.

"For me, this job with Penney Candy has been the most fun I've had since Henry and Claire died. And you know what?" she challenged, her voice rising. "If my money bothers you, Johnny, well, that's *your* problem, isn't it? I have no intention of handing over my share of Henry's business to Reed, just because he thinks I owe him—or to satisfy your starving artist's ideals and temperament. If you can't love me because we're happy together, *fine!* Better to find out now rather than after I've lost my heart and soul to you."

Despite her best efforts, a sob escaped her as she left his room.

Within the hour, Johnny informed Edgar Penney he was leaving. In the room next to Tess's, the candy magnate wheedled and pleaded, appealing to Johnny's sense of wonderment—displayed in every room of his home—but to no avail. Gazara seemed determined to make all of them as miserable as he was. After he'd hauled the last of his trunks outside to await the stagecoach, the slam of the door reverberated throughout the house. *Like the closing of a crypt,* Tess thought glumly.

The halls rang with silence as the evening stretched on. The potent aroma of peppermint seeped out of Edgar's bedroom, accompanied by none of the usual sounds of sex play. Not wanting to think about how Blythe, Daphne, and Edgar were consoling each other, Tess wandered the house's mazelike halls to drink in the details of Johnny's artwork, the joy and childlike spirit that shone in each of his sparkly murals and friezes. While she understood his desire to stretch his abilities, to have his work *seen* rather than buried here beneath the Colorado snow, it saddened her that he'd left under such a cloud.

A cloud of his own making.

Tess fingered the curlicues of an ornate stained-glass ribbon tied around a Pinwheel Pop. The coils of candy seemed to spin as she watched, like a never-ending rainbow, even though reason told her the image wasn't moving. It was Johnny's mastery of blending colors and glass facets to create the illusion of movement. She could practically *taste* the grape, cherry, orange, lemon, and lime.

And what flavor would the blue be?

Tess blinked. She'd heard that question spoken quite plainly, yet no one stood anywhere near her.

A giggle bubbled up from deep inside her. This place *was* magical, and it had taught her something very valuable, too. Never in her life had she stepped outside the social expectations of the Memphis elite, yet she'd run away from a businessman who coveted her money, traveled to a place totally unknown, on a whim, and had fallen for an artist who'd seduced her with the rise of an eyebrow. And today she'd told both of them she didn't *need* them.

What a liberating thought!

Tess realized then that her time and her future were her own. She missed Claire and Henry, yes, but she'd gotten beyond their loss, had shed her widow's weeds for an outrageously revealing elf costume, to entertain children far needier than she. She'd blazed a new trail without a staff or a husband to direct her. And it felt good. It felt *damn* good.

Something primal shifted within her. Tears trickled, but this time it was sheer joy at her own accomplishments that made her swipe at her eyes and head for her room. Why remain here, in a house without windows, to endure the endless boredom Daphne and Blythe had described? She had a mansion in Memphis, sunny and comfortable even in December. And if she left tomorrow, she could be home for Christmas.

Home . . . I want a home where love lives again.

Well, what would that matter if *she* didn't live there, too?

* * *

Edgar sat at his desk, already writing out her paycheck when she entered his office the next morning. He wore his red, fur-trimmed Santa outfit, with the hat angled jauntily over his brow. "I'm well aware you don't *need* this money, Tess—because I asked Spec Penrose to find out about you the day you arrived," he added with a catlike grin. "But I insist on paying you for the wonderful way you've spread Christmas joy to our orphans. Godspeed, Tess. We're going to miss you terribly."

Tess took the check and then gaped. "You can't be serious—"

"My generosity comes with an ulterior motive. And more than a little magic." He leaned on his desk, fixing her in his gaze. "I also know, of course, that you and Johnny have been very, very naughty. But it's so nice to see both of you *happy*."

"Are you sure about that?" she countered. "The minute Johnny learned I had money, he turned tail! He didn't like it when I told him it was *his* problem, either."

"Precisely why I brought you here, my dear. Remember that magic I mentioned in my ad?" Edgar's grin flickered. His flawless face had an ageless, childlike appeal, and she still had no idea how old he was. "Never stop believing in the magic of Santa, Tess—the goodness that comes of giving and receiving. Trust me, my dear. Johnny will come back to you, and it'll all work out. Always does."

Johnny's handsome face flashed before her: his playful, dusky smile . . . that body made to fit against hers . . . kisses that drove her over the edge. Oh, how she wanted to believe in Santa's magic! But if she was to make her train, she couldn't let Edgar talk her into any more visions of sugarplums. "Thank you again for all—"

"Before you go," he said, nodding toward her check, "might we discuss a bit of business?"

14

_____

"Merry Christmas, Warren! Thank you so much for fetching me at the station."

"Thank you for filling me in on your adventures, Miss Tess. It's so good to see you smiling again." Henry's former driver embraced her, his eyes shining. "I shall call upon the attorney immediately to initiate those dissolution proceedings on your behalf. After the way Mahaffey's treated you and the Delaneys, it'll be my pleasure to watch him squirm."

Tess smiled sadly. "I didn't want it to come to this."

"Of course you didn't. You don't have a contentious bone in your body." The stalwart man glanced toward the house, which stood dark and silent in the gathering dusk. "Are you sure you'll be all right? I can notify Margaret of your return."

"Please." Tess gripped his thick fingers between hers, imploring him to believe she was rational. _Strong_. "After the extraordinary suggestion Mr. Penney made, I have a lot to ponder—a whole new purpose. And it excites me!"

"I can see that. You're sparkling like a diamond on the Colorado snow."

She grinned, recalling those deep drifts and their blinding whiteness in the sunshine. "Have a wonderful day with your family tomorrow. I've enough here from the butcher and the bakery to last me for days, and I can't wait to set my plans in motion."

The old fellow bussed her temple fondly. "Henry would be so proud of you, Miss Tess. I'll check back in a couple of days, then. Merry Christmas, and God bless you!"

"Oh, He has, Warren. He and Santa both have. Thank you again."

She stood at the curb, waving until his carriage rolled out of sight. Then, shopping bags in each hand, she gazed at the three-story brick house that seemed to glisten as the twilight gathered around its gables. *Home!* How wonderful this place looked—and how totally different she felt since the day she'd sneaked out to avoid Reed Mahaffey's courtship.

She relished the thought of quiet meals alone with time at her desk putting pen to paper, conjuring the magic Edgar Penney had challenged her to create. She could spend her days visiting orphanages all over the South with bags of his imaginative candy, watching those dear faces light up as Edgar's confections and financial assistance brightened hundreds of little lives. Plenty of children right here in Memphis would benefit, too.

Tess stepped quickly toward the porch. She had a fire to light, and her stomach rumbled for the ham and pastries and fruit she'd bought, and—

That's odd. Why would Margaret and George hang a new wreath on the door before they left?

Gazing at the fresh greenery, she noted its adornments of red, gold, and green . . . squares and globes wrapped in shiny paper, which stopped her heart. A sparkly red envelope was wedged into the center. What on earth could this mean?

She dropped her bags to read the message, written in the same calligraphic script that graced the Naughty or Nice game papers: *It's Christmas Eve, Tess. If you want a Naughty Santa to pay a visit, light a candle in your bedroom window. Be Nice and take off your clothes. Midnight.*

A gust of wind whipped the note out of her hand and down the street before she could catch it. Her heart pounded. Had she really seen Johnny's writing—heard his voice murmuring those provocative words—or was it wishful thinking? She looked around the yard, but except for the wreath and those sparkling candies, she had no proof of his presence.

After the way he snubbed you, why are you so shamefully eager to see him?

What if Reed bought a box of those candies in Denver and he's trying to trap you?

You still have money—even more now, from Edgar—and Johnny despises that! Why do you think anything will be different? What'll happen to your plans for all those orphans?

Tess had no answers. But the way her insides clenched, the way she gazed out every window of the house, hoping to catch a sign of him, spoke volumes, didn't it?

Johnny returned at eleven forty-five, to stand in the shadow of the tall hedges. Even in the glow of the winter's moon, Tess's house looked warm and welcoming. Its brick and stone details, the symmetry of its walls and windows, appealed to him. He'd come to Memphis expecting to despise Henry Bennett's overblown mansion, but its simplicity, its quiet solidity, had drawn him in by surprise. A peek in the windows had hooked him as surely as Edgar Penney's peppermint opium. Mrs. Bennett's palette of cocoa and cinnamon and sage felt as comfortable as a favorite armchair, while the understated furnishings bespoke a family who felt no need to flaunt their affluence. Clean and neat, solid yet soft.

It was a far cry from Francine DuPont's overblown, opulent showpiece full of gilt and gewgaws. Tess lived in a home—a *home*—where a family had lived and loved every day until those dearest to her had departed. This morning he'd gazed into each lower-story room, steeped in sensations that had startled him at first. It was downright unsettling, how *settled* he felt as he beheld Tess's belongings.

Why would she take me back? The question punched him in the gut, for he'd so stupidly assumed she was like other women with their wiles. All he had to show for his bluster—his rudeness to her—were trunks of useless, shattered glass . . . something akin to the way he felt about himself when he'd left Edgar Penney's sugar-coated catacomb of a house. He'd told Tess that the candy master had enslaved Daphne and Blythe with his opium, yet he now felt like an addict who'd stepped out of a den and into daylight for the first time in months.

It's Tess who makes you feel alive again. Whole, and worthy of that higher-minded work you aspire to.

Humility. Could he muster enough sincere humility to request a fresh start? A woman who'd invited dozens of little children to bask in her warmth—who felt such compassion for them as she handed out candy—deserved a man who allowed her light to shine without demanding center stage for himself.

And what good are your stained-glass designs without light to show them off? To make their true colors glow?

What a startling thought! If he could word such an idea into his plea for another chance, perhaps Tess Bennett would reconsider.

A tiny speck of light appeared in the window above him. A candle! And then her face appeared in its glow as she searched the yard.

Johnny wanted to shout and sing. Tess had read his message! She would hear him out! He bolted toward the front door and then remembered his mission: He was a man wooing a woman, not some feckless adolescent racing to get laid. He sucked in the cool night air, giddily climbed the front steps yet fought the deep fear that she'd be naughty instead of nice. If Tess Bennett had any idea how much *power* she had over him . . .

As he reached for the doorbell, he didn't want to consider the consequences of failing to impress her. *Why the hell did you decorate this wreathe with candies from a sex game? If she thinks you only want her body, only came here to plunge into her—*

The door flew open before his finger found the button. His heart shot up into his throat. By the glow of her candle, in her silky white peignoir, Tess resembled an angel. Serene and mysterious, she stood before him. Just watching. Waiting, with an expectant expression on her lovely face.

Tess bit back the "Merry Christmas!" she'd been ready to exclaim. Not a good idea to appear too eager, considering Johnny Gazara had so much explaining to do. The silence stretched between them. She ignored the chill of the night air, willing her body to remain absolutely still.

"Tess," he finally murmured. He sounded strangely distressed. And very needy.

She nodded, watching him.

He licked his lips. His eyes roamed over her, lingering on nipples that ignored her order to remain calm and disinterested.

"I-I've behaved like the lowest kind of toad—"

"They say you have to kiss a lot of those to find your handsome prince."

"And I'm so damn sorry for those awful things I said before I left Edgar's, and—"

Tess pressed her lips together. In a deep scarlet shirt, and with his onyx eyes shining in the candle's light, he glowed like an ember. Saint Nicholas, indeed—but not the kindly, bearded fellow children imagined. Oh, no—a saint was the furthest thing from her mind right now!

"If you'd give me another chance, I'd treat you like a queen,

Tess," he babbled. "I've been looking around Memphis these past few days for design work."

Tess fought a mischievous grin. An idea blossomed, full-blown and beautiful. Had Edgar Penney planted it there, perhaps? He had that magical way about him.

"Well, well, well," she murmured, gesturing for him to come in. "I happen to be looking for a new *partner,* because Edgar has donated a small *fortune* toward spreading his generosity—and expanding his candy business—into the South. But if my money upsets or offends you, Johnny—"

"I want *you,* Tess! Not your money," he rasped. "You know that, I hope?"

Wasn't *that* a refreshing admission? It sent visions of Reed Mahaffey racing from her recent memory, so all she had to contemplate was this handsome, repentant man with ebony hair and long, sensitive artist's hands.

Johnny pushed his windblown hair back to focus on her, his face alight with a love so fierce it frightened her. "How many times have my words come back to haunt me these past few days—from that first time when you asked what I wanted for Christmas?" he recounted in a strained voice. "I wanted to be home—with you, Tess. Yet when any other man admired you—and why wouldn't any man wish for you, under his tree?—I acted like such an ass!"

Tess's lips quirked. "I *like* your ass, Johnny."

"And why on God's earth would I compare you to any other woman?" he continued urgently. "I got so damned— What?"

She laughed softly. "I like your ass. Even when you act like one."

Johnny's laugh billowed to fill the foyer as he reached for her. Then there were only his lips, moving around words she no longer heard for the pounding of her pulse, and then they were pressing into hers with an urgency that said all her Christmas wishes were about to come true.

Tess eased away, breathless from his kiss, yet needing to test her idea on him. No sense in pursuing this reunion if he refused to take part in her new dream. "Will you be my partner in this new business venture?" she heard herself asking. It seemed a miracle her mind could form coherent sentences, the way his gaze and scent aroused her. "I want to build a candy castle. A place for homeless children to live," she gushed. "And inside, I see lollipop walls and candy cane gates and—"

"The way Edgar decorated his house?" Johnny queried with a quirk of his eyebrow.

"No, the way Johnny Gazara envisions it. But if you'd rather design cathedral windows and—"

"I'd rather rip that robe off you and make you holler my name until it echoes all over this house, Tess."

Her mouth fell open. Her pulse thundered to that primal beat this man had ignited in her the first time they'd met . . . every time they'd come together. "Ah. Pleasure before business."

"And love, pure and simple—and hot and complicated." His eyes burned into hers as his fingertips coaxed the filmy robe from her shoulders. "And naked. Always naked."

"Naughty or nice?"

"Nice and naughty, Tess." He slipped his arms around her and stopped an inch short of kissing her. "Your candy castle idea intrigues me . . . because it's perfect for you—and who else could possibly design a structure to match your imagination?" he teased. "So let's do it! And meanwhile, what do you want for Christmas, little girl?"

Sheer joy filled her soul. And what this man made her *want* was something she realized she could have forever, if she said the word. "You?" she teased.

"What do you *really* want, Tess? Tell me in no uncertain terms."

She giggled. This man had a way of making all the trimmings and trappings superfluous, didn't he? "Take me upstairs, and then *take* me," she murmured. She stood on tiptoe to whisper into his ear, "Fuck me senseless, all night long."

Johnny kissed her hard, crushing her close. "Now you're talking!"

And as he carried her up the stairs, Tess knew they'd need no candy-wrapper instructions, no rules or props or anything but their naughty thoughts to guide them through nights of passion into years of love like this house had never known.

And wasn't that nice?

STOLEN CHANCES

CHLOE HARRIS

1

Winston Matthews charged from the study wanting to punch something repeatedly and hard enough to break his hand. The old man could do whatever he damn well pleased. Winston didn't need his money or want anything to do with his position or connections. But nobody, not even his bloody father, was going to tell him he could never see his mother and sister again.

His father had all but ruined him coming home to Belize Town for the Christmas holidays. At least now he didn't need to wait for Twelfth Night to set sail. Perhaps he could leave as early as tomorrow. But then, his mother wasn't feeling well, so like it or not, he'd have to swallow his pride and stay.

Winston resisted the urge to roar his frustration at the stuccoed ceiling. What would all their illustrious guests think?

After two long, deep breaths, he plastered on a smile and made his way downstairs to join all the frivolity at the Christmas Eve ball.

The string quintet was jingling a merry tune for a country dance when Winston entered. A few of the guests sat catching their breath or stood in clusters watching the dancers, his mother among them. As soon as she saw him, she excused herself and came toward him.

"Winston, my dear boy." She proffered one hand in greeting, and Winston took it, wrapping it around his arm. The dark circles under her eyes were proof she didn't feel as well as she let on. "I'm so glad you're here. I understand you arrived early this afternoon?"

"Yes, but Father asked to see me right away. That's why I couldn't come to you sooner. I'm deeply sorry."

Her thinned lips curled into a pale smile. "Don't be. I know perfectly well he can be overbearing. But let's not talk about it any longer. You look extremely well, Winston. A little too tanned, but your"—Dolores Matthews paused and opened her fan, clearly searching for an innocuous enough word—"your lepidopterist studies keep you outside for long stretches of time, I suppose. How are your endeavors coming along?"

Winston fought not to smirk. "Mother, there's no need to beat around the bush. I've been first mate on a merchant ship for half a year already. It's nothing to be ashamed of."

"Nor punishable by law." Dolores gave a relieved nod.

"That, too, yes. Never mind that being privateer is sort of a family tradition." His father had branched out, so to speak. He had known who to bribe and who to cheat or kill, or both, here in British Honduras, and he got a title and the post as governor-general in return. "But I turned my back on all that." And all the blood and corruption his father dealt in.

"Thank goodness you did! The laws are horrible nowadays. I couldn't bear the thought of you—"

"Let's not talk about my wild youth any longer, shall we?"

"Your *wild youth*? I'll say. You sound like you're ready to settle down. Knowing that would infinitely please certain guests. Lady Louise Barnes, for instance, confided in me that she and her incessantly giggling daughter hoped to meet you tonight." With a slight tilting of her head, Winston's mother indicated where not to look right now. "Or Lady Georgiana Woodford—I suppose she's in the next room at the buffet—has brought her two lovely daughters with her. They're both out in society now, and Lady Woodford is trying very hard to land a son-in-law or two. Then there's Lady Amelia Shutterford—"

"Mother, please. I do appreciate your efforts, but marriage is a port I seek to avoid for a while longer still."

Staring into the crowd, Dolores sighed. "You might not want marriage, but your sister is certainly thinking along those lines."

Following her gaze, Winston saw his sister at the far side of the room, more or less hiding behind a lavish arrangement of silver saw palmetto leaves intertwined with Mexican cedar and Santa Maria, one of many arrangements used to decorate the house for the holiday in the absence of holly and mistletoe. She listened to the music and was apparently fawning over one of the musicians.

Dolores nodded gravely. "Yes, Charlotte is not being very subtle about her fascination with the lead violinist. Angelo della Pietà, or whatever his name is, is said to have accompanied Vivaldi round Europe after having been his last student."

When Father found out about Charlotte's infatuation, the stargazing violinist would find himself in the gutter with a knife between his ribs. "Maybe he prefers men," Winston suggested.

His mother tapped his shoulder with her closed fan in a mock scold. "Well, whatever his preferences, I could certainly do with a glass of punch now."

Offering his arm, Winston accompanied his mother to the adjoining room. There some guests were seated, some standing, chatting in between bites of roast goose, shellfish Christmas pudding, and mincemeat pies, washing it all down with champagne or punch. The wall opposite the huge terrace doors was riddled with Winston's ostensible pedigree. Every time Winston looked at it, he had to suppress a bark of laughter. One of those so-called ancestors looked like Edward Teach. Father had probably thought it a practical joke to acquire that painting.

Lady Barnes had followed them. Winston noticed her alarmingly purposeful stride toward them. Her gaze was fixated on a point next to his right shoulder, and when he looked back, he saw Lady Woodford and her daughters making their way over as well, with Lady Shutterford and her daughter close behind. All of a sudden, Winston felt like a tasty crab circled by hungry seagulls. He quickly scanned the room for a means of escape.

Hope came in a hysterical shriek that drew his attention. When he looked toward the commotion he could see Lady Shutterford had punch from her stomacher down to her skirts, and all the color had left her face in mortification. Winston should definitely go fetch the smelling salts. But something stopped him, something that made the small hairs at the back of his neck rise.

Winston watched Lady Ponsonby, who was the unfortunate guest responsible for the mishap, patting at the wet blotches with her lace handkerchief while repeating how utterly sorry she was. Then another lady caught his eye. With a casual stroll, she walked by. One moment a little too interested in the ruby necklace around Lady Ponsonby's neck and in the blink of an eye later, unfazed by the impressive piece of jewelry.

Having lived among thugs and thieves for quite some time, Winston immediately recognized the lovely young woman for what she was: not just any houseguest but a crook who had just marked her prize. How had she come by an invitation for the holidays?

It didn't matter really; she was here now and Winston had to do something about it. Stop her, possibly distract her and protect the other guests without raising suspicion.

Winston excused himself before his mother could protest his leaving and made his way through the crowd standing at the terrace door. He only just avoided stepping on one or two toes and shoving one of the guests. His mother, it seemed, had chased after him and chose that moment to call his name—and Winston's target stopped in her tracks.

Turning, she perused the crowd. Her loveliness took his breath away. Her eyes were big and her nose small in just the right ways. Her plump lips glistened like she'd just bitten into a ripe fruit. Or more like he'd just kissed her senseless. What else he could see of her was just the way he liked his women. Keeping her busy all night, Winston thought with a sly grin, would be a real hardship.

When her eyes traveled up his body, he could feel them linger here or there. What would her hands feel like when they whispered over him? Would she be a shy and quiet lover, or would she moan in abandon when he made her crest with his mouth before he buried himself deep inside her? If she was as good at her profession as Winston thought she might be, she'd most likely be whatever kind of lover she thought he wanted her to be. That had definite possibilities within itself.

"I don't mean to be rude, but"—Winston cleared his throat, his voice no more than a lust-induced rasp—"there seems to be no one to introduce us. Nonetheless, I must ask you to dance with me right away."

"Your boldness is unbecoming, sir." Her words were like stab wounds of icy scorn, but interest flared in her eyes.

"Sorry to offend you, but I beseech you to rescue me." Winston bowed and let his gaze wander up and down her body, leaving no doubt about his intentions.

Just as she was about to answer, his mother called his name again. The echo of her summons sounded suspiciously like Lady Barnes and Lady Woodford together.

"Mr. Matthews, I presume?"

Winston could see the transformation in the lovely little thief. She suddenly became much more interested in him. If he played his cards right, she'd think him a better quarry than Lady Ponsonby's ruby necklace. "I am he, Lady . . . ?"

"Latimer. Beatrice Latimer." She leaned to the side a little, checking the crowd behind him to see who had called his name. "They are eagerly awaiting your return, Mr. Matthews."

"That is why I implore you to help me. You must understand the predicament I'm in."

"Your predicament?"

"Yes. Those ladies over there." Winston leaned closer and lowered his voice. He caught a whiff of bergamot when one of the light auburn curls piled on her head teased the tip of his nose. He loved the feel of a woman's hair and was glad the West Indies was too hot for wigs. "They wish me to marry one or all of their daughters, and I'm afraid they'll stop at nothing to achieve that."

"I see." Beatrice Latimer, if that was even her real name, looked in their direction one more time, then back up to him and smiled. "In that case, you do need to be rescued."

"Very much." Winston offered his arm. "And quick, if you don't mind."

"Of course," she said, and bit the inside of her cheek as she looked down. "We shall leave at once."

"Jolly good." Passing his mother, Winston bowed in her direction but ignored the preying women who surrounded her. "Accompanying me out of the room will suffice if you're not inclined to dance. We could take a turn in the garden, or if you'd rather not, I could show you my family's art collection in the long gallery upstairs."

"The art collection?" Despite her flirtatious tone, she didn't look up at him. Her gaze seemed to jump from one guest to the other, as though she was measuring them. Was she looking for an accomplice? Unexpectedly, she looked up at him, batting her long lashes that framed arrestingly stormy gray eyes. Winston had difficulties remembering where his train of thought had left off. "Sounds fascinating, Mr. Matthews."

Upstairs, her stare flitted around the hall, from the column that hid an alcove to the bust at the opposite wall, back to the painting on the left and the three-branched brass candelabra next to it, then back to the heavy mahogany door barring the entrance to Winston's room.

"On second thought, though . . ." Winston halted, looking left and right as if he'd heard something. He moved aside and felt with his free hand behind his back for the handle on the door. The hinges grated as it swung open. "This way, please," he whispered, and guided her into his room.

"Where are you taking me?" Even though the light of the torches outside flickered through the windows, it was still too dark to see her clearly. Nevertheless, Winston could hear her breath hitch and the unmistakable quality of a knowing smile tinge her words.

"This is my room, my lady."

"Your room? Impossible!" Beatrice turned on her heels and made a halfhearted effort to leave, but he caught her by the elbow and held her back. "I must leave at once. What will people think?"

"I thought your kindness would expand even further and you'd be willing to help me with another dilemma as well." He eased a little closer until all his senses were flooded with her fresh orangey scent.

"Another dilemma, Mr. Matthews?" She leaned her head back and looked up at him.

"Indeed. It is imperative I'm not seen any more tonight." In the pale flickering light from outside, Winston could see mirth curling one corner of her full lips. He let his knuckles explore the other half of her lovely face that was cast in shadows. Her pale skin, unmarred by powder or rouge, was as soft as velvet.

"Very ungentlemanly conduct." Beatrice leaned into his touch. The erotic tension in the room escalated.

"Of course!" He let her hear a distinctive and purely masculine chuckle as he stepped up to her, closing the remaining handful of inches separating them and letting her feel how much he wanted her. "If you're looking for a gentleman, you won't find one in here."

"A shame, really. And what would you suggest we do until the early morning hours?" Her words were low, full of seduction. Undulating her body, she increased the pressure against his arousal.

"Oh, I can think of a lot of things, Lady Latimer, and they all require *some* privacy." He lifted her in his arms and turned so that her back was against the wall. She slung her legs around his waist, pushing her female softness against his cock.

"Let me thank you properly, shall I?" Rolling his hips, Winston let her feel his hard member through all the layers of clothing separating them still. One hand sneaked up the inside of her skirts and along her thigh until he found her moist core. There, he toyed with her hardening nub in between gentle squeezes, and she went pliant in his arms. Her lids went half-mast as her head sank back against the wall.

Carrying her to the settee, he set her down and knelt in front of her. As he loomed over her, he studied her lovely face, her half-closed lids heavy with desire, her quick pants that spoke of her need, her supple lips. Winston knew they'd feel magnificent wrapped around his cock.

Lowering his head, his tongue swept over the trembling beat of her pulse. Next, his lips wandered up her neck to nuzzle the underside of her jaw. His hands slid down her waist and traveled lower still, purposefully grasping the hem of her skirts. He pushed them up until they bunched at her midriff. Taking her tight little ass in his hands, he dragged her closer to the edge of the settee.

Beatrice purred as she spread her legs wide and tilted her hips. Helpless at the marvelous sight, Winston bent to her. His tongue flicked over his lips, savoring the spice of her sex in the air. The perfume of her rich cream drew him, enchanted him, made his mouth water for more. Her slight quiver of anticipation in response had need thrumming through him. When he opened his mouth for a taste, he dragged the flat of his tongue over her with slow deliberation. His body caught fire as the first trickle of her honey-sweet musk exploded in his mouth.

"Oh," she breathed, and ended in a blissful sigh. "Winston!"

Loathed to stop, he bent back just long enough to reply, "At your service, Beatrice."

"Less talking, if you please."

A woman after my own heart. Winston smiled against her moistness. Spreading her folds with two fingers, he buried his face fully against her.

Winston licked and swirled his tongue over her, thrusting it deep from time to time. Arching her spine off the settee, she bent her head back in pleasure, her soft moans and whimpers spurring him on.

His entire body reacted to her lascivious response. He felt he could go for hours on end, making her as wild with desire as he already was. It didn't take long until she writhed on the settee, her pants changing to little whimpers of pleasure.

Immediately after his tongue left her, his mouth settled over her clit, continuing to pleasure her. He thrust two fingers deep, palm up. Slowly at first, his fingers pumped in and out of her while he continued to softly kiss and suckle her sensitized clit. Crooking his fingers lightly, he thrust harder into her each time until she rocked away from him on the settee only to close the distance for his intimate kiss when his fingers retreated. Faster he pushed into her, and when a fresh gush bathed his two fingers sheathed in her, he added a third.

Suddenly, Beatrice lifted her thighs and draped them over

his shoulders while her hands fisted in his hair. Her hips jerked forward, slamming her sex into his lips, and she hooked her ankles against his back. The next moment, as her gasps turned to pleading whimpers, the undulating movements of her hips became frantic. She rolled her eyes upward and gasped, then moaned. Winston felt her climax, felt her squeezing his fingers tight, felt her clit jerk against his tongue.

"Goodness me!" Beatrice wheezed out a slow breath. "You're incredibly good at that."

Winston could only chuckle while tenderly lapping over her one last time before he was released from the firm grip of her thighs around his head.

Limply, her legs fell from his shoulders. Winston kneeled up, reaching down to free himself while licking her juices off his lips. Just as he leaned down to carefully position himself, she came alive again, whipping up her arms and locking them around his shoulders, her legs crossing at his waist.

"Kiss me."

Happy to obey, Winston dipped his head and took her mouth in a sweet slide, sealing her lips with his. She immediately opened and allowed him entrance, and when her tongue shamelessly rubbed along his, he heard himself moan. Their kiss was greedy and full of voracious desire, tongues dancing and swirling to the relentless pulse of their need for each other, for more.

Everything about her, her skin softer than her silk gown, her orangey scent now completely suffused with her feminine musk, was driving him wild. The head of his penis nudged into her warm, wet entrance, and Winston was trapped between wanting to pin her down and shove his cock inside her hard and fast, or holding back, drawing things out with a slow and steady pace.

Beatrice's hand left his shoulder and groped his buttock. Nails biting into skin, she demanded he fill her. Gladly, he obliged, rolling his hips up. He stuffed her inch by inch, to let her slowly adjust to his width. Arching his hips, he drove his shaft even deeper into her slick cunny. When he was as deep as he could go, she broke their kiss and gasped.

Winston took his time easing his cock out of her. He felt her whole body shudder with pleasure as he rocked gently against her and slid back inside. He fully intended to savor this, to enjoy her. Her hips bucked up against him, urging him on, but he didn't waver. One thorough, deep, silken stroke after the other, his hands clamped over the tops of her thighs to keep her locked in place for his unhurried, measured thrusts.

Eyes closed, her head fell back. The flickering light sneaking inside their cocoon from outside let Winston see rapture written on her face. He could feel it in the gripping spasms around his pulsing cock, and he could hear it in the wicked little cries that left her.

No other woman Winston had enjoyed had felt so good, so perfect, so hot around his cock. An orgasm the likes of which he'd never experienced before simmered right beneath his skin, hot and blinding and exhilarating. He had to concentrate, not allow himself to come undone and give in to the raging torrent of prolonging pleasure and craving completion.

But he feared the battle was already lost. A fresh gush of her honey wet his cock and trickled down his balls, bathing him in her scent, marking him as hers. His rolling thrusts deepened. Rough, long strokes had her whimper and moan. Pumping hard and faster still, he lunged in and out of her. She moved with him, meeting him stroke for stroke, the smacking sounds of skin on skin the only music they could hear.

Burning waves of desire spread through him. Her tight, hot pussy created sublime friction against his cock. Prickling tendrils of pleasure slung around every limb of his body. The surge of ecstasy blazing through him was fierce.

He slammed his cock into her, grunting with the effort each

time, and she responded in kind, crying out in rapturous frenzy each time she ground her cunny against him. The next moment his orgasm hit, violent and blistering, as hard and fast as he fucked her, and with each wave that washed over him, Winston felt stunned, his strength leaving him. He braced himself against the settee to keep himself from crushing her, his hands resting right and left of her waist.

When their breathing returned to normal, Beatrice began to laugh, quick exhalations of breath just short of a hoarse giggle.

"Can we do it again?"

"As you wish." Winston still fought to get air into his lungs. "I might need a moment, though."

He hooked his index finger into the crisscross of ribbons and bows at her stomacher. "I'm sure your bosom is as delectable as the rest of you, but there's too much between my lips and them still. So, if you don't mind . . ."

"No," she positively purred while grabbing a hold of the bows over her stomacher. Swift fingers opened them quickly, then ripped open the corset that lay underneath. "I don't mind at all. Hope you don't mind my getting you naked first."

Even if he'd wanted to, he couldn't protest. Winston's mind had gone completely blank when he beheld the most glorious tits he'd ever seen.

2

Rosie Archer opened her eyes, instantly conscious of her surroundings. She always woke quickly and fully aware. Leading the kind of life she did, it had become a skill that had served her well. When your identity changed frequently, it was essential not to be foggy or forgetful in the morning—especially if you weren't waking up alone. Not answering to the right name or being confused and saying something completely out of character could eventually get you brought in front of the magistrate—or worse.

For the moment she was Lady Beatrice Latimer, spending the holidays all the way through Twelfth Night at the home of the governor-general of British Honduras. She and the governor-general had several of the same nefarious contacts, so it had been easy to find a way to procure an invitation. He was as well known and popular among the underground as he was among the elite. The guest list was prestigious, so she'd expected to gain a top-quality bauble or two.

Currently she was sore in just the right places and stretching her limbs lazily in the bed of her host's son, Winston, the one and only heir to the governor-general's vast fortune. This was the third night they'd spent together, and she wondered if she'd get lucky enough for him to want to continue their liaison through the whole holiday season. It might make it harder for her to scout and procure a good piece like that fabulous ruby necklace, but now the possibilities were much broader.

Speaking of broad . . . Rosie glanced at the man beside her. He was still sleeping soundly. Careful not to wake him, Rosie eased her way up to a sitting position. He barely moved when she tucked the silk pillow behind her and leaned against the carved mahogany headboard.

The sheer white curtains swayed a little in the fading night breeze from the sea just beyond the Matthews' mansion.

With a content sigh, she stretched again. Arms over her head, one hand kneaded the lower arm of the other. Then she repeated the languid massage on the other arm. Leaning her head to the side, she watched his muscular chest rise and fall with the deep breaths he took. The sheets pooling around his narrow hips barely covered Winston's truly imposing and most awe-inspiring asset.

There'd been nothing mediocre about his performance either. He was an extremely talented and generous lover. She'd marked a few sons of wealthy and titled men before, and in her experience they tended to be immature and selfish lovers, happy to find their own pleasure quickly. That was nothing at all like the man beside her. With Winston it seemed as if her pleasure was as important to him as his own.

That first night had been a pleasant surprise—not at all what she'd expected. She'd already settled on a prize for this fortnight's undertaking. Lady Ponsonby's exquisite ruby necklace had caught her eye right away. It was worth a fortune, and even more if you had a matching piece you never intended to sell at any price.

But then Winston had come along. He'd seemed like any

other gullible mark when she'd first met him—with the added bonus of him being as tall as an oak and handsome. His dark blond lashes could make any woman burst with envy. And the heat in his gaze ... Rosie shivered with the memory of his hazel eyes glittering with lust. They'd called to something in her she couldn't put her finger on.

The first slivers of the morning sun peeked through the sheer white curtains, making his thick hair shine like white gold. The tentative rays crawled farther into the room, revealing how impersonal and nondescript it really was. It could have been anyone's room. Any guest's room. Her own room didn't look that different.

That was peculiar.

Winston shifted in his sleep. Rosie turned back to him and realized he was tanned. Why hadn't she noticed that before? His skin was sun kissed not only on his face, which did happen to the few who weren't careful when living in the Caribbean, but also on his arms and across his whole torso. Fashionable gentlemen never let themselves tan at all. Not even here in the West Indies if they could help it. Not ever. They wouldn't be caught dead resembling the working class.

Their hands wouldn't boast calluses from manual labor either.

That was a little too curious.

Maybe he wasn't who he pretended to be? Could he be putting on an act as well?

She'd heard stories of people being lost at sea or separated from family for long periods of time and someone else taking their place and pretending to be them. But if that were the case with him, it would have had to have been very recent for him still to be so tanned.

But if something like the return of the long-lost son of the governor-general had happened recently, she'd have heard about that. It had to be something else, but what?

218 / *Chloe Harris*

Goodness gracious, what if he was the competition?

Up to now, Winston had turned out to be something altogether very different at every turn. That gave her a strange, uneasy feeling she wasn't sure what to do with. Her innate ability to quickly read people kept her dry, fed, and clothed. But he wasn't the open book he should be. That was putting her off balance.

Winston Matthews didn't make sense, and that was dangerous for a woman like her. She was going to have to keep a very close eye on him. But with his strong body, his soft hazel eyes, and his amorous talents, it wouldn't be too bothersome of a chore.

Rosie carefully folded the sheet back. Let the other ladies lie abed until noon enjoying their holiday. She had things to do. This was work for her, after all. Looking at the gorgeous, mysterious man beside her, she couldn't help but think how much she did so enjoy her work to the fullest. She left the bed and the room without waking him—another skill she'd perfected along the way.

Tugging on the scratchy lace at his sleeves, Winston cursed what polite society regarded as proper clothing for the third time this morning. His coat was much too narrow and would surely tear in two as soon as he hitched his shoulders. The white necktie throttled him so much that he'd probably swoon like a damsel any moment. A crude curse slithered from his lips as one of his ridiculous pink heels caught in the carpet and had him stumble like an oaf round the bend.

Winston righted his clothing and resumed his stiff stride down the corridor. His wardrobe wasn't the only reason for his foul mood. He'd awoken to a warm and soft empty pillow that still smelled of Beatrice, only she was nowhere in sight.

He'd been looking forward to a morning of seduction. Spooning her, his arms around her. Sluggishly entering her while still half asleep and snuggling into that warm, wet tunnel. Hardening fully. Enjoying a laggard fuck to start the day properly.

No such luck; she had left him sometime in the early morning hours.

He couldn't really say why he hadn't liked waking up alone, other than the obvious missed opportunity. Maybe it was his suspicious nature. He'd hate to find she'd already done something to make him turn her over to the authorities. He didn't want to part company so soon. He'd enjoyed their time, and not just the sex—positively mind-blowing with the demanding little minx—but also her company. Her wit. Her sense of humor. Her refreshing lack of inhibitions.

If he did say so himself, luring that pretty thief to his bed had been an exceptionally good idea. An affair would be the perfect solution to keep her away from the others and by his side. Also, she'd be tucked in safely where he could warm her all night long should she wish it. She may need a bit of convincing to see they could both only profit from it.

Approaching the stairs, Winston heard a ruckus beneath him. By instinct, he halted in his tracks and leaned into the shadows of the corridor. Checking the mirror set into the chest piece of the polished plate armor at the top of the stairs, he tried to find out what was going on below.

Was it another party already? A strange place for it, though. There was no laughing either.

The mirror didn't help much; it was only useful when just one person tried to sneak up the stairs. In that case, the dagger hidden behind the bust next to Winston usually proved indispensable. Seeing as it was neither night nor an assassin out to kill him or one of his family, Winston stepped out into the light.

None of the guests hunching in solidarity with whoever was the center of attention took notice of him. The blob of people moved a little to one side, then to the other, low chatter accompanying much patting of shoulders or hands to soothe the agitation.

As soon as Winston was within hearing range, he could make out the words "ruby" and "necklace" and saw Lady Ponsonby bobbing her solemn head while dabbing at a tear.

Oh, bloody hell! That didn't bode well.

The people parted and Winston entered the sea of worried glances. Subdued apprehension pressed against him like a strong current, but Winston pushed forward to stand next to Lord Ponsonby, who was just then scratching the bald patch at the back of his head.

While the tang of nervous sweat from Lady Ponsonby was strong, there was no mistaking the sweet bergamot caressing his senses. Winston's pulse leaped to a drumroll, and tender warmth spread in his chest as he realized Beatrice was among the pandemonium, in its very center, holding Lady Ponsonby's hand and murmuring, "Don't worry. I'm sure the necklace shall be found in no time."

However gentle her words were, her glare toward him certainly wasn't. "Mr. Matthews, one of your family's guests has suddenly found herself bereft of a special piece of jewelry this morning. The very same ruby necklace she'd worn to the Christmas Eve ball, in fact." Beatrice narrowed one eye at him as if he had something to do with all of this.

Was she ruthless enough to take the necklace while he was sleeping and somehow act as if she was angry and suspicious of him?

Winston couldn't believe it. But the necklace was gone.

If she'd taken it, Winston hoped to be able to tell when she looked him in the eye. But she was good; he couldn't see any trace of remorse or triumph on her features. And if her pursing her lips in distaste was anything to go by, all he could tell was that she was trying to antagonize him.

"Silly twit," Lord Ponsonby grumbled to his wife. "That

collection has been in my family for generations, and you're losing it all piece by bloody piece."

Beatrice took Lady Ponsonby and together they ambled into the garden.

"Not to worry, Lord Ponsonby." Winston bowed, hand over heart, even though he would have preferred to slap the man. "I will personally start looking for it right away."

Already on his way out, Winston swore to never again make the mistake of letting Beatrice out of his sight. Nothing good could come of it.

3

Steadying Lady Ponsonby's shaking hand, Rosie guided her out onto the back terrace leading to a bowling green, bordered on both sides with logwood tree–lined paths. The gardens were similar to a few others she'd seen in the West Indies—European staidness and order imposed on what was once a jungle.

The paths converged at the entrance of a passion vine–covered maze at the far end of the lawn. On the other side of the east path, the kitchen garden was hidden behind a cordon of starflowers and sweetleaf. Rosie and Lady Ponsonby decided for the west path into the formal garden and took a seat on a stone bench beneath a groomed cashew tree.

Rosie took a long, deep breath. "My, don't the lime trees smell divine!"

Lady Ponsonby looked up from her lap. She seemed a little confused by the innocuous comment. "Oh . . . what's that, dear?"

"The trees. Smell lovely."

"Yes, yes. A little overpruned for my taste but very nice." At that, she made an effort to appear cheerful, but unease eclipsed her smile.

Rosie patted the other woman's hand in sympathy and waited for her to begin the conversation again. Patience was the key to trust—and Lady Ponsonby's trust was essential to her goal.

Rosie could only hope she would be able to keep her patience where Winston was concerned. She'd counted on easy work for the holiday season, but it seemed she was going to have to deal with competition now. It was just as well. Christmas had never really meant anything special for her. She'd never had anything close to what anyone would call a traditional Christmas celebration. The extra challenge was just the thing to distract her from all the silly merriment.

A small cough beside her brought Rosie's attention back into the garden and to Lady Ponsonby, whose clammy hands jerked in Rosie's warm palms like she wanted to say something.

"I'm afraid I've ruined everyone's holiday."

"Nonsense!" Rosie assured her. "You haven't ruined it; you've made it. You know how people are. The holidays would be unremarkable and boring for them without a little excitement. I do hate that it was at your expense. Was it a very special piece?"

"Yes, part of an old family collection, you see. My husband wouldn't have been quite so angry if a matching ring hadn't also gone missing some years ago."

"Oh, dear, then I will make it my mission to do everything I can to help you find it." Rosie didn't say anything about giving it back once she found it, though.

"Aren't you so kind, Lady Latimer, a true spirit of the season." Lady Ponsonby's smile looked much more genuine this time.

"It's nothing, really. Now you must think where or when did you last remember having it."

"I wore it our first night here, then put it on again right before I came down for the ball last night, of course." It was apparent she had repeated this several times recently. "I just don't know what could have happened."

That wasn't what Rosie was asking. "Yes, but try to trace all your steps last night in your mind and feel the necklace on you. Was there a time during the night you remember touching it or feeling the weight move when you danced? Or perhaps you felt it pull when someone bumped into you?"

Rosie could see Lady Ponsonby tracing her footsteps in her mind. She pursed her lips, then frowned and huffed. Suddenly something must have dawned on her. She paled, her eyes wide, and she unconsciously touched her throat.

Rosie's stomach gave an excited flutter while she tried her best not to appear too eager when Lady Ponsonby leaned in a bit closer. "Darling girl, if you would promise to keep this private for the moment . . ."

Rosie sensed her trepidation the minute Lady Ponsonby stopped midsentence and looked over Rosie's shoulder.

"Mr. Matthews!"

Rosie inwardly sighed in frustration as she turned toward Winston with a pleasant smile. His acute sense of timing was not appreciated nearly as much this morning as it was last night. But she had to give him credit; he was good.

"Lady Ponsonby."

"How much you resemble your father!" Lady Ponsonby let them hear a slightly nervous cackle of laughter before she cleared her throat. "I wanted to thank you for all your concern earlier."

"It was my pleasure and my duty, Lady Ponsonby." His large frame provided almost as much shade as the tree they hid under. He seemed to know it and bent down on one knee to converse on their level.

"Mr. Matthews, have you met Lady Latimer? She also so sweetly offered to help."

Winston gave a slight bow toward Rosie. "We met Christmas Eve, yes. Good morning, Lady Latimer."

"Good morning, sir."

"I trust you slept well last night after the excitement of yet another ball?"

Insufferable. That angelic smile might fool others, but not her.

"I certainly did, yes. I feel quite refreshed this morning."

"No tossing and turning?" He bared impossibly white teeth. "Wonderful. Then you were up and about early enough to witness the disaster?"

"I'm not in the habit of sleeping late, so yes, I've seen it all." Let him think she'd caught him red-handed. Maybe that would rattle him.

"Perhaps also how it came about? Any detail you could bring yourself to remember would help." With his eyebrows raised, he clearly expected to hear something like *I've seen you take it, you charming*—no, no, make that *you cunning giant of a man.*

Instead, it was Rosie's turn to curl her lips into a secretive smile. "I was just asking Lady Ponsonby the same when you interrupted us."

With his head bowed, Rosie thought she could see him bite his cheeks to hide a grin. "Lady Ponsonby, I hope you don't mind if I ask Lady Latimer to take a turn around the gardens with me. Perhaps we can compare notes on how best to help you find your precious necklace."

"Such sweet, young people." She tapped Winston on the knee. "Yes, do go on. I've had enough excitement this morning." Lady Ponsonby certainly looked eager to leave. "I believe I'll take a rest until luncheon." She rose and Winston stood, holding out his arm for her to take it.

Rosie had a funny feeling Lady Ponsonby was indeed eager to leave. Not to rest, but to follow up on that last thought she never had a chance to share. Blast the man. Winston had certainly put a nice wrinkle in her plan.

Lifting his arm a notch as if to remind her he held it out for her still, the wry smile on his face a little too self-assured, he prompted, "Shall we?"

Rosie stood without his help but placed her hand on his forearm when they walked from the formal garden back to the path that led to the maze.

Something about him was intolerable and appealing at the same time. Maybe because he represented an extra challenge? Or because he wasn't the usual competition? If he'd taken the necklace, it was obvious he was trying to keep her from getting any evidence. But keeping close to him and finding out more about him was just as good for her as far as she was concerned.

"Tell me, Mr. Matthews—"

"Please, don't you think we're past that formality, Beatrice? At least away from company."

"All right, then, Winston. What do you normally do to pass the time here at Government House? When the calendar isn't full of holiday festivities, I mean."

"Not much really—I'm not home very often."

"Oh? Where do you spend most of your time?"

"Business takes me all over."

Business? Most men in his position were men of excess and leisure. "Business for your father?"

"Good heavens, no!" He must have recognized her triumphant look at his slip and quickly looked into the sun, raised his chin a notch, and took a calming breath. "I mean, I have my own pursuits."

"How very industrious of you." *And vague,* she thought. This was going to take a bit more cunning.

"Thank you, my lady."

When she'd watched him first come down this morning, he'd looked at home. Commanding and handsome, without a doubt every inch born for this world. But there were other times she'd catch a glimpse of something in his eye, or something in the way he moved and suddenly it seemed like the opposite was true—like someone untamed and dangerous was hiding just below the surface.

It was as intriguing as it was unnerving. It almost reminded her of those old stories of fairy glamour. But she guessed in a way that was true of her, too. What was Beatrice Latimer other than fairy glamour? Glamour was ethereal, fleeting and insubstantial. Wouldn't it be nice one day to have something solid, something lasting and strong to stand on instead of constantly dodging quicksand?

They reached the maze and he led her inside, easily making his way through the twists and turns of purple-flowered vines. When they reached a temple tree in the middle of another crossing in the maze, Winston halted, turned on his heel, and flashed a crooked smile. The next moment he pulled her closer, kissed the tip of her nose, and nudged her through a fissure in the vines. She emerged in a charming little secret garden with a gazebo in the middle of the maze, she supposed, a bed of heliconia on one side. On its other side, pipe vines crawled up and created extra shade.

Rosie turned back, studying the hidden entrance. She heard muffled footsteps on the moss-soft soil, and out of the shadows Winston emerged. Mischief glittered on his face, making him look even younger but also naïve. Her heart lurched in an odd way and began to beat even faster.

"Where have you taken me?" Was that her own voice sounding so breathless?

"I thought we might need some privacy. To compare our notes." His eyes weren't exactly hazel, but more green when the sun shone into them. And tender. Trusting, even.

"To what end?" Rosie could easily see why she'd thought him easy prey. But she knew better now; he wasn't a man to be trifled with. Just like his father. How much were they really alike? One thing was for sure: Winston didn't like his father. But did that mean he was better or worse?

"I hoped we could work together to find the culprit much faster." Why would he want to pretend he didn't have the necklace unless he wanted to send her and everybody else on a wild-goose chase?

What if he really didn't have it? But that didn't make sense. Or did it? Why couldn't she shake the feeling that there was something she failed to see?

Good heavens! This man had her off kilter like nobody before. She should walk. No, run. Accept defeat and be gone from here.

But that would inevitably mean she'd failed. She couldn't have that.

Rosie was so wrapped up in her thoughts that she didn't even protest when he led her into the gazebo.

She'd get to the heart of the matter by any means necessary. So, if that required her acting the not-so-overtly-skeptical damsel for a while, so be it. She'd find the necklace and cut and run.

When she sat on the wooden bench in the middle, she voiced the first thought that came to her mind. "Lady Ponsonby seemed more panicky than sad that she lost a precious piece of family heirloom."

"You noticed that, too? I think that's highly suspicious."

"It's true, you know. She was about to reveal something . . . vital, I guess, before you came."

"Damn!" Winston balled one hand into a fist and hit the palm of the other. Grinding his molars, he leaned forward, elbows braced against his knees. "Shouldn't have followed so soon, but I had to get out of there or I would have punched Lord Ponsonby."

"I was surprised that she seems to be only in her midforties rather than in her sixties. So much younger than I initially thought."

"She is. It's not surprising, though. She's shackled to an old man with spindly legs, a bulging stomach, and the temper of a billy goat with constipation."

"Yes, he's awful, isn't he?" Rosie shook off the unpleasant shudder down her spine.

"I've been told he lost a small fortune yesterday at cards."

"And you think he lets it out on her now?" Suddenly, Rosie gasped. "What if he's taken the necklace, made it look like somebody's stolen it, and pawns it as soon as they're back in—" Wait, that couldn't be. Winston had taken the necklace when she'd gone to her room to freshen up and get ready for the day. She looked up at him. "I forgot. Where are they from?"

"Boston, I believe. That's a valid theory. But I think it's not that complicated."

"Really." Rosie crossed her arms in front of her chest.

Avoiding her focused glower, Winston rubbed his chin. "I don't think Lord Ponsonby is capable of such deception. He'd simply take it—off her neck if need be—and sell it and that's that. The culprit we're looking for is much smarter."

Was he really that arrogant? He suddenly wasn't as appealing as he was mere moments ago.

"Somebody versed in society, capable of sneaking in and out of rooms without being seen, deceiving people and them being none the wiser for it."

"Nonsense! If you ask me," she said, her voice low, "I think we're looking for a man who is cunning and reckless enough to do it."

His eyebrows bounced up on his forehead. "A man?"

"Yes." Rosie nodded. "Why not? You don't think so highly of your peers?"

Winston barked with laughter.

"Who else but a man could do it? All the women are asleep until late, and then they take even longer to make themselves look presentable for them. Who else but a man knows what such a necklace might be worth if Lord Ponsonby hadn't bragged about it at the card table?"

"I never said—"

"No, you didn't, but he could have! He's the type."

"Beatrice." Winston caught her hands in his and kissed the knuckles of first one, then the other hand. "There's something I need to tell you."

Aha! She had him now.

"I've enjoyed our time together very much." Like the first night, he brushed her cheek with his knuckles. It seemed too much effort to resist the comfort this small gesture brought. But just as she came to her senses and was about to protest, she heard a woman's voice coming from outside in the maze.

"So, you haven't really been able to get a hold of him?"

Placing his index finger over her lips was enough to silence her. She gave a minuscule nod, and Winston beamed. If only that small curling of his lips didn't make her breath come so hard.

"No, I told you. But neither have you," another woman replied.

Winston's fingers snaked around her neck, and when the tips pressed into her nape, Rosie let him nudge her to him. His lips sealed her mouth. A spark sizzled down her spine, and her body melted into his, her fists loosening. He tasted so sweet, like honey. He even smelled like honey. She splayed her fingers and let her hands roam his chest up to his shoulders, her fingers burrowing into the thick mass of blond hair, loosening his braid.

"The maid told me she'd heard that he's not the typical bachelor."

"If he's into men, well, that's something we can work around. But, please, don't tell me he's a monk."

His hands around her waist, Winston lifted her up. Rosie came to sit astride him without so much as a protest. The slight risk of being detected added something new to their lovemaking.

His busy hands sneaked under her skirts, tracing the inside of her thighs in tickling circles. A funny tingling started in her belly and spread through her body into her limbs. Maybe this was a little too dangerous. Rosie began to struggle off him, hissing, "What do you think you're doing?"

But Winston only shook his head, dragging her even closer. His kiss now turned heated in single-minded seduction. While one hand snaked over her thighs, his fingers sliding down her crevice, the thumb of his other hand found her clit and flicked over it. The same instant he thrust one finger into her from behind. Rosie yelped, then moaned into his mouth.

"Did you hear that?"

"What was that?"

Mortified that whoever was outside had heard her, Rosie began squirming against him, but soon her motions turned from wiggles of protest to her grinding her hips into his ministrations. God help her, but the thrill of being right next to those women outside made his caresses a hundred times more intense.

She broke the kiss. "Winston, please, what are you doing?"

"Just what you want me to do."

"I don't—" He thrust a second finger into her, and Rosie felt his digits were welcomed by another moistening gush. "Oh, God!" She shivered, breathing hard against his lips.

"Shhh, love." Winston spoke just loud enough for her to hear. "We don't want them to find out, do we?"

Every nerve ending in Rosie's body was alive and on fire. Swallowing another moan, she increased her gyrations on his fingers and she saw his lips quirk. Like he knew what was going on inside her. She'd only ever experienced a similar rush when she was in the middle a particularly difficult coup. Oh, this man and what he could do to her . . .

"Maybe someone is on the other side of this huge loop?"

"Probably. They're certainly not here. Soophieee, darling, where are you?"

He never changed the rhythm of his fingers thrusting deep. Slowly but steadily they invaded her, crumbling her defenses until she pushed back, shivering at his wicked gentleness and sobbing for more.

Winston's whisper was a seductive croak. "You know what would feel even better in you than my fingers, don't you?"

Rosie shook her head. "No. I mean, yes. But no. I'll be completely mussed."

"Not if you stay on top." She swallowed a whimpering moan as his fingers retreated.

A breath later, she felt the fat plum of his cock nudge into her entrance. Throwing her head back, Rosie pressed her lips together when she felt a high-pitched gasp form in her throat.

"He does look a bit the brute, though."

"Regrettably so. My daughter was devastated to find him lacking the usual refined looks of a man-about-town. But I told her that beggars can't be choosers."

"Aah, yes." Winston was gritting his teeth to obstruct his groan. "That's it." His large hands caught her hips under her skirts, and then he slammed up into her, all his rigid length filling her in one hard stroke. "Much better, innit?" He sounded as breathless as she felt.

Heat and strength stretched her. Fully, completely. Fiery sparks, centering in her belly, rushed through her bloodstream into every nook of her, numbing her mind, stealing her thoughts, and leaving only hunger and need behind. She couldn't stop herself from moving, rotating on him. Impaling herself, her sheath swallowed him only to release him just a little before she sank down on him again. The risk of discovery was a powerful aphrodisiac, pushing her to the edge.

"Clara is quite taken with him, though. She seems to fancy this animalistic ruggedness."

"Ooooh, here's a thought."

"What?"

"He's like the fur-clad brutes of old, clubbing the men to death and ravishing the women." The woman giggled.

"*Mmm, positively delectable!*" The other woman's giggle joined the first one's.

Rosie's whole being bubbled with glee. When he wrapped her in his strong and powerful arms, she was driven to grind her core against him even harder, squirming and shivering as he hugged her. Trying her best to stay quiet only made her mind focus more on the feelings driving her to want to scream.

"*Don't let our daughters hear that.*"

"*Never! Not that they'd know what to make of it, haplessly innocent as they are.*"

Rosie's breath came in small gusts. When she heard herself moan and whimper softly, Winston sealed off those little noises with his lips and drank in her groans like a man dying of thirst. The little spark at the bottom of her spine ignited, and she felt her orgasm building, strong and scorching and blinding, arduous pinpricks twining around and into her.

"*Have you heard of Isabel's streak of bad luck?*"

"*A streak?*"

"*Yes, the latest scandal in Boston. Her daughter is said to have caused it. That's why she and her husband are hiding here for the holidays while the daughter is off with relatives in France. She'll be lucky to find anyone for the poor girl to marry before her misstep is too large to conceal.*"

"*No! Delicious bit of gossip that is.*"

As Rosie felt herself beginning to spasm around him, Winston purred into her ear, the sound as erotic as the precious strokes of his cock. Before long, he caught her hips in his hands, pressed his feet down, and braced his back against the bench. He used the leverage to push up into her, shoving his cock into her again and again. Too slow, but relentless. Too hard, but not nearly as rough as she needed it to be.

"*Yes, and then this morning's incident.*"

"*Somebody has robbed her of her necklace, I hear?*"

Her climax twinkled in blistering sparks, built to tower over her, and suddenly crashed. Ecstasy threatened to burst from her in a scream. Rosie bit her lower lip and caught her breath. She bit even harder until she tasted her own blood, but she didn't make a sound, not one whimper, nothing, even when he rocked gently against her as though trying to keep her body from ceasing to ripple and spark with rapture.

"*Indeed. Oh, there they are! Sophie, dear!*"

"*Oh, Mother, this maze is awful. I'm afraid we're totally lost!*"

"*There, there. We'll find our way out in no time, won't we, Clara?*"

However much Winston tried to draw out her pleasure, inevitably Rosie recovered. Contented, her mind drifted back into her body only to find herself weak and stunned. The fervor of their passion combined with the thrill of remaining undetected added a new intensity she'd never experienced before. All she could do was cling to him, dig her fingers into his shoulders, and let him hold her in his safe embrace.

"*Of course we will, Mother. I've just told Sophie the juicy bit of news.*"

"*What news?*"

"*That he's a pirate!*"

"*Oh, Clara, wherever did you get that?*"

A dirty snicker erupted from the other woman. "*That would certainly explain a lot of his brutishness.*"

Winston rained tiny little kisses on her, first on her earlobe, then on her cheek. Up to the corner of one eye, where he kissed a tear away, then over her eyebrow. The root of her nose. A chaste kiss on her lips. His gentleness woke something in her, some sensation alien to her. Something that made her choke, made her want to cry and burst into laughter at the same time.

Leaning back, Winston caught her gaze. "Usually I'm more in control of myself."

With a satisfied hum, Rosie let herself sink onto one shoulder. "Believe me, I remember. Only too well."

"I'm sorry I came in you."

"That's all right. Don't worry. We're safe. For now." Apparently she'd lost her usual eloquence sometime during this encounter.

"*Silly thing. I've heard he's so unfashionably tanned because of his lepidopterist studies.*"

"*And where did you hear that?*"

"*Why, I overheard him and his mother talking days ago. At the Christmas Eve ball, I think.*"

"*Sophie! You mustn't listen in on other people's private conversations!*"

Rosie kept her voice as low as possible. "Are they talking about you?"

"Humpf. 'Fraid so. Remember the Christmas Eve ball when I said I needed to be rescued?"

Rosie leaned back. "Yes?" Now that she looked into his gentle eyes, Rosie knew it wasn't true what they said. He might look like a brute, yet he was anything but.

"I didn't jest."

"And here I thought you were desperate enough to lie to lure me into your bed."

"So you spent that first night because you pitied me?"

Rosie smirked. "Something like that."

"*There! I seem to remember entering this maze there!*"

"*Where?*"

"*Over there!*" Their voices began to fade.

Rosie tilted her head and held her breath as she listened closely to see if she could hear any more. Nothing more than the occasional humming insect or the fingertips-rubbing-on-steamy-glass cries of quails could be heard.

"Are they gone?" She still didn't dare to speak louder than a husky whisper.

Winston gave a slow nod. "I think so."

His arms tensed around her, the loose embrace suddenly becoming so tight it made breathing a bit difficult, and for a fraction of a second, Rosie thought she could see him make a conscious effort to release her. Then his hands snatched up and cupped her cheeks, keeping her captive for another one of those unbelievably gentle nibbling-sucking kisses that rendered her boneless and that he did so well.

Her pliant body sinking into his, she gave in with a sigh, opening herself to his exploring, expert kiss. What was one more second or two before she had to leave and—

She forgot those trivialities in the face of his tenderness. A man who knew how to employ his lips, teeth, and tongue was really the best thing in the world. Even better than lemon sorbet.

"Oh!" Reality caught up with her when she felt his flaccid cock slip from her.

"Here." Winston reached into his pocket and produced a handkerchief that boasted no lavish frills and laces, as would be expected of a man of mode. "To clean." He cringed a little, visibly embarrassed.

Rosie slowly stood, wiping herself clean, while Winston remained seated, buttoning his britches. Task accomplished, he threw his head back, his fingers combing the mane. Turning this way and that, Winston looked for the leather band that had kept his hair in check before.

"Where—" He jumped up, bent over the bench, and searched the ground. He stood again, one arm hitched into his waist, while his other hand rubbed his chin in thought. "Beatrice, I really wanted to ask you something."

Her skirts were back in place. She brushed some fold out as she looked up at him. "Yes?"

It was now or never, Winston thought. "I think we should spend the rest of the holidays together."

Judging from how her mouth opened and remained a little agape, Winston might have been wrong about the right time and place. He quickly got down on his knees and searched underneath the bench. "There are many reasons." No leather band under the bench either. "For one, I'd love to fall asleep again with my cock tired and spent and still in you." She'd crossed her arms by the time he was finished wiping dust off his knees. "For another, I'd like to wake up again with my cock hardening in you."

"Typical. Is there any *real* reason?"

Maybe a charming smile to entice her was in order. "Yes, of course! If we stay close, we can find the necklace faster. Plus, you'd continue to rescue me from those evil mothers looking for a son-in-law."

"Of course. And I'd also help you keep your sexual appetite in check when it comes to their innocent daughters."

"I'm not some kind of sex fiend."

"Yet it seems the only thing you're interested in."

"No. Everything about *you* raises all sorts of healthy appetites in me. I feel . . ." Should he say *not so alone?* "Connected. Does that make sense?"

She took three steps, strolling out of the gazebo with her head bent. "I need to think about it."

"What's there to think about?" Winston followed her, walking in a circle around her. "Don't you want the sole heir of the governor-general of British Honduras at your beck and call?" At that, he left her while he squeezed himself through the fissure in the vines to see whether there were any other guests in the maze or if they could just simply walk out unseen.

"There was a time I thought I did," he thought he heard her murmur behind him.

"What was that?"

"Oh, nothing. If you'll excuse me, I need to freshen up."

Stepping aside to let her through, he felt slight panic rising in him. She was going to leave him, but he needed her by his side to make sure she behaved. He had to think on his feet now. "Beatrice, I need to go to town later in the day for a bit of Christmas shopping. Care to join me?"

"I don't know. I'm not one to make much of a fuss over the holidays. The shops will be crowded and . . ." She seemed so pensive all of a sudden.

"But you must! Mother isn't well and I'm tasked with all the new year's presents for the servants and the few tenants in charge of the orchards. I have no idea what to get the women or any of the children. Besides, don't I deserve a boon for such a pleasant morning in the maze?"

She sighed and laughed at the same time. "Humbleness is a virtue, you know. I'll go. Only for your mother's sake—and for the sake of the poor servants who would be stuck with your bad choices in gifts."

"Jolly good," Winston drawled, and put on his brightest grin.

She halted and turned, squinting as if she tried to see into his mind and read what was there. "That's twice you've said that. It does sound strange coming from you. I'd expect it from a commoner, or even a sailor. But you?"

"I'm more than meets the eye." Winston shrugged, surrounding himself with an air of casualness.

"That I've already figured out. The rest is a bit hazy still."

And that was exactly how it should be, Winston thought. He figured if he kept her guessing enough, she wouldn't read him as quickly as others and lose interest in him.

4

The streets and waterways of Belize Town were crowded as usual. Rosie preferred to stroll on foot through the white-washed and clay-roofed market as they were, but many others came and went by both small and large boats. The merchants were more than happy to serve customers via land or sea.

Again Rosie was struck by the contrasts of this place. The shops, stalls, and carts all decked out in their Christmas finery seemed almost mocking amid the crumbling ancient ruins and warm sunshine. It addition to the decorations, every merchant had a sign or ad offering advice on the best gift ideas. Rosie wondered if Winston had really needed her help or if he'd had other motives for asking her along.

Winston looked around, his eyes darting everywhere in the crowded market. His expression could only be described as overwhelmed. "Where in the world do you suggest we start?"

"Why don't we window-shop first? Take a turn around the whole market before we buy anything?"

"Really? What would that accomplish, just walking and not buying anything?"

She could easily tell he was not one of those peacocks adept at shopping. Most likely his valet and his mother before that bought all his clothes and most everything else for him, not that he didn't look just wonderful in those valet-bought clothes.

"Well, think of it as a battlefield and we're preparing for battle. The first thing any good warrior would do would be map the scene, then develop a strategy and decide on the best places for attack." He just stared with almost the same expression, so she tried to explain more. "You wouldn't want to attack the first spot you come to when there's a much better spot farther afield but all your ammunition is spent by the time you get there."

He continued to stare and blink for another second as if she'd sprouted two heads or turned purple. Finally his concerned look turned into a broad smile "I surrender to your shopping expertise, Captain." He even bowed, sweeping his arm wide, indication she precede him. "Please, lead the way to victory."

"Cheeky!" She gave his arm a light slap as she passed him.

Soon they made one complete loop past all the shops and stalls and now stopped to peruse the massive window display at the British Mercantile.

After discussing tactics for this first skirmish, they ambled in. Everything a good British citizen far from home might want was inside. A display of finely crafted Barlow jackknives right next to a magnetic compass in a cherrywood box with brass repoussé and chasing caught her eye. She smiled and tugged Winston's arm, pulling him toward the case. "I can't think of a boy on earth who wouldn't be happy with a knife like that as a gift."

Rosie watched Winston's eyes almost twinkle, perhaps with the memory of his own first jackknife. It was hard to imagine such a large, fit man as a small boy. It must have been nice to get such a treasured holiday gift.

"That compass . . ." Winston's words trailed off, but she

thought she caught him looking longingly at the piece before he shook himself like he'd just woken from a dream. "I completely agree. A boy's greatest treasure is a good knife. I knew bringing you along was a capital idea." Winston waved a salesman over and placed his order.

They continued to meander through the large store, also picking out four sets of silver sugar cutters tied with a cream-colored silk ribbon to a brown-paper-covered loaf of the finest quality sugar and several leather and silver mugs called blackjacks. The salesman went to the back to gather everything they'd bought and package it together so they could take it with them instead of arranging delivery to the house some time later. "It just feels more like Christmas this way," Winston explained with a wink.

Rosie thought it was as good a time as any to try and add more pieces to the brawny, handsome puzzle beside her. "You know, most men in your position would have sent the housekeeper or possibly his valet on this errand."

"Who doesn't enjoy a bit of holiday shopping to get in the spirit of the season?"

Most people would, she wanted to agree, but she wasn't sure she'd ever actually felt the spirit of the season. "Still, you must care for your mother very much."

"I do. She's a good woman who hasn't had the easiest of marriages or the best of health. And I suppose I agreed to come out of guilt, too. I haven't been around much in the last few years."

There again was that vague mention of him having his own mystery pursuits outside the family. They had had this conversation before, and she didn't expect him to tell her much more this time than he had before—but she had to try. "You mentioned business before, not content to be a man of leisure and the future governor-general?"

"I have no intention of being the governor-general ever." The answer was abrupt.

"Well, you are right. You most certainly aren't like most men. But doesn't your family expect you to be?" If he felt some guilt for whatever it was he was off doing, perhaps she could play on that.

His answer was delayed by the salesman's return. He handed the brown-paper-wrapped package to Winston and they headed back out to the street.

Rosie was surprised when he chose to continue their conversation as soon as they emerged into the sunshine. "I'm sure they are still hoping I will do what's normal for a man of my station. Along with every mother hen in attendance at the house at the moment. But let's just say I'd like to keep what little soul I have left instead."

Rosie raised an eyebrow at such a dire prognosis. "That bad, is it?"

"It can be."

Rosie pointed to a stall selling the perfect present for some of the younger females on the list. Beautiful little knitted bags trimmed with ruffles or netting and beads. They were very well done with intricate patterns of birds or flowers or fruit.

"Lady Latimer, I concede to your womanly expertise on this one. Pick out the five you like the best." He bowed and stepped back a little.

Rosie trailed her hand lightly over the delicate purses. She tried to pick out ones of equal quality but different enough so one girl wouldn't feel like another's was better or too similar.

An odd memory surfaced. Girls she knew when she was younger would make similar things and take them to the back door of millinery shops, hoping to make a few coins or, perhaps even better yet, be hired on in some capacity. Rosie had had higher ambitions than being a dressmaker's maid. With the help of a good teacher, she'd taken a different route altogether.

She found the perfect ones, and Winston paid the tanned young mother bouncing a babe on her hip. What she would have given to have gotten a gift like that, just once . . . It was of no matter. She had much finer things than these now.

Winston surprised her by holding up his hand as the woman gathered with her free hand the bags Rosie had chosen. "Very fine choices. But, tell me, which one do *you* like the very best?"

Rosie thought for a moment and picked a simple white and navy one with a bird in the center surrounded by daisies and fine white netting with pearl-like beads for the trim.

"This one is yours, then." Winston's large hands almost looked obscene picking up the dainty object by its thin twisted silk cord.

"Oh, no, I couldn't." She didn't like him being so nice to her.

"Of course you can. It's just a small token to say thank you for the help."

Rosie took the bag, folded it gently, and placed it in the larger one she was carrying. She turned her head away and started down the street with a barely audible "Thank you," coughing the unwanted emotions away.

When she had the unexpected sentimental outburst under control again and tightly locked up deep within her, she turned the conversation back to him. "So, Mr. Matthews. If not the governor-general, what do you want to be when you grow up?"

"Having been raised in both England and the West Indies, it's hard not to develop an affinity for the sea. There is a magic to being at sea that calms me, makes me feel at home. And there is still much money to be made in trade and shipping."

"New money. My, my, Mr. Matthews." She teased. "Not afraid to get your hands dirty, are you?"

"No, actually, I'm not afraid at all to get my hands dirty in all sorts of ways, half of which you couldn't imagine." His hand swept lightly across the small of her back.

Oh, but she certainly could. Before her cheeks turned bright red with the scandalous thoughts swirling in her head, Rosie searched the vendors' carts for a distraction. "Oh, look! These bayberry candles would be a very nice gift."

Even when she was low on funds, Rosie always bought bayberry candles over tallow when she could find them. They burned better and longer than tallow with a much more pleasant scent, yet they were still a good deal cheaper than beeswax. The bundles of six candles tied with a dark green velvet ribbon and decorated with a sprig of the berries would make a nice gift without being so extravagant the receiver would be afraid to burn them.

Winston bought ten bundles, and they both laughed when the old woman with very few teeth who sold the candles chanted, "A bayberry candle burned to the socket brings food to the larder and gold to the pocket."

Their next stop was a tobacco shop. She thought it would be good for his shopping ego to make at least a few purchases from an establishment where his own expertise far exceeded her own. All men, it seemed, knew their cigars. Rosie closed her eyes and breathed in the warm, dark scents while Winston made his own purchases.

She hadn't liked the thought of Christmas shopping, but it had turned out to be a very pleasant day indeed. Satisfied with their shopping, they headed for a small outdoor tea shop for refreshments. They sat in the shade at a small, brightly painted table, eating bite-sized mincemeat pies and sipping dragon fruit, lime, and mango punch.

"You know, Beatrice, we've done hardly anything but talk about me on our outing. Tell me something about you."

"Like what?" When working, Rosie always tried to keep personal details at a bare minimum. Even with a well-thought-out cover, the less information given, the better was always the rule.

"Like what gifts did you enjoy getting for Christmas as a child?"

Even with all her experience as a charlatan, Rosie wasn't sure what to say to that. The truth was, she'd never gotten any. Maybe it was the holiday spirit that permeated the market despite the heat or some ridiculous sense of gratitude for such a small, silly gift she'd just received, but she gave him something as close to the truth as she'd ever dared. "I hate to dampen any of the merriment of the occasion, but I'm afraid I didn't really get holiday gifts as a child."

"A lady of your station and who I'm sure was equally as beautiful as a child as now, why ever not?" Winston wasn't joking. He looked genuinely saddened.

She hated that. "When my father came to the West Indies, I was left behind with a puritan aunt who didn't pay much attention to me or celebrate Christmas as most puritans don't. After she died, I was sent to a girls' school where almost all of the students went home for the holidays. There was a fine meal for the few of us who stayed but no gifts really. I wasn't reunited with any family until I came of age." The truth was, there were no parents or aunt. Although St. Nicholas's Hospital for Better Education of Gifted Young Women was something of a school, it was more of an orphanage. They did have a fine meal every year provided by a local ladies' charity auxiliary.

But Rosie wasn't bitter. She'd learned a trade she excelled at and made her way quite well enough.

Winston set his cup down and took her hand. "But you're not with your family this year either?"

She gave his hand a slight squeeze, then let it go. It was harder somehow to tell her story with him touching her. "No. Mother went back to England for the winter, as funny as that is, and I agreed to accompany Lady Ellenton here as her companion." She had actually uncovered that the elderly lady's original companion was in need of some very quick cash, and Rosie had bribed her into not coming so she could take her place.

That twinkle from earlier was back in his eye, like some great idea had suddenly dawned on him. "I will make it my personal mission to make this your best Christmas ever, then."

That was not a great idea. In fact, it was a very, very bad one. "No, really. You shouldn't bother. It doesn't matter to me. Isn't finding Lady Ponsonby's necklace your current personal mission?"

"But how can I resist the challenge? I live for a good challenge or two at one time as the case may be." He chuckled at his own wit.

Rosie really didn't want anyone, least of all Winston, trying to make up for something she'd convinced herself didn't matter anyway. But she wanted to keep the mood light. His charm was contagious. "Oh, I can tell that you do. Why not try three or four challenges all at once?"

They laughed then, finished their punch, and left the restaurant to head back without more discussion on the matter.

During the lazy ride back in the open carriage, Rosie knew she should have protested more, but the thought of experiencing a happy holiday with someone like Winston suddenly had an appeal. Rosie wanted stability more than anything in the world. The reason why spending the holiday with him held a draw for her was because somehow it felt real and solid, even if she didn't understand why it did. She'd never had a safe, stable life, never been able to depend on anyone but herself. But she'd convinced herself she liked it that way.

To her, money was the only thing that mattered, the only thing that equaled power and safety. She was constantly searching for the one mark that would give her the big payoff—that would let her retire. But there never seemed to be a last one—

only the next one. She'd thought maybe the necklace was it, or maybe it was Winston.

Rosie had to admit, it was a lovely holiday so far, all due to Winston. And now he wanted it to be her happiest holiday ever. Did he really? And, more importantly, did she want that, too?

Rosie shook off the sentimentality. It was too dangerous in her line of work. Early in her career, she'd learned too many harsh lessons about trusting people to believe his motives were anything but ulterior. She was getting sloppy, and it had to stop. He had taken her far off her target. That had most likely been his plan all along.

She was going to find the right time to prove he'd taken the necklace and get herself back on track with her original goal.

Winston couldn't say why, but he felt like hopping up the stairs and whistling a tune. Instead, he took two stairs at a time, eager to get to his room. He needed to freshen up and change for dinner and the party that was to follow.

I've heard of a girl . . .

When he'd given her that purse, Beatrice had been mortified and she hadn't known how to react but to run to the next stall.

Who lives by herself . . .

Winston didn't think the memory would ever fade. He'd nearly felt sorry for her then and there. But he'd enjoyed her predicament too much. He had witnessed the struggle on her face when she was torn between a giddy grin and an embarrassed frown. Evidently, she hadn't seen that many Christmas presents in her life, if any, but now because of him she had at least one.

Waiting for his boat . . .

He didn't really have any idea why it felt so special for him when he knew it shouldn't matter all that much.

To come home . . .

He knew he ought to do the right thing and have the authorities deal with her, yet somehow he always managed to find an excuse not to do so.

She was a beautiful, albeit sly, thief. He wanted to do the right thing, but maybe there were reasons behind why she did what she did. *Complicated* didn't even begin to describe all the feelings at odds and chasing themselves merrily in his brain. He'd have trouble sorting them out if he ever sat down to analyze them. Luckily, he wasn't the brooding type but more a man of action.

Such is love . . .

What he felt for her—this glowing and pulsating warmth in his chest, this urge to lay the world at her feet just to see her smile once like she had when she'd murmured that hasty "thank you" and stashed the purse away—was this love? Was he falling for her?

If so, they didn't have a future together, he grumbled in his mind as he walked down the hall to reach the alcove that would allow him to slip into his room undetected.

He'd reached the door to his room, but his gut told him to enter from the hidden passage behind the tapestry. It was just a funny feeling, foolish perhaps, but he hadn't made it this far without learning to trust his instincts implicitly.

His thoughts turned back to Beatrice like they always seemed to since he'd been home. She had to change. She couldn't go on like this. It needed to stop. Sooner or later, it would kill her, either literally if she got caught, or it would gradually snatch away a tiny piece of her soul each time she had to lie to survive.

He eased the door open, the hinges too well oiled to make a sound. His hand was about to sweep a bit of the tapestry aside to catch a glimpse of his room, but Winston halted and frowned. He was keeping his more-than-shady past hidden from her, too. If she was hiding behind her own mask, then so was he. How much longer would they keep up lying to each other? He wanted her to trust him, but that was something he couldn't force. He also wanted to trust her. Maybe he should take the first step? But there was no neat and tidy way to broach the subject except saying, *I'm utterly sorry. I happen to know you're not who you are, but rather a thief who has stolen Lady Ponsonby's necklace. Would you kindly hand it over so that we can give it back?* Not bloody likely.

For that matter, how much longer was he going to deliberate on whether to talk openly with her while hiding behind a dusty tapestry in his own room?

The lid of the chest at the foot of his bed snapped shut. Winston's head reared up and he narrowed his eyes, his nostrils flaring as he searched the room for the intruder from behind the moldy embroidered drapery.

He couldn't believe it. Short of rubbing his eyes with the heel of his palm to make sure he really saw what he thought he did, his jaw went slack. Beatrice was standing in the middle of his room, blowing a stray strand of hair from her face. She was still facing the chest. Arms akimbo, she suddenly turned on her heel like the jerky needle of a compass, like she was trying to decide where to continue.

"Looking for something?" Winston barely kept the growl out of his voice as he stepped out of his hiding place and strolled toward her.

Whirling around, Beatrice caught her breath. She quickly recovered and raised her chin in defiance. "As a matter of fact, I am. Where's Lady Ponsonby's necklace?"

Astonishment throttled him so hard he felt his eyes bulge.

"Come now, you've heard me. Let's stop the pretense."

"Gladly. Why are you searching my room when it's you who has stolen it?"

"Me?" She gasped, quivering with indignation. "Never. You've taken it. Hand it over and I'll take it to Lady Ponsonby."

"I didn't take it." Winston willed her to hear the sincerity as he spoke.

"Of course you did!"

"I didn't!"

"Did too!"

"Beatrice, you're not who you want me to believe you are. For all I know, even the name you've given me is a false one. I know you're a thief. A grifter who has set her mind on that ruby necklace. So where is it? Hand it over and *I'll* take it to Lady Ponsonby."

At least she now had the decency to pale. "You're not who *you* pretend to be!"

"What makes you say that?"

"You aren't the typical spoiled and self-absorbed son of new money. So who are you really? I think you're the thief here."

Winston tried to bridge the sudden distance between them by reaching for her. " '*He's the type*'—isn't that what you said about Lord Ponsonby? You can read people so well, but for some reason you can't read me. Why?"

Turning her back, he could see her shoulders hunch as she crossed her arms in front of her. "I can't trust my instincts around you."

"But why not?"

"I. Don't. Know."

"Unfortunately for you, I am no thief, just the son of the governor-general."

She snorted, and Winston knew she didn't believe a word he said.

"But why are you tanned all over ... um, well ..." She blushed. "Almost all over."

He couldn't stop his crooked grin from spreading. "Paid close attention, did you?"

"Stop that. I am terribly vexed right now."

"All right, if you have to know, I have unusual sporting hobbies and it does get very hot there."

"Vague. Again. *There?* Where *there?*"

"At sea, of course!"

"What do you mean, *of course?* You're a sailor?"

"I am."

"And you've known about me . . . since when?"

"Even before you gave me that name. Is it your real name?" She shook her head.

"I thought so." His words came out on a long breath. "What's your real name, then?"

"I don't need to give you any details."

"Fair enough."

"I don't understand." She kept shaking her head as she stepped away from him. "All this time you've played me for a fool? And now you're adding insult to injury by insisting on not having the necklace? Who do you think you are?"

"I was hoping you'd realize in time—"

"What? The error of my ways? What, are you a saint now, too?"

"Beatrice, or whatever your name is, can't you see? It's not right. If you don't stop here and now, I'll make you stop."

"Not right? Not? Right? You have no idea what's right and wrong. There is no black and white in my world. Only live and let live. That necklace would help me survive another year—or even two. What is it to Lady Ponsonby but a trinket? For me it's sustenance. For you that may be wrong. But it's what my life is all about."

"Don't force me to call the authorities."

"Are you threatening me?"

"Consider yourself duly warned."

"Consider yourself the worst of asses. I'm done with you."

"Beatr—"

The door swung shut with a loud bang. The remaining silence cleansed the turmoil in his mind.

She was right. Winston groaned and rolled his eyes up. He not only was an ass, the worst of the lot, but also he was a hypocritical ass. Not so long ago, he'd lived on the edge as well. Every time the sails were set, he gambled with his life, since all the man-o'-wars haunting the oceans made the trade unpleasant at best, impossible at worst. He was more likely to get caught and hoisted from the deck by his neck and hung for piracy than come home alive. But it had been too much fun contributing to the losses of his father's numerous endeavors.

Clearly, an apology was in order. How could he make amends?

He didn't want to lose her company so soon. Her being with him felt right. Caring for her, thinking of ways to give her a nice Christmas without her pride getting in the way had provided him with a new purpose. She'd never had anyone care for her, spoil her, or even try to understand what it must have been like for her, and Winston wanted to give her all that.

But she'd probably not even allow him to grovel at her feet at this point.

5

Rosie slammed the door to her room shut. She liked her freedom and independence just fine and certainly didn't need a man telling her what to do.

Well, good riddance!

Instead of stomping her feet, pouting, and whining like a spoiled child, Rosie pictured her fury frothing and rising in a pot like boiling milk. As she'd been taught by Miss Olson at St. Nicholas's Hospital, she breathed in deeply and pictured letting go of all her rage with the long exhalation that followed. Sometimes more than one calming breath was required. This was one of those times.

So Winston knew she wasn't who she pretended to be. If he'd known she was lying all along, why would he believe her if she told the truth now? She certainly wouldn't in his place. Her stomach clenched as a fresh bolt of defiance energized her. Furious, she paced the room.

There was only one way to prove she hadn't taken that necklace. She had to find it, now more than ever.

But why would she want to prove anything—to him? It wasn't important what he thought of her.

He expected her to do "the right thing." There was no wrong or right way to be a thief. There was only a good way and a bad way, and she was bloody good at it. She was who she was, and Winston could bloody well go to hell.

This might be his world, but this was her life and her profession and she didn't want or need to change. She loved what she did. She would stick to her original plan, find the necklace and be gone before he knew what hit him.

It shouldn't matter that she felt like she'd be betraying him if she took the necklace. She'd had to betray countless people before. Winston was no different, was he?

Good grief, even she was sick of her own whiny thoughts. Rosie rubbed her nose, halting in her frenzied pacing.

She needed to pack. Throwing open one chest, she gathered her rosewood hairbrush and comb and threw them inside.

Rosie stopped and took a deep breath with both hands on her stomacher. This was ridiculous. Maybe the spirit of the season had finally gotten to her, but she couldn't live knowing she'd betrayed him. She had to keep telling herself it would be just what he deserved. She just needed to focus and stop being such a sentimental fool. She must not let all the *Christmas* in the air get to her.

She'd laid out a fine muslin nightdress and hadn't worn it once, having spent every night . . . She mustn't think about it. Or his gentleness. Or what strange feelings he'd kindled. Folding the nightgown, she held it to her chest. She chided herself for having let her guard drop, her mask slip. What had given her away that he'd known?

Opening the paper wrapping of a dress, Rosie glimpsed inside. The soft nightgown slipped from her fingers as she looked at the exquisite yellow and lime sack-back gown she'd had especially made for this holiday. She hadn't had a chance to wear that either. Her fingertips hovered over the delicate goldwork embroidery shaped like tiny sparrows on the flounces trimming the petticoat.

How had he, in merely a heartbeat, smashed to rubble the walls that she'd spent years erecting between herself and the rest of the world? How incredibly arrogant had she been to believe herself immune to his charming wiles?

Winston Matthews was every bad thing she could think of. She'd believed all those lies he'd fed her. In her mind, she'd even made him out to be some virtuous and noble man trying to find his way in the world. But he was just another typical son of another typically conceited family of new money.

The ruby necklace wasn't the only bauble of considerable worth here. She could probably settle for something else. She'd just have to find it. And for that purpose she'd better get downstairs. She'd show him just what a good thief she really was.

Looking her best and hurrying at it was not Rosie's forte, yet she managed to take the fastest bath in her life, and with the help of the maid she'd been assigned, was ready in no time at all. She turned in front of the polished mirror, looking at herself from all sides. They'd done quite well all things considered. The pearl-crowned pins seemed to have been strewn at random in her hair. She wore most of her hair up while some wild curls fell down her shoulders, adding to the overall impression of methodical unruliness.

The tight corset pushed her bosom up so high that she looked more than well endowed. The décolletage was almost indecent and would certainly serve its purpose. At the back, the yellow box pleats on the shoulders fell loosely to the floor in a slight train. Open in front to better show off the goldwork on the stomacher, the lime-green petticoat boasted the same ruffles and golden sparrows as the gown. Flounces spilled from the elbow-length sleeves. Rosie should have worn a wide pannier with it, but it would only hinder her in maneuvering quickly from room to room without being detected, so she settled for a moderately wide hoop instead.

As she descended the main stairs, some guests halted in their conversations as they looked up at her. Others let their words trail off. A moment later, mouths were clapped shut collectively.

Maybe, Rosie thought, cringing inwardly, she'd overdone it. While being the reason for slack jaws and rude staring was quite flattering, it was not the desired effect.

Just as well, Rosie decided as she saw Winston standing with his back to her in the middle of the room. She didn't want to delve too deeply into why showing him what he could no longer have meant that much to her. What counted was that she got a ludicrous amount of satisfaction out of imagining he was among those pining after her.

Her feet carried her closer to him on their own accord. Just before she reached him, she saw Lady Ponsonby in the far corner, and instantly she changed direction. She hadn't had time to talk to her again and find out just what she had been about to tell her in the garden.

A hand gripped her elbow and tugged a little too hard, forcing Rosie to stop. She almost got a crick in her neck from looking up at Winston. One would think she'd have gotten used to it by now. But somehow he was much more imposing, and those icicles of aloof contempt she'd mentally surrounded herself with chipped off and clinked on the floor.

Something was wrong, her instincts screeched. Panic rushed through her body. Rosie swallowed hard, trying to understand her sudden queasiness or why her heart attempted to jump out of her chest right that moment.

"I believe we haven't met. Yet."

Realization dawned only when she registered the callous almost-smile on the pleasant mask of a predator who looked like an older version of Winston. His nearly golden eyes made it impossible for her to move, to breathe. This man, no doubt Winston's father, exuded danger from every pore—and it was not the kind that made one's groin hum in approval. Attempting to extricate her arm from his grasp, Rosie prayed her anxiety wasn't etched on her face.

"Father."

Rosie barely restrained a whimper when she felt Winston's warmth by her side. She steeled herself when relief threatened to cause her knees to buckle.

Something happened between the two men. Winston's warning glower suddenly made his father's scowl pale to insignificance until the older man's fingers loosened and slipped away from her. Her lungs fired sharp protests at her and she remembered to breathe.

Lady Ponsonby at the far back of the room came into focus once more. At first, Rosie couldn't put a finger on what she saw on the woman's face, but then understanding hit her. She couldn't keep her curious gaze from bouncing back and forth between Lady Ponsonby's dreamy yearning and Winston's father, who didn't even notice her.

Winston's father broke eye contact. "My study tomorrow morning, son. It seems I've underestimated you." He gave his son a curt nod and bowed slightly to her.

Winston's eyes roamed her body like he wanted to make sure she was all right and in one piece. A slight frown appeared on his forehead. "Lady Latimer. If I might have a word with you—in private?"

Rosie blinked. As soon as she recalled what had passed between them earlier, she tried to muster some of that anger. But it was in vain. She was usually able to stay calm in any dangerous situation, but right now she felt too rattled to pull together her scattered wits. All she wanted was to get out of here, so she laid her hand on his proffered arm. "I believe you've mentioned something about an art collection in the long gallery upstairs?"

* * *

Her light touch on his arm left him as soon as they reached the deserted long gallery. Two floors down, the musicians started playing a country dance, its echo reverberating from the high ceiling above. Winston watched her walking toward the balustrade. Her back to him, she braced her arms against the wooden parapet.

"I wanted to apologize," he stated plainly. "You were right. I'm a complete ass."

"Winston—" She looked over her shoulder at him.

"No, please. I need you to hear this." He took a step toward her but thought better of it. Turning his back, his gaze lingered on the numerous tapestries and paintings of strangers.

He knew what he wanted to say; he just hoped it came out right. Resting his hand against the cold stone wall, serenity settled over him.

"Not so long ago, I led a less-than-perfectly-acceptable-and-law-abiding life myself among the meanest of thugs, the wickedest of whores, and the shrewdest of tricksters. I believe I felt at home with the worst of those miscreants because none of them asked anything of me. We all preferred to be left alone, respecting each other's privacy. That's why I knew what you were the moment I saw you." Winston let his gaze sneak away from the empty cocoon of a clothing moth on the Flemish tapestry to take in the vision of her. She still kept her back to him, but her shoulders were squared now.

"It's true? You're a pirate?" Her whisper was carried to him as the music below died.

"Not anymore, no. I'm now first mate on a merchant ship. In time I will have my own ship."

"Does that mean you believe me when I say I haven't stolen the necklace?"

"I do, yes."

The silence between them was unbearable. Winston had to

get closer, yearning to be near her as if her warmth and bright-ness could scare away the worries inside. "Will you . . ." Her bergamot perfume permeated the air and drew him closer still. "Do you accept my apology?" He buried his nose in her hair, pursing his lips to kiss one of the pearls in it. "I had no right to be such a self-righteous prig. I'm sorry. I was worried you'd get caught when I wouldn't be there, because"—Winston swal-lowed—"I've come to care about you a lot . . . perhaps too much."

She looked over her shoulder at him, and for the first time, Winston saw her unmasked gaze, raw vulnerability laid open. He understood how crucial this moment was. With one more step, he closed the distance between them completely and rested his hands next to her on the parapet.

"I don't know how you do it. How you always throw me off guard. It's a mystery to me how you can so easily shatter the barriers I've set." Winston felt her body give a little. "And yes, I accept your apology."

"Will you tell me your real name?"

She turned her head forward again, watching the guests below. "I'm Rosie Archer."

Winston felt the corners of his eyes curl upward. Rosie was a lovely name, fitting such a delicate and precious woman. "You look stunning tonight, Rosie. I must say I felt an unfamil-iar, territorial violence churn in my gut when I saw every man in the room lusting after you."

Her breathy laugh was low, sensual. Winston's cock stirred. "Now, we can't have you bashing their skulls in. They didn't do anything but look."

"Reason enough for me."

"I sought to impress but one man."

"Did you?" Winston could see her heart banging heavy in her chest as the globes of her breasts, pressed against the stiff corset, quivered seductively with each drumming beat.

"Yes." The word came out on a shaky puff of breath. "Did it work?"

His swelling cock sought to snuggle closer to her buttocks.

"Aah," she sighed. "It did."

"I want to take you. Here. Now. Soft and slow."

Tilting her head back, he saw the surprise in her huge eyes. "Here?"

"Yes." Reaching down, he began to pull up her skirts inch by inch.

"No." She licked her lips, her lids sliding down. Her body gave a light shiver when he touched the soft skin of her naked thighs. Winston loved how much she was thrilled and aroused by the forbidden.

"I will be clever enough so those illustrious guests two stories down will see only you, so if you act like nothing's going on, they won't know."

"They will hear!"

"So you'll have to be silent."

Rosie moaned.

"But you'll have to watch out for anybody who might come this way."

Alarmed, her eyes snapped open.

"I don't want to be interrupted once I'm in you." Fingers splayed, Winston spread her cheeks, the tips dipping into the welcoming moisture spreading over her sex. "I'm not going to stretch you with a finger—or two or three—before I bury my cock in you so sluggishly you'll think you'll go insane by the time I'm halfway in unless I fuck you faster."

More of her dew wet his fingers.

"Once I'm up to the hilt in you, I'll make you glow. Breathe in, slide in. Breathe out, ease out."

"Glow?" Her breathing was reduced to short, sharp puffs.

"When people look at you, they'll know. You'll glow like a

woman who's just been fucked well." With one hand, he reached for the fly of his breeches, popping the buttons open one after the other. "You're so wet, Rosie. I can't wait any longer, but I will if you tell me to."

"No!" Rosie hissed over her shoulder. "Do it already!"

Winston clucked his tongue. "Wanton." Rolling his hips up, he sank inside just as he'd promised. She stretched around him, the muscles quivering just before they opened and allowed him in. He pushed a little more. Obediently, her pussy swallowed his cock, gripping him and trying to suck him deeper inside. But Winston held back and fed her bit by bit only.

When he was halfway in, he heard her whimper. She balled her hands into fists and he burrowed deeper. A shiver raked his body at the exquisite torture for both of them. The desire to take her hard and fast, slamming his cock inside her as far as it would go, was almost overwhelming. Gritting his teeth, he held back.

Finally, when he'd driven his cock into her up to his balls, he gripped her hips to hold her in place. Then he began to move out, counting. *Twenty-one, twenty-two, twenty-three.* And he slid back inside. *Twenty-one, twenty-two, twenty-three.*

"Are we still safe?"

"Uh-huh." She thrust her bottom out, meeting him halfway. Winston held her tighter, fucking her just a little faster.

"Good. I want to come in you. When we return to the party, I'll have you walk around well oiled and smelling of sex. Of *me.*"

Winston gritted his teeth to hold back the groan when her body quivered, her pussy starting to flutter. The spasms around his cock made his sliding back inside a little harder, and he sank deeper in a relentless stroke, quickening his rolling thrusts only just.

"With every trickle down the inside of your thighs, you'll

remember this, remember how I made you come up here while watching the people below and how they will never know what happened here. Between us."

This was wicked beyond anything he'd ever done before. His head spun. She was so wet. Felt so good. When she caught her breath, her head fell back to rest on his chest while he continued to rock gently against her.

Next she leaned forward with a low moan, thrusting her hips up more to meet him stroke for deliberately slow stroke. Her body stiffened, and Winston knew she'd crest any moment now. When her orgasm hit, his Rosie didn't make a sound other than a tiny sob.

Winston whipped up one arm and, hand cupping her chin, he brought her closer for a kiss. When his lips settled on hers, he instantly thrust his greedy tongue into her mouth, purring as she answered in kind.

Her pleasure ignited his own. His climax burst upon him with such ferocity he couldn't have prepared himself for it. He buried himself deep in her in one last thrust, closing his eyes to fully experience her pussy contracting around him and milking him. He saw bright dots swirling before his eyes as he spurted into her.

Winston lost track of time. He didn't know when his frenetic heartbeat returned to normal or when her rapid and shallow breathing slowed down. When his cock slipped from her sheath, he opened his arms, giving her room to gather herself, and stepped back to right her petticoat before he closed his breeches.

Somehow he didn't want to return to the party only to have to deal with superficiality, conceit, and deception. He'd much rather spend the evening in—

Rosie gasped loudly. "Oh. My. Goodness!"

"What?" Winston grasped her upper arm and turned her to

face him. As far as he could see, nothing was wrong with her. "What is it?"

"I just realized something."

Winston waited for her to elaborate. But nothing came. She just stared into the distance, her eyes wide and unblinking.

"Rosie?"

She shook herself out of the snail shell of her thoughts. "Yes, sorry. When we were downstairs in the room, I saw Lady Ponsonby. At first I didn't understand, but then I realized sparks flew between her and—well, actually no. Only she threw sparks in your father's direction." Wrapping both her hands around one of his, she looked up. "I'm sorry."

"For what? I have known since I was a boy that he wouldn't kick a woman from his bed unless she was my mother."

Rosie winced.

"And what is it you've just realized?"

"That if you don't have the necklace, because you're no thief, and I happen to know I certainly don't have it, maybe it hasn't been stolen. Only misplaced."

Why would Lady Ponsonby take the necklace off and forget where she put it if it were so valuable? Unless . . . "She didn't take it off."

"No, she didn't." She shook her head.

"She lost it during her tête-à-tête entanglement with Father."

"That's what I was thinking, yes. It must be what she'd wanted to tell me in the gardens."

With that new information, finding the necklace should be easy. "Now all we need to do is find the perfect spot for a discreet dalliance."

Her smile was so bright it was blinding. "So, where should we start?"

"We?" Winston saw the beginnings of a scowl on her face and hurried to add, "Don't you want to get back to the party?"

"And do what? Roaming the house in order to solve a mystery promises to be much more fun." At that, she stood on tiptoes for a moment, impatient to start what appeared to be a much more exciting adventure than a dull party. Once more, a smile spread over his features in response to her charming giddiness.

Rosie fell into step beside him. "Where do you suggest we start?"

"There's an alcove on the second floor of the west wing that's perfect."

"Could people pass and interrupt?"

Winston had never thought about it, but now that she mentioned it . . . "If someone lost their way, yes."

"Then we needn't bother."

Winston felt the question on his mind wrinkle his forehead.

"Lady Ponsonby isn't as adventurous as . . . erm . . ."

"You?" Winston offered, slowing his strolling down the stairs to match her speed.

Rosie snorted a laugh. "As *us*. Isn't there someplace more private you can think of?"

When he reached the end of the stairs, he stopped in his tracks. There were many places they could have gone to. When Winston was still a boy, he'd occasionally caught servants in alcoves, under stairs, and other places providing enough shadow and privacy for a quick humping and groaning and sweating.

But where would his father take his paramours except for the town house he provided for his current mistresses or the local bawdy house? It had to be somewhere he felt safe and secure enough to take her. His father was mistrustful and easily suspicious. He always had an eye in the back of his head.

Except for one room where he felt completely at ease. Nobody dared enter there.

"His study," Winston murmured, catching Rosie when she

teetered after his unexpected turning into a different hallway leading to the aforementioned study.

When they reached it, Winston found the door locked. Just his luck, he thought, and looked around to find suitable tools to pick the lock. Rosie was quick to help; she had one of the pins from her hair in one hand and fished for something between her stomacher and corset. She produced what looked like a stiletto.

"May I?" Elbowing him aside, she knelt in front of the door, her gaze fixated on the lock.

Winston watched out for her while she stuck the instruments into the lock. She had the door open on the third attempt. One last look left and right to make sure nobody had seen Rosie slip inside, and he followed, careful to avoid making any noise when closing the door.

The study was darker than he'd anticipated, with only a sleepy crescent moon illuminating the interior. But Winston knew the room well enough to maneuver around without bumping into furniture.

Now, where would he hide if he was about to ravish a married woman? Where would they be least likely discovered?

His gaze was drawn to the one large window in the right corner, half of it hidden behind a curtain, the other half kept secret by the bookshelf right next to it.

"There," Winston whispered, and pointed to where he thought they should start searching.

Rosie pressed herself against his back. "It's perfect. Let's go find ourselves a ruby necklace."

In three strides he was there, lifting the first cushion on the windowsill. Before he looked under the second pillow, he felt eyes on him. But only Rosie was there in the room with him, so he tilted his head in her direction.

She approached him with a seductive swagger to her hips. "I

think it would be much easier if we did what they did to find the necklace faster."

All of a sudden, his hands clawed the cushion to keep from shaking. Stretching her arms, she put her hands flat on his chest, pushing him into the wall behind him. Rosie laughed at what had to have been one of the dumbest expressions he'd ever had on his face in his life; then she ripped the cushion from his death grip.

Throwing it onto the floor to kneel on, she busied herself opening the fly of his breeches, the tip of her tongue burrowing into the tiny crevice in the middle of her upper lip.

Dumbfounded like a randy boy who was about to feel a woman's mouth on his cock for the very first time, Winston could only stare, watching her reach into his britches to free his cock, which was already as hard as granite at the prospect of such delight.

"Rosie, you"—Winston exhaled audibly as she pumped his cock—"you don't need to do this."

"I know." She met his gaze just before she bent to lick around the head of his cock. Winston felt his knees wiggle at the sight of her mouth so close to his—

"Fuck," he snarled as the tip of her tongue swirled over and into the tiny slit in his head. He felt a drop of precum erupt.

Then her lips were on him and Winston forgot to breathe. Her hot, wet mouth engulfed him and sucked him deep into her throat. He didn't dare move his hips and drive his cock too deep into her warm and talented mouth.

Her hand closed around him and followed her lips up and down, up and down his cock. Sucking, licking, trailing loosely and sucking again, slowly licking all his strength and reason away. There was nothing slow or playful about her sensual foray.

His eyes rolled up as the determined rhythm of her mouth and tongue brought him to a fever pitch. He was ready to burst right about now. Desire swamped him as the pleasure in him kept on building with every touch of her, every caress of her lips and teeth and tongue, until he was sure he might go out of his mind.

Lifting her chin, Rosie met his gaze. Hunger beat at him, merciless and unyielding, urging him to move, to drive his cock into her mouth and spill his seed down her throat.

With a groan, he cupped her head between his hands, and even though it felt like ripping his soul out, he nudged her away from him.

Biting her lower lip, she stood, raising her arms. "Lift me up. Against the wall."

"Rosie." Winston felt his voice degenerated to a croak. "I can't."

She gazed at his hard cock. It was plain to see that he *could,* because he didn't think he'd ever been so hard, or so horny for that matter, in his life.

"No, I mean, if I take you now, I'm not sure I can draw it out long enough for you to enjoy it as well."

Rosie laughed and jumped into his arms, wrapping her legs around his waist and rubbing her pussy against his cock. "Winston. I know there's not a selfish bone in you. I know you're a generous, giving, and nearly indefatigable lover. Let me do this for you. Just for you."

"I . . ." God, it was hard thinking with her rubbing her wet folds against him, teasing him by taking just a little of his head inside every now and then. Hard and fast he needed her. And now. "Are you sure?"

"Yesss!"

He didn't need more. He plunged into her and pistoned away, trying to not care whether he fucked her in the right angle that he'd bump against that spot inside her that would make her wild, make her purr and scratch and moan in ecstasy.

Instead of holding her tight in his arms, he opened them and braced himself against the wall. She probably held on to him for dear life with her arms and legs crossed at his back. He was pumping hard, his rough thrusts jolting her each time. He loved those little noises and wicked little cries that left her throat.

Heat. Pounding her. His cock viciously hard.

The desire to crest gripped him. He tumbled into another shuddering, earth-shattering climax. And the tremors kept coming, his mind splintering to pieces.

Despite having difficulties getting enough air into his lungs, Winston groaned, wrapping his arms around her as he spoke. "Rosie. You're . . . you're like a part of me I didn't know was missing." Whether it made sense to her or not, to Winston it did.

He set her down and let her stand on her own only when he was sure her knees wouldn't give out anymore.

"What's that?"

"What's what?" Winston followed her gaze.

There, behind the third cushion, wedged into a crevice in the windowsill, something shiny and sparkly reflected the moonlight.

6
_____

Awake and fully dressed in a navy ribbed silk traveling dress and matching jacket, Rosie took a flint and steel and lit the low-burning, cut-glass lamp on the bedside table. Wanting to make sure the light didn't wake Winston, she stopped and watched his barrel-like chest rise and fall with a low and steady, peaceful rhythm. Peace was not something she could relate to at the moment at all.

Her stomach fluttered, her heart raced, and her mind was alive with countless thoughts all jumbled together. It was hard to reconcile the man she now knew with the presumptions she'd had when she'd turned around that night of the first ball and saw him standing there. It was ridiculous now to think of him as an easy mark, as a spoiled, lazy heir who would be simple to manipulate. He was none of those things.

But much more disturbing than that was how different she was. The change in her own mind was frightening. For the thousandth time that night, she wished she'd never come here. How one man, one arrogant, strong, cunning, caring, and generous man could rock her to her core in such a short time was deeply touching and horrifying at the same time.

And now she was about to do something she'd never thought she would do since she stepped out of St. Nicholas's Hospital for the last time. Rosie opened the small velvet bag she'd brought, picked up the necklace from the table, and slipped it inside. She cinched the drawstring and placed it around her wrist before she picked up the lamp by its ornate base and moved through the room without making a sound.

She shut the door as silently as she could. Careful not to run into any other guests on their own clandestine missions, Rosie looked up and down the hall. She made her way down the noiseless dark hallway.

Necklace in hand, part of her tried once again to convince herself to take it and be gone by morning. But somehow, no matter how hard she tried, she just couldn't do that to the only man who had ever showed her caring and trust.

Loyalty and, dare she think it . . . love . . . had been just concepts in storybooks. But now, this Christmas, she understood them. Understood how they could make you do things you never thought possible. She'd never thought twice about Christmas before, never even liked the holidays because she never appreciated why everybody was so falsely happy all around her. To her, Christmas had only ever been a time of year where it was easier to make others believe her stories. But suddenly nothing seemed as easy—or important—as it used to be.

But what motivated her wasn't just her feelings for Winston. It was Lady Ponsonby herself and what Rosie thought might be a glimpse into her own future. She thought she empathized with Lady Ponsonby now. She could be sweet but was also a lonely and jaded woman. Her husband had a substantial fortune and gave her an easy life, but he was mean and never there for her. They lived separate lives, and Lady Ponsonby sought to make her life more bearable any way she could, even if that

meant cheating on her husband just to not feel so alone for a little while.

Rosie had been taught not to let people close, but seeing
how Lady Ponsonby's life had turned out, she wondered if she
was going to be as unhappy one day. Money, of course, made
you comfortable. But what did you do all by yourself after
that?

If she betrayed Winston now, she'd very likely throw away
her only chance to be free of the instability of her life. And also
possibly to be truly happy. If she walked away, she might end
up as Lady Ponsonby, alone in her gilded cage, or worse, alone
in jail for her thievery.

Rosie came to the end of the hall where it intersected with
the wing her room was in. She stopped. A turn to the right led
to her own room—and her packed bags. Straight ahead led to
Lady Ponsonby's.

She almost laughed at herself. She was both literally and fig-
uratively at a crossroads.

She could either choose to give Winston and the unknown
new world he offered a chance, or go with what she knew, what
she was comfortable with. But now she knew that with the lat-
ter, she could end up being another shallow, vain, and lonely
shell like so many others who yearn for hedonistic, temporary
distractions to ease their loneliness. That made the world she
knew much less attractive than it had once been. Damn that
man for turning her life so topsy-turvy she wasn't sure which
way was up.

A thought struck her almost like lightning. The lamp shook
in her hand and she swayed on her feet. For the first time, she
realized that all the money in the world couldn't buy her what
Winston offered so freely. Love, real safety, and peace of mind
had no price really, did they?

It wasn't just because he made her feel special and he tried so
hard to make this Christmas good for her. It was everything

about him. His loyalty to his mother and his independent spirit, how his strength made her feel small but cared for and safe in his arms.

Rosie looked straight ahead. Then she continued toward Lady Ponsonby's suite.

She was going to give love a chance. She had faith in Winston, trusted him, and wanted to learn to have faith in other people, too. Even though she was scared to death, she was ready to try and see where their love might lead them. She was going to fight to have the man of her dreams, who loved and adored her. And, because she couldn't shake everything about her old life just yet, a man who gave her stability with his wealth as well.

This Christmas was already very special for her, and all because Winston showed her how different it could be. She wanted to give him something back to show her willingness to let go of the past and try to have faith in him and others.

Yet when she reached Lady Ponsonby's door, she hesitated. A last bit of doubt crept in, and she fought the urge to turn and run or just slip in silently, leave the necklace, and go.

Rosie took a deep breath and quietly knocked. She'd wondered if maybe the lady wasn't alone, but no quick scurrying at her knock could be heard. She knocked one more time, and without waiting for an answer, she entered the rooms.

"Lady Ponsonby, are you awake?"

The window was open to the bright moonlight. Rosie heard rustling and then saw the woman trying to sit up. "Yes? What . . . Who's there?"

"It's Beatrice Latimer." Rosie moved closer to the bed as the older woman sat up. "Sorry to disturb you, but I must speak to you for a moment."

"Dear girl, what is it? What are you doing here?" She got out of bed and put on her dressing gown, then sat back down on the bed.

Rosie set the lamp on the bedside table. "I have something for you."

"Yes? What is it?" Lady Ponsonby slid over on the bed and patted the mattress for Rosie.

She sat gingerly on the bed with her feet dangling off the side and handed the older lady the velvet bag. Lady Ponsonby opened the bag and looked in, then looked at Rosie, not quite believing what she saw. Looking back down, she pulled the necklace from the bag. "Oh, dear girl, thank you so much! Where on earth did you find it?"

Rosie wasn't sure how to explain it, but for once decided to try the truth and see where it took her. "It was found in the main study under the cushions of the windowsill. The one by the bookshelf when you first walk into the room."

"Oh." Lady Ponsonby bowed her head and let the necklace fall back into the bag. The bag fell onto the bed. "And since you're bringing it back in the dead of night, I suppose you know how it got there."

Rosie touched the other woman's knee lightly. These were the kinds of problems the truth could cause. She never wanted her to think she was being accusing or judgmental. Telling the truth correctly was something she was going to have to work on. "I do, but only because I was there to do much the same thing. You'll find no stones coming from this glass house."

Lady Ponsonby looked up with a small smile and placed her hand over Rosie's. "Thank you. I don't know what to say."

"There is something else." Rosie pulled her hand back and reached into her pocket for the ring that matched the ruby necklace.

Funny, Rosie thought. It had been one of the first truly valuable things she'd taken when she'd first started in the business. She guessed that was why she'd kept it. She must have taken it from Lady Ponsonby personally, since she'd mentioned she'd been the one to lose it. But Rosie hadn't recognized Lady Ponsonby at all.

It almost seemed like fate had intervened to have the first and last thing she'd stolen—or tried to steal—be part of the same set and returned together.

She pulled out the ring. Lady Ponsonby recognized it right away. "What . . . where . . . where on earth did you get this?"

"I've had it for quite a long time. I don't remember from where, but when I saw the necklace, I knew it might be part of the same set."

Lady Ponsonby blinked in astonishment. "Yes, they were made for my husband's grandmother along with the matching earrings and a bracelet. In her later years, she'd taken to wearing pink wigs and quit wearing the ruby jewelry because she thought they clashed with her hair. She gave them to me as a wedding gift."

Lady Ponsonby shrugged and laughed. "Those wigs where as horrible as she was and looked atrocious with her skin tone."

They both laughed so hard that Lady Ponsonby had to dab tears from the corners of her eyes. At least Rosie thought they were from laughing.

"You know what," the older lady said, giving the ring back and closing Rosie's fingers over it. "You've had it for so long. It's yours now."

"To be honest"—Rosie opened her hand again and held the ring out to Lady Ponsonby—"I was hoping you'd say something like that, because I was wondering if perhaps there is any way you might want to buy it back?"

"Buy it back? Is there something you need money for?" She looked very worried then. "Oh, has the man you were meeting done something dishonorable?"

In fact he had, many times. Rosie had enjoyed those things very much. But that truth wouldn't help anyone. "No, no.

Nothing like that. There is just a special Christmas gift I was hoping to buy."

A very sly, conspiratorial smile showed on the other woman's face in the lamplight. "For Winston?"

"Yes." She knew just what she wanted to get him to show him how she felt.

It had been a hell of a morning. When Winston woke and she wasn't there and neither was the necklace, he thought the worst and was devastated. All morning he'd wavered between hating her for doing this to him, hating himself for falling for it all, and holding out hope that some way, somehow there was an explanation.

But now it was almost afternoon, and any hope he'd had in the morning was all but gone. He'd spent several hours with a painted-on, brittle smile when sitting in his mother's morning room to help with preparations for the rest of the holiday.

He'd promised his mother he'd come by this morning, but sitting in one room talking about New Year's and Twelfth Night was the last thing he wanted to be doing. He more than welcomed the distraction when Lady Ponsonby walked into the room. He hoped she was here to speak to his mother, and he started to rise, but she waved him back to his seat.

"Here you are, Mr. Matthews! Dolores, I hope you won't mind if I have a short word with your son?"

Unfortunately for Winston, with her usual perfect grace, his mother agreed. "Of course, Isabel." She patted Winston's hand. "I think we're done here anyway."

Winston stood, bowed to his mother, and led the other woman from the room and down the hall to the main staircase.

"Lady Ponsonby, is there something you needed?" To be honest, she was the last person he wanted to see. He knew it wasn't her fault, but still she played a significant role in the drama that was Rosie's world. But again he reminded himself that Rosie's life wasn't very different at all from the one he'd led. Dangerous, unpredictable, but with money to be made. They were well matched, and that made him want her all that much more.

"Mr. Matthews . . . I, well . . . I just wanted to . . ." It was obvious this wasn't going to be an easy conversation.

"Yes, what is it?" The minute the words were out, he knew his tone had been too harsh. But he'd lost his patience along with everything else. "Forgive me, Lady Ponsonby. It's just been a bit of a morning."

They'd reached the top of the stairs and stopped. "I just wanted to thank you for whatever part you may have played in the safe return of my jewelry."

"Think nothing of it." He wasn't paying attention at all and was already starting to walk away when he realized what she'd said. "Excuse me, what was that?"

She hesitated and seemed unsure of how to phrase her words. "The ruby necklace was found and returned, and I just wanted to thank everyone who might have had a hand in its return."

He had a sudden urge to hug the older woman, to throw her into the air and let out a hoot that would bring the roof down. Rosie hadn't left him; she'd done the right thing! As it was, he tried his best not to smile and simply said, "I can only say that if I did have a hand in it, it was my pleasure."

She gave him a sly smile of her own and a curtsy before she turned and walked away. And even with his heart drumming in his ears, he could have sworn he heard her say, "I can just bet it was."

He spent the rest of the day searching for Rosie. First, he checked her room and discovered most of her things still there. He could not fathom how he could have been such a fool. He could have spared himself almost a whole day of grief if he'd just checked there first thing. He promised himself he would never immediately think the worst of her again.

But he still needed to find her. There was so much he needed to tell her, so much he wanted to plan with her. He wanted far more than just the holiday together. Another week or so wasn't enough time for everything he wanted. He wouldn't stay in his father's house any longer than he had to, but wherever he went, he wanted her there. Making love on a rolling sea had an appeal that couldn't be found anywhere else, and he couldn't wait to introduce her to its special brand of delights.

He looked in the gardens, including both mazes and even the kitchen garden with no luck. Back in the house, he checked the main sunroom, the music conservatory, the library, the long gallery, and a half dozen other places.

Now he was beginning to worry that something bad had happened. Maybe she'd been exposed as an imposter or maybe someone she'd cheated had finally tracked her down. One thing was for sure: They both had pasts that could cause problems for their futures. But whatever they might be, Winston was prepared to handle them. If only he could find her.

He was getting desperate. He even contemplated knocking on the study door and asking his father if she was there or if he'd seen her. His father had approached her the night before. Maybe he suspected something. But when he stopped his father's secretary on his way into the study, the man assured him his father was in with his solicitor and they had been the only occupants all day.

On his way to find Lady Ponsonby again to ask her if she knew where Rosie might be, he was waylaid by some of the other male guests.

"Matthews!" Lord Rutterford slapped him heartily on the back. "We've hardly seen you all week. Where have you been hiding yourself?" It was clear by the way he swayed ever so slightly on his feet that they'd already abided in some liquid merriment.

"I've been catching up on family things, running errands for Mother. If you'll excuse me—"

"Oh, no, no, no," Mr. Anderson chimed in. "We have you now, my boy. Can't say no to a guest during the holidays. You must be our fourth for some cards."

Lord Rutterford and Viscount Wingate both nodded and hummed in absolute agreement.

His mind was too preoccupied to find an excuse, and he had no choice but to join them. "Of course, gentlemen, lead the way."

He spent a miserable tea time loosing at cards, distracted by everyone who entered the room and every shadow that passed by the doorway or the open windows.

There was still no sign of Rosie by the time he'd left to dress for dinner and no sign of her as he stood against the same railing where he'd taken her to watch the merriment of yet another holiday dance in the ballroom below. He smoothed his hands against the polished wood and remembered how she'd looked, how she'd felt. . . .

Where the hell was she? He was about to leave to check the dining room where the dinner buffet had been laid out when he felt someone behind him.

"The music seems even livelier tonight, doesn't it?"

His intention when he turned was to make sure she knew how angry he was. He wanted to punish her for all the anguish and worry, the miserable drunken card game, and everything else he'd been through all day. He meant to demand she tell him where she'd been and make her swear never to do that again.

But he didn't. When he faced her, all those thoughts were gone. Rosie radiated pure, unadulterated loveliness. She wore a pewter satin gown over a claret-red silk petticoat. The way she held her hands behind her back emphasized her soft breasts pillowing above her stomacher, which was decorated with clusters of embroidered poinsettias with pearl centers. Her hair was a perfect pile of curls, and she beamed with happiness.

There was no power on earth that could make him say anything to take that happiness away. "Is there music playing? Everything else, even the music, seems dulled to almost nothing when compared to your beauty."

"Ah, spoken like a man who knows how to charm every woman he meets." It didn't seem possible, but her smile was even brighter now.

"Not every woman, just you. Only you."

"I think I like the sound of that."

That was very good, because Winston didn't think he was ever going to want another woman again. "You'd better get used to it. I don't intend to let you go for quite some time." He didn't want to say forever just yet; he didn't want to scare her off.

"Planning to keep me close to keep everyone else safe from my designs on all their treasures?" Her voice was soft and teasing, but he knew she wanted assurances, and he was more than happy to give them.

He moved toward her and placed his hands around her waist, pulling her close. He took a deep breath of her sweet bergamot scent. His heart careened and he kissed her neck. "To hell with anyone else. My motives are purely selfish and, truth be told, slightly obscene at the moment."

"Do tell, Mr. Matthews."

He felt her pulse quicken beneath his lips.

"I can do better than that." He tried to close what little space was left between them, but she pulled back.

"No, wait. I have something for you first."

She took a step back and revealed a small package wrapped in green paper with a gold ribbon that she'd hidden behind her back. She looked so proud of the gift she was giving that Winston's hands shook at the honor of receiving it. He carefully pulled the ribbon loose and opened the paper.

"It's the compass from the mercantile shop." That's where she must have been. She'd gone to town on her own to buy a Christmas gift for him to surprise him. "I can't believe you even noticed it when we were there. Rosie, did you? I mean, I hope you didn't."

She laughed and rose on her tiptoes to kiss his cheek. "Don't be silly. Of course I didn't! I even paid full price. I didn't even try to negotiate or anything."

It was beautiful. The compass was made of the best-quality polished brass, cherrywood, and beveled glass. She'd been very generous. "Rosie . . . I . . . there is something you need to know. If you think all this will be mine someday, it won't. When I first arrived, my father made it quite clear I was cut off completely. It was only on my mother's urging that he ever let me stay."

He thought she'd be shocked, angry, or at least pull back to discuss it, but she hardly even acknowledged it. "I am very glad he let you stay. My holiday would not have been merry at all without you."

"You really don't mind?"

She placed her hands on the outside of his where he still held the compass. "Honestly, I thought I would. Part of me is still trying to tell myself I should, but somehow, unbelievably, I don't." She shook her head, laughing at herself. "Besides, I know you're a man who is not afraid to get his hands dirty, and I'm not the kind of girl who minds dirty hands."

His mother was wrong. None of those simpering society ladies would have ever been right for him. Rosie was what he needed. Rosie, who he could tell all of his truths to. Rosie, who he accepted for who she was, good or bad. And first mate or gentleman, she accepted him. "That's very good, because I've got big plans for us, Rosie girl."

"I can't wait to hear."

The ball must have been hitting its stride below, because the music swelled louder than before with a lively dance tune. Winston carefully set the compass on the carpet beside them, then swept her off her feet by her waist, twirling her to the music. "First, we'll have our Christmas dance."

Her laughter warmed every inch of his body. "And after this?"

He set her back on her feet. Her breasts nestled against his chest and his groin snug against her hips, he held her close enough to feel his arousal. "I'm going to take you back to my rooms, then slowly and carefully unwrap the very best Christmas present of all. And I'll spend a very long time enjoying every inch of it."

Her breath hitched as he bent to place a kiss on the top of her breast, drawing a little circle with his tongue. "And then?"

He continued to place small kisses, licks, and soft bites along every inch of exposed flesh. "And after the last ball, I'm going to take you to sea and show you all the extra pleasures an ocean voyage can provide."

"And then?" This time her voice shook a little with uncertainty.

He stopped what he was doing and looked into her eyes. He knew what she was asking, and he could only hope she liked the answer. "And then if you still want me, we'll find our own way together." Winston drew a quick breath. "You know, I did a lot of thinking today. If I hate the way my father has done things so much, then instead of running off to sea, maybe I should come back and try to do something about it. Maybe British Honduras does need another Matthews as governor-general. And maybe I could use your help to achieve that." He cradled her lovely face in his hands when her eyes swelled with unshed tears.

"I think you are a good man, Winston Matthews. And I think that is a very good plan."

With a groan of hunger, his lips latched on to hers in a heated kiss that seared him inside and out and shook him to the core. Relishing in the passion that instantly built around them so high it would drown them when it broke, his tongue swirled around hers, greedily devouring what she gave. He kissed her with everything he had, not caring at all who below might look up to see them. He poured all the emotions of the day into the kiss. Winston interrupted their feverish kiss and leaned back just far and long enough to draw much-needed air into his lungs. His tongue brushing over her lower lip, he tasted her shallow pants, soft moans full of passion, sighs that spoke of her desire.

She fisted her hands in his hair and pulled him close, moaning into his mouth. His heart quickened. His body tensed. He was on fire, but she ached for him, too, squirming against him as she did, her hips pushing into his groin, rubbing seductively against his already rock-hard member.

Only when he was in danger of throwing her down and taking her then and there, whoever heard them be damned, he pulled back, wheezing in another lifesaving breath.

"Is this what love feels like?"

Blinking her eyes open, she thought for only a moment before she answered, "I've never felt it before, but I'm sure that it is."

He was sure that it was, too. "Merry Christmas, Rosie."

"Happy Christmas, Winston."